The Beyondness of War.

The third book in the Peter Parker series.

Project Red Book Part 2.
The Simurgh.

Russell B Smith.

Contact - Olmi Publishing© -
<u>Olmipublishing@yahoo.com</u>

A word about the Author.

I live in breath-taking Abruzzo, Southern Italy. The views of the magnificent mountains, rolling countryside and the Adriatic Sea are a great inspiration for my work.

I have been here for several years now with my Wife and ten dogs, enjoying the atmosphere, the people and the wonderful traditions of this little-known Region of Italy.

I would normally write adult fiction, of which the Peter Parker series is one, although I do occasionally write for children.

My latest children's book is "Popysan the Green Dragon". Have a look at that book and the other books in this series on Amazon.

I also have a Facebook page, Russell.B.Smith Author, this contains my latest releases and information, such as the map relating to the Peter Parker books.

MAP.
There is a map of the area available on the Facebook page @Russell.B.Smith Author.

Books by Russell B Smith.

The Peter Parker Series.

The Beyondness of Things.
Published December 2020, available from all good book shops and from
Amazon books as an e-book or in paperback.
ISBN 978-1-8383146-0-6

The Beyondness of Fear.
Published April 2021, available from all good book shops and from
Amazon books as an e-book or in paperback.
ISBN 978-1-8383146-2-0

The Beyondness of War.
Published 2023, available from all good book shops and from
Amazon books as an e-book or in paperback,
ISBN 978-1-8383146-4-4)

The Beyondness of Peace.
(Expected 2022/23)

Children's books.
Popysan, The Green Dragon.
Published March 2021, available from all good book shops and from
Amazon books as an e-book or in paperback.
ISBN 978-1-8383146-1-3

The Lee Hunter Crime Files.
Five Murders and Counting.
This book is available from all good book shops and from
Amazon books as an e-book or in paperback.

ISBN 978-1-8383146-3-7

Bodies on the Ninth.
This book is available from all good book shops and from
Amazon books as an e-book or in paperback.
ISBN 978-1-8383146-6-8

Characters and places.

Flight Lieutenant Peter Parker. (*Louis Dubois.*
Undercover name in France)

A Spitfire pilot in the RAF.

Susan Walker.

Peters Wife in England.

Doctor Claude A Durand.

French Scientist. The target for Peter when he returns to France.

Code name 'Red Book'.

Madeleine.

A woman Peter knows in France.

Philipe.

Former member of the French Resistance.

André.

Former member of the French Resistance.

Laurent.

Owner and barman at the Bar Le Chat. Former member of the French Resistance.

Pierre Dupuy.

Local Vet and leader of the local Resistance.

Monique.

Second in command of the local Resistance.

Marcel.

Local Resistance fighter.

Lieutenant-Colonel B.R. Smith.

Peters Special Operations Executive (SOE) handler.

Wing Commander Richard James. R.A.F.
C.O. 694 Squadron.

Bob Swanbourne. Wing Commander James Navigator/bombardier.

Jacques Forelle. Former Police officer in Saint Aderald, now a Manager in the Prison in Chênes.

Sister Beverley Jane. Catholic Sister and local District Nurse.

Didier Allard. Owner of the Hotel Paris.

Leo Monet. Chief of Police in Chênes.

Hauptman *(Captain)* **Karl Wagnor.**
Officer in charge of the local German SS.

Private Lena Webber.
A young female German soldier befriended by Peter.

Lieutenant Schneider.
Karl Wagnor's Security Officer at the Manor House.

PLACES.

Saint Aderald.

The local town in France.

RAF Burton Wood.

Peter Parkers home base in Kent England.

Bar Le Chat.

Bar in Saint Aderald, where the German Officers meet.

Chateau Du Beck.

Town in western Belgium.

Bar Saint Stephen.

The bar in Chateau Du Beck.

The story so far.
Following The Beyondness of Things.

Peter, along with what's left of the local Resistance group, escaped back to England and safety. This followed a tumultuous operation, with Peter and his group assassinating the senior officers of the German Security Police, in a cunning and carefully planned operation.

Upon returning to England, he is once again recruited, by the British S.O.E. and is ordered to return to France, for a second, larger operation, despite his objections and the desperate pleadings of his Wife Susan.

Unfortunately, Peter and the group are discovered and attacked by the German Army, in a carefully planned and executed operation. The members of the group, including Madeleine, are separated during their escape, and do not meet again throughout Peters hurried and desperate flight from France. Eventually, he returns to England, Susan and their baby, however the war is not yet over, and Peter can't forget his life of adventure and excitement with the French Resistance and with Madeleine.

Following The Beyondness of Fear.

Ordered to return to occupied Europe, Peter Parker has once more to jump into the dark of the night and an uncertain future in north-western France. He has to find and bring back to England a missing French scientist who holds the future of the war and victory in his hands. The problems are, no one knows where he is, and the German SS are also hot on his heels.

"It's a quick 48 hour job" he was told, but things go terribly wrong from the start and Peter finds himself in a nightmare of deception, lies and double agents. United with some old friends, they have to find the scientist before the SS do, or victory for the Allies will certainly slip away. He finds himself cornered by the evil Karl Wagnor of the local SS and is operating in occupied France without a contact or a radio, will he succeed, the future of the war and freedom itself depend on it.

He finally finds and gets back together with Madeleine in an incredible mission to find or kill Doctor Claude A Durand (Red Book), will they accomplish what seems to be an impossible task, will they both survive?

By 1943, several major milestones had been reached by the Allies, in their pursuance of victory in World War 2.

In North Africa, British and American forces had defeated the Italians and Germans by 1943.

An Allied invasion of Sicily and Italy followed, and Mussolini's government fell in July 1943, though Allied fighting against the Germans in Italy would continue until 1945.

On the Eastern Front, a Soviet counteroffensive launched in November 1942 ended the bloody Battle of Stalingrad, which had seen some of the fiercest combat of World War II. The approach of winter, along with dwindling food and medical supplies, spelled the end for German troops there, and the last of them surrendered on January 31, 1943.

Source: History.com.

"The difficulty is not so great to die for a friend, as to find a friend worth dying for."

Homer

Chapter 1.
RAF Greenford.
Southern Kent, May 1943.

Wing Commander Richard James stood in the briefing room, in front of the members of RAF 694 Squadron. He was a relatively young man to be a Wing Commander, around 5 foot 11 tall, average build, brown hair, clean shaven and but with a steely determination obvious on his face.

He was the kind of man that just wouldn't quit, no matter what the circumstances were. He had this almost immortal quality. He had proved himself in battle many times with extraordinary talents at the controls of his aircraft, and with his honest leadership skills that had established him as a popular leader with his men.

Number 694 Squadron had been equipped some months ago with the latest version of the twin engine De Haviland Mosquito fighter bomber, and they were making the best of their aircraft's superior performance in sweeps across northern Europe. They had sallied forth many times, tormenting the German Airforce, industries and troop concentrations. The squadron had gained an enviable reputation for daring do and accomplishing every mission asked of them. Wing Commander James called the briefing to order and pulled aside the large curtain that had covered today's mission into occupied France.

"Right you lot, pay attention, it's now 07:00 and we leave at exactly 08:30, everybody sink watches in 3,2,1, mark. Now, we have two aspects to our mission today, one is to bomb the railhead here, and the other is any targets of opportunity on the following return leg home. The weather guys report clear skies with a modest southerly wind, no prospect of rain or low cloud"

Wing Commander James tapped the map firmly with his long pointing stick, turning in order to make sure they had all been paying attention.

"Now it's fair to say the railheads are a very important target, so we need to make sure we hit them and hit them hard. I know you guys want to be off shooting up any German lorry or troop carrier within one hundred miles of where we are supposed to be, but we have to knockout these railheads. If we don't, the top brass have made it very clear to me that we will be going back there tomorrow, to finish the job, do I make myself clear?"

There was a general mumbling from the group of pilots and navigators.

"Never mind mumbling, first we hit the railheads, then we can go on a jolly and beet up anything with a German flag on it, do I make myself clear?"

The was a resounding "yes sir"

"Right, so I don't expect to turn around mid flight only to find that my ten aircraft have suddenly reduced to three, do I?"

"No sir"

"Good, because if I do, you lot will be delivering red cross parcels in some far-off place, on the other side of humanity, got it?"

"Yes sir"

"Now, we approach the first target, from the northwest, it's just over the border in Belgium, we go in low, keep your eyes open, we expect some German fighter response, mainly as we leave the target area.

Once we have dropped our bombs, we first turn southwest, along the French Belgium border and then directly north and home for tea. If we see any enemy activity on the ground, strafe and destroy, there might be a lorry convoy or two heading west, in particular toward the army base near to Saint Aderald, any questions?"

There were no questions, the young men from 694 Squadron were ready for the fight, they couldn't wait to leave. They almost ran out of the briefing room, off to the mess for breakfast and then on towards their aircraft to begin the mission.

Wing Commander James turned to his navigator, Bob Swanbourne, who was waiting patiently by the mission board.

"The chaps are the best you know Bob, they just need a little firm handling from time to time, but I bet they get the job done. I hope without any issues though, I am sick of writing letters to missing crews' families"

"Richard, they are fine, just ease up on yourself, sometimes you push too hard, you don't need to take complete responsibility for everything you know"

"I know Bob, but these guys are just babies, four of them are nineteen, two more have just turned twenty, the oldest is only twenty-five. When I was their age, I was still chasing girls and getting drunk in the Nags Head, not killing or being killed, it's no start to life"

"You are right Richard but it's what we have, they will be fine, just look after yourself, before the stress or this dam war kills you"

Wing Commander James laughed and smiled at Bob Swanbourne, "come on Bob, breakfast and then off"

The twin Rolls Royce Merlin engines roared into life on each of the De Haviland Mosquito fighter bombers. Due to some unrepaired aircraft damage, a shortage of spare parts and three pilots on the sick register, Wing Commander

James only had nine operational aircraft, including his own. This was going to be a lightning operation, low level, in and out before the German air force could react.

The Mosquitos ran down the runway in three groups of three and moved elegantly into the air, the Op was on. The Germans called them the Moskitoschreck, or Mosquito terror and they were on their way.

Chapter 2.
The French Belgian Border.
May 1943.

The day was glorious, warm sunshine, a bright blue sky, you could see for miles. Birds swooped taking insects in flight, and the occasional bee buzzed, there was a gentle fragrance of early flowers, summer was really here, and it was splendid.

The two German soldiers had been very thorough so far, they had searched in every compartment of their little car. They were now both looking in the back, any minute now they would lift up the rear seat and discover the hidden radio. How could they have been so stupid to hide the radio in such a place, even the laziest guard would find it, and the game would be up!

Peter reached around to the back of his trousers and took hold of the handle of his browning 9mm pistol. Slowly and very carefully he clicked the hammer back and slid off the safety. It was obvious to him that his pistol would not provide enough fire power for himself and Madeleine to escape. He was certain that he could catch one or two of the soldiers off guard, but they would soon be shot down.

He figured however that it would be a better end than rotting in some Gestapo dungeon somewhere in Germany. He had already tasted that outcome in the manner house on his first visit here, he wouldn't be doing that again.

He looked across at Madeleine, she glanced back, there was a certain look of resignation on her face, he smiled at her, she looked down at the ground then back with a smile and a blown kiss. Peter felt strangely relaxed, their outcome had been decided and they were about to die. Perhaps it was a relief, all the torment of the last couple of years would be washed away in a blaze of gunfire. No more the fear of being court, no more the decisions that would cost people their lives.

He looked around at who might be his first target, the officer standing only feet from him, he would be an easy kill. There were two motorcycle guards, they were looking west into France, perhaps they could make a run for it before they turned their machine guns on them. What about the two soldiers searching the car, they could be well away before they got out and opened fire. All this would be pointless though as there were two other heavily armed soldiers on the other side of the road. They were looking directly at Peter, he would be dead before he even got one shot off, never mind five or six.

Peter looked back at the car, the two soldiers were opening up the back seat, once they had it out of the tight confines of the car, they would certainly see the radio hidden underneath. It was no more than two or three seconds later when a shout went out from one of the soldiers in the car.

"Sir, sir, a radio, there is a radio hidden in the back of this car"

The officer looked first at Peter, then towards the soldier in the car.

"Well Frenchie, if indeed you are French, we seemed to have a radio hidden in your car, let me guess, how on earth did that get there?

Peter looked firstly at Madeleine and then back at the officer, he slid the Browning out of his waistband and readied to fire. He just about levelled the gun at the German officer when the whole ground erupted into shards of stone and earth. Dust filled the atmosphere, grit stung his eyes, complete disorientation enveloped him. Then the air ripped hot once again, from absolutely nowhere, there came the noise and screaming engines roaring overhead.

He instinctively threw himself to the ground, shocked but utterly oblivious as to the reason for this explosion of clamour and debris. He crawled towards Madeleine, she was likewise prostrate on the ground, with a look of utter terror on her face.

"Peter, what the hell is going on?"

Before he had time to answer, there was another cacophony of noise, further eruptions of earth, small stones and gravel. He threw himself over Madeleine, in some vein attempt to protect her from whatever was exploding all around them.

There was however something very familiar about the noise, he screwed up his face, trying to understand what it was. In an instant, he recognised the distinctive rattle of a 20 mm cannon and 303 machine guns.

"Crawl over to the car, if I am not mistaken, we are being strafed, and that engine noise was a Rolls Royce Merlin, the same one I had in my Spitfire. Go, and keep low, this might be our chance to get out of here"

He looked up, the two De Havilland Mosquitoes were climbing hard and turning to starboard just as hard as they could. There engines were screaming with the stress as the pilots opened up the throttles.

"They are coming around for another go, we need to get to cover, next time we will be minced by these guns. Run for it, get into that ditch whilst we still have time, run and run hard"

They got up and ran, their lungs bursting with the effort, hearts pounding with the terror of this situation. They threw themselves into its muddy depths, it wasn't deep, but it gave them some protection and perhaps comfort from the aerial onslaught.

"Stay down, lay as flat as you can, don't move until I tell you to, understand?"

She didn't reply, but he didn't have time to check, he had to find out what was happening at the border post and to the German soldiers who were manning it. The dust was still hanging in the air, giving a slightly yellow tinge to everything, it stung his eyes as it blew in the direction of the ditch. He blinked several times in an attempt to clear the irritation, just in time to see the Mosquitoes levelling up for another run.

"They are here again, keep your head down, here they come!"

He ran back to the ditch where Madeleine was laying and instinctively threw his arm across her back, protecting her as best he could, even though he knew it would be in vain against the hail of lead from the aircraft. The guns snarled and the engines roared as the two De Havilland Mosquitoes screamed overhead. As soon as they passed, he put his head above the side of the ditch, the scene was one of complete chaos and destruction.

He caught site of one of the motorcyclists riding off on the French side of the boarder. His sidecar, complete with machine gun and soldier bouncing as he sped west away from the death from above. The other motorcycle, lorry and their little car were in flames, full of holes, flames issuing from every door and smashed window, black oily smoke whirling into the air. There was still debris and dust in the air, it would be some time before this cleared but he couldn't see anyone moving in any part of the scene in front of him.

Peter strained his neck and hearing to try and work out where the two aircraft were now and more importantly, were they be coming back? Try as he might, he could not ascertain where they were, the smoke from the burning vehicles simply blotted out most of the sky.

He turned to Madeleine, she was right behind him, covering her head with her hands, she was visibly shaking but mercifully, seemed unharmed.

"Wait here, no matter what happens stay put, I am going to find out who is still alive and if I can get that radio out of the car"

Before she could reply he was gone, Browning 9mm pistol in hand, he charged off towards the burning car, into the dust and carnage. It was immediately obvious that the radio was beyond rescue, the car was burning with such ferocity that he couldn't get withing twenty feet of it.

On the plus side, the German officer who ordered them out of the car was obviously dead, smashed full of holes, he was barely recognisable. Three soldiers were running away from the scene, they clearly didn't care for Peter and Madeleine, self preservation was their main aim. The two men that were searching the car were no more than blackened manakins, trapped inside.

He scanned the skies again, the two aircraft were no more than two small dots heading north. Without hesitation, he ran back to the ditch and Madeleine.

"Right, out, we need to get away from here before those men regain control of themselves and come back for us"

Madeleine scrambled out of the ditch, she was covered in mud and clearly in shock,

"Where are we going?"

"Well three of the Germans have run north and they are still running, don't suppose we will see them again, the motorcyclist has gone west, so let's try south, at least until dark"

"What about our clothes, food and that radio?"

"Cinders, nothing more than ashes, we need to get away Madeleine, we will think of a plan, but first, we need to get away from here"

He took hold of her hand and they started to run, without looking back, and just as fast as they could. They took off across the fields, some with early crops, other with livestock grazing. On and on they ran, scrambling through hedgerows, across ditches and over farmers gates. They soon slowed, exhausted, looking about, it seemed that no one was in pursuit.

"Do you think they will come looking for us Peter?"

"Well, they will have returned to the checkpoint by now, I am sure. Perhaps they think we burned in the car but to be honest, they will be looking for us, I don't doubt that. The advantage we have is they have no idea where we went, or in which direction, so long as we play it safe, and stay out of the way, we should be ok"

The smoke from the checkpoint was still visible, whirling in black vortices into the faultless blue sky. It marked the point of the attack and the place where their opportunity for escape had come, thanks to the attack from the RAF. They were a mile or two away, no one knew where they were and things seemed quiet, at least for now.

"Sorry Peter, this is as far as I go, we need to rest, in case you hadn't noticed, it's been a hell of a day"

Chapter 3.
Home for Tea.
May 1943.

"Shooting skip, that Gerry lorry went up like a roman bloody candle, must have been full of ammo. I like hitting these border posts, plenty of Germans and no air cover"

"Can't agree more Bob, well that's the last of the 30mm, time for home, give me a compass heading, petrol is low so direct course please"

"Two minutes skip"

Before Wing Commander Richard James could reply, the nose of his Mosquito exploded into a million shards of metal, sending bright red slivers bouncing off his cockpit windscreen. A split second later the grey spectre of a Focke-Wulf FW190 fighter flashed over his cockpit, it's BMW 801-c1 engine screaming as it did so. He immediately turned hard right and pushed the nose down in order to gain speed, opening up the throttles as he did so.

"Where's it gone Bob, I can't see it?"

"Don't know skip, it's underneath us, keep banking, I think our wingman has gone down after him"

"How did he manage to creep up on us, where was our wingman, he supposed to be watching our tail? I will have bloody words with Jacko when we get back, he should have been watching!"

The airframe of the Mosquito strained and vibrated violently under the extreme strain of the turn, juddering and groaning, but it held together.

"Get them on the radio Bob, where the hell have they gone? They were watching are arses, dam fools, they better get back here and bloody quick"

The annoyance in Richard's voice was clear, the fear was not, he remained calm and calculating, "getting angry will only get you killed", he often remarked.

"Can't skip, that 190 took our radio out, eyes only I am afraid"

Before long the right-hand engine started to smoke, slowly at first but the unmistakable dark grey smoke of burning oil began to flow from the Rolls Royce Merlin engine cowling, and soon after a fire alarm flashed in the cockpit.

"He's nailed our starboard engine Bob, what's it look like, can you see the damage?"

"Looks ok skip, some smoke, oil, should get us out of here"

Wing Commander James craned his neck looking almost 360 degrees, searching for their assailant. If he didn't find that 190 soon, he would be on top of them before he could manoeuvre out of the way. With a damaged nose and righthand engine, the 190 would always have the upper hand. Also, where was his wingman, had he gone after the 190 and been shot down, had he gone missing some time ago and been unable to radio the alert? This was the confusion of conflict, the fog of war, unanswered question, unexpected situations, it was the survivors who always came up with a plan.

"Still can't see him skip, no wait, the 190, break left, break left"

Wing Commander Richard James threw his aircraft hard over, switching from a right hand to a left-hand turn, this made his vision blur for just a second, darkness closed in, but he stayed in complete control. However, he could feel the lack of sharp handling, his experience told him that Focke-Wulf FW190 must have done a lot more damage than first thought.

"It's rolling Bob, it doesn't feel right, there is more damage than I can see, where is that 190 now?"

"Took him by surprise that switch, he has rolled away to port, but he will be back I am sure"

It was at that precise moment that Wing Commander James felt an almighty bang and heavy vibration. His once smooth aircraft now felt completely different. Rattling and vibrating, noises issued from all over the airframe, he instinctively knew that this was very serious indeed.

"That sounded terminal skip?"

"I think that was part of the tail coming off, don't seem to have much rudder control. I am going to pull up Bob, see if we can climb, just in case we have to jump"

He pulled up and the aircraft started to climb but as he did so, he noticed another FW 190 some 1000 feet below.

"That kind of explains a bit Bob, there are two of the bliters, look down there, climbing towards us, a second 190"

The Mosquito was climbing as hard and fast as it could but the damage to the right-hand engine and airframe was drastically affecting it performance.

"Bob, we aren't getting out of this, those two 190's will be on us soon, we have a knackered engine and goodness knows what else. There is no 30mm ammo left and very little petrol, a bit of a fix you might say"

"Looks that way skip"

Wing Commander Richard James pushed his aircraft down and left, trying to gain as much airspeed as possible, he was aiming right at the second FW 190. He closed to within two hundred yards and opened up with what remaining ammunition he had in the 20mm canon.

The first few rounds missed but with some subtle adjustments, he walked the deadly cannon shells right onto his target. The 190 exploded into a storm of metal shards, oil and burning fuel. One check of the altimeter though showed that they were so close to the ground, that it would be almost impossible to pull up in time.

'Hold tight Bob, this is going to be close, the bloody knackered starboard engine is not firing properly at all"

Bob Swanbourne looked nervously at the rapidly approaching ground, normally he would be confident of getting out of this scrape, but with only one good engine.

Another rake of bullets clipped into the starboard wing, this time the engine stopped and quickly burst into flames.

"That's it Skip, that bloody 190 has done us properly this time"

"It's ok Bob, I can get us out of this, but we will have no altitude left, I suspect we will be ditching in one of those fields down there"

James pulled back hard on the controls, the whole aircraft shook and rattled fiercely, some more of the damaged nose split off and crashed into the windscreen. Bob Swanbourne looked out over the wings, they were bent upwards with the unimaginable strain, and that starboard engine was by now fully engulfed in flames.

"Skip, we need to get down, that engine is going to burn through the wing any minute now"

"It's ok Bob, we have time, don't worry old chap, I will get us out of this"

The nose started to come up, it was clear that the skill of the pilot was beginning to take effect. Right in front of the aircraft was an old railway goods yard, it looked abandoned, with an overgrown grass covered track, leading towards the west. Not far on the left-hand side was a signal box that was adjacent to a more used railway and not far past that, a river.

"Down there Bob, those fields in between the railway and the river, I will put her down there. Brace yourself, this is going to be rough, best of luck Bob"

Chapter 4.
There must be another way?
May 1943.

The night-time closed in over Peter and Madeleine, like a blanket of purple and black. There were no visible lights in any direction, they felt alone. They had managed to find some shelter in the remains of an old farm building, it had no roof and only three dilapidated walls, but it kept the chilly night breeze at bay. They dare not light a fire, so they held on to each other for comfort as well as warmth.

"Tomorrow we will try and find something to eat and drink, we might be able to catch a lift towards Saint Aderald. Who knows, but we need to stay positive Madeleine and we need to stay sharp!"

"But Peter, our whole plan is now in ruins, we have no food, no radio, no transport, goodness only knows where we are? How on earth are we supposed to get to Doctor Claude Durand and more importantly get him out, we can't even call the RAF for transport back to England?"

"I know it looks desperate Madeleine, but we have to find a way, let's just take it a step at a time, find something to eat, and find out where we are"

"Why don't we catch the train at the station near saint Aderald, travel north. We can change trains and get back to my uncle and aunties in Belgium, we can try and start again"

"It's a good plan but we haven't got time, it would take days, even weeks to get back to where we were at the border crossing, even if someone else gave us a car and the Germans didn't catch us on the train. No, we have to press on, how about your parents, could they help us?"

"Peter, it's a lot to ask, you know how my father thinks about all of this resistance thing. He has seen what the SS do to people, especially those who help out, that's how he lost his best friend"

"I know but we will need a lot of help, as well as luck, we can't use Philipe, Laurent or André, the Germans will be watching them night and day. Neither of us can go wandering into Saint Aderald, we would be spotted straight away, I don't see what else we could do?"

"There must be another answer Peter, there must be another way, I can't ask my parents"

"I am not sure that there is, there might be someone we could call on though, let's see how it goes"

The next few days would prove some of the toughest Peter had faced. They had to try and live of what they could find, beg and steal from the farms they came across along the way. The nights seemed long and cold, no fires to keep them warm. Some farmers were keen to help with what they could, others simply slammed the door in their faces.

They headed west, eventually, they would reach the Rivière Reese, from there they could move along its length until they reached more familiar ground. It seemed an easy plan, just keep walking and they would be in an area where they might call upon friends but there seemed little hope of that at this present time.

They passed the long nights reminiscing, talking about friends, Saint Aderald and the Bar Le Chat. They laughed at Laurent and his illegal stills and Philipe and his hatred for the Germans.

They smiled but inside they were both very frightened indeed. Already their plan had failed, and they were barely in France. There was so much to accomplish, including finding the scientist, it just felt impossible and all this with the SS hard on their heels.

They slept but only in fits and starts, this would be their lives now until either they were killed, or they managed to succeed in their mission. The truth though was clear, the more likely end to this adventure was capture and death, there seemed little or no alternative to that!

Chapter 5.
It's Been a Hell of a day.
May 1943.

The De Havilland Mosquito had skidded to a stop in the corner of a large field, it was covered in holes from the bullets fired by the two German aircraft. Wing Commander James had managed more of a landing than a crash, wheels up and level as they hit the ground. The aircraft bounced violently several times before it stopped, having completed several pirouettes.

The starboard wing had been ripped off an lay a few yards to the right along with the smoking engine. The canopy was covered in soil and debris and there was an alarming smell of petrol, but at least they were down in one piece.

"Right Bob, out, I don't like the smell, we need to get away soonest"

He pushed open the door and jumped out, there was an increasing amount of smoke, thick and pungent, burning rubber and oil made the atmosphere hot and choking. He turned to see the rear part of the aircraft starting to burn and on the other side of the fuselage, flames beginning to dance from the ruptured fuel tank.

"Bob, get out now, she is going up, get out"

There was no movement from the cockpit, other that swirling smoke filling the interior of the aircraft. James pulled himself back inside, only to see Bob Swanbourne still sitting in his seat, harness still fastened.

"Bob, get a bloody move on or we are goners for certain"

There was still no movement from his Navigator, and by now the cockpit was full of chocking grey smoke. Wing Commander James coughed violently, his eyes streaming, he pushed up into the cockpit, undid the harness and began to pull Bob Swanbourne out of the burning aircraft.

He dragged him out and down onto the ground. With adrenaline pumping he hauled him away from the scene of the crash, still unable to open his eyes due to the clogging smoke. Eventually, he sensed the air cooling and clearing, his coughing calmed just a little and his eyes began to clear.

He looked down at his Navigator who lay motionless on the ground. To his absolute horror, James saw that he had several bloody bullet holes in his right-hand side, his whole uniform was bright red with blood.

He knelt down next to him, but his body was motionless, his face had a grey pallor, that look was something Wing Commander James had seen many times before during his time flying Lancaster bombers. On more than one occasion he had returned to base with crew members already dead, and that colour and look on their faces meant only one thing.

"Oh Bob, I am so sorry, I guess when you said, 'Skip, that bloody 190 has done us properly this time', you didn't mean the aircraft. Bob, why you my friend, why couldn't the bastards have got me instead. Now look, what am I supposed to do without you looking after me, Bob, my old pal. You deserve better than this, dying in a bloody field somewhere in France.

Listen Bob, I don't seem to have a choice old pal, I can't bury you here, can't take you with me, I need to get away, but I guess you understand that hey! Look I am going to have to leave you here, they will take care of you, decent burial and all of that.

I will talk to Jenny, tell her what happened, there won't be any anonymous letter, not from me or the RAF, I promise. I will tell her the truth, exactly what happened, I know you would want that. I will make sure she is taken care of Bob, I promise you, she won't want for anything, rest assured"

With tears streaming down his face and an absolute crushing sense of lost, Richard James stood up and surveyed his surroundings. His aircraft had come to a stop on the edge of a ploughed field, it was now completely engulfed in flamed, with ominous spitting and crackling noises coming from within.

He looked around, a hundred yards to his left was a river and to his right, a railway with a signal box. There didn't seem to be any immediate cover, so getting away from the huge black smoke signal that his aircraft had now become, was his number one priority. He pulled the body of Bob Swanbourne as far as he could, and far enough away so as not to be affected by the fire and possible explosion.

"OK Bob, I am off now, got to get away from here before Gerry picks me up, which by the looks of things, won't be too long. It's been a hell of a day I guess, let's hope things get better from here, take care old pal"

He took one last look at his old friend and set off towards the river, expecting to be captured at any moment.

It didn't take him long before he reached the banks of the river, the flow wasn't particularly fast, but the river was very wide. It had that oily run that warned of deep water and hidden dangers, Richard James stood on top of the steep bank gazing onto its depths.

"I know that look, been fishing too many times not to take the hint, that water is not one you would ever be able to swim across, I wonder if there is a boat nearby?"

As much as he looked, he could find nothing that would assist him crossing the river, there was no way he was risking swimming, so he turned south, "there is bound to be a bridge at some point!"

He walked on during the last light of the day, he could hear vehicles in the distance and the occasional dog barking. It was clear that the Germans had found his burnt-out aircraft, but at least they hadn't found him. Keeping the river to his right and the railway to his left, he progressed on until dark.

"Right, this is as far as I go, if I continue thrashing about in the dark, I will certainly end up in the river, I need to find a place to rest for the night"

He lay down on the ground, it was slightly damp but at least it was covered in a thick sword of grass and moss. He felt comparatively safe, at least for the time being, as the darkness threw a shield of anonymity around him.

As he began to relax slightly and opened up his senses into the night, he heard talking, it definitely wasn't French and there seemed to be three of four different voices. He reached for his .380 calibre Enfield revolver, but then thought better of it, "won't be much good against their machine gun!"

Holding his breath and his nerve, he stayed completely still, laying totally flat on the damp grass. The voices came and went for most of the night but thankfully came nowhere near Richard. He occasionally fell asleep but never for more than a few minutes. Any noise would wake him with a start, each time he reached for his service revolver, but each time it was a false alarm.

Eventually, the light began to return, slowly at first but then with more rapidity, the warmth that it brought was a welcome relief from the damp cold air that persisted near to the river. He shivered with the cold and the dank, he needed something to eat and a hot drink, but there was little chance of that anytime soon.

He dragged himself upright, the crashlanding of the previous day had caused stiffness and aching all over his body and in particular in his back. Stretching out he looked around, the early morning mist was very beautiful and added a certain charm to the view, but he was acutely aware of what that mist might hide.

Right in front of him was the confluence of another river to the one he had been following from the previous day. It caused a great sweep from left to right as it gently merged into the other flow.

He could see to his left, emerging from the mist, the railway and a short distance away a bridge for the railway to cross the river.

"OK, if I can make that bridge, I might be able to move about the landscape a little better, I have been trapped up against the river for far too long"

Slowly he edged towards the bridge, "perfect place to wait in ambush for a downed airman" he thought, "if it going to happen, it's going to happen here"

He climbed up from the riverbank and onto the simple steel girder bridge, it was just one track wide but was clearly in use. He expected to be cut down in a hail of bullets at any moment, but nothing happened. Keeping as low as he could and despite his aching back, he crossed the bridge and immediately slid down the riverbank and into cover. The feeling of relief at crossing the river and more importantly at still being alive was intense.

During the rest of the morning, he headed south along the railway. There were several close encounters with the searching soldiers but the thick undergrowth surrounding the tracks proved a very effective hiding place. By late that evening he had reached another bridge, this time where a major road crossed over the rail tracks. It was under this bridge that he decided to spend the night, it perhaps wasn't the best place to hide but he was exhausted and needed to rest.

Chapter 6.
Meeting.
May 1943.

Peter and Madeleine had been slowly and cautiously following the road from the Belgium border for the past few days. It had been hard, with little food or anywhere safe to rest. They had benefited with a lift from a rather smelly Belgian lorry driver delivering wood. Despite his odour problems and his foul language, he had managed to get them much closer to their goal than they could ever have managed on foot.

The Riviere Un was now in sight, all they needed to do was cross it and find the track that led over the railway line and towards an old footbridge. This bridge crossed the Riviere Reese and would lead into the old watermill where Peter and the two American airmen were ambushed on a previous mission.

Once there, they would find at least some protection from the elements and maybe some of the hidden provisions left behind after the previous attack. At least it would be a starting point for the rest of their mission and a relatively safe place to hide and just as importantly, one step towards their goal.

They days consisted of slow movements, hiding in ditches, and reacting to the slightest noise or activity. They moved from place to place, waiting, observing, using their sense to evaluate their next move. They could not afford to take even the slightest risk, discovery would end in only one outcome, being tied to a post and shot as spies.

"There seems to be an awful lot of German activity Peter, surely they are not still trying to find us, I thought you said they might presume we were killed in the attack?"

"I am not sure they are looking for us, did you see that thick black cloud on the horizon a few days ago? Well, I think that was the crash site of one of the aircraft that attacked the border post. I did wonder at the time if they had managed to shoot one down, there can't be much else around here that would burn like that, it must have been. Poor blighters, I guess that's another couple of 'missing in action, presumed dead' telegrams. This bloody war asks too much of us all Madeleine, too much of those serving on the front line, too much for their families and too much for society. Who the hell thought this was a good idea, what a terrible mess we have got ourselves into and for what?"

She didn't reply, she was thinking about what Peter had just said, and of those people who were no longer alive because of the war, so many good people, so many waisted lives. He was right, for what, it was a terrible mess and no end seemed to be in sight.

They continued to walk along the main road, on constant alert for German patrols but nothing appeared. It was however a pleasant day, warm sunshine and a cloudless blue sky. It could have been much worse, rain, cold and mud, at least they were thankful for that small mercy.

Peter looked very French in his workman's clothes, his blonde hair shining in the bright spring sun. He was tall and strode along in a purposeful and confident manner. Madeleine on the other hand moved with a certain grace, her hair flowing in the breeze, her eyes sparkling. Peter looked across at her, she was wearing a red dress, it reminded him of their first meeting in the barn and her red coat and beret. He reached out and took hold of her hand, she squeezed his tightly, they were both grateful for the comfort this simple gesture brought.

"We will get through this Madeleine, I promise"

"I know, but what will it cost us Peter, how many more lives will it take, how many more families will be torn apart?"

"My boss would say, 'that's war, it's not supposed to be bloody pleasant, you just have to get the job done'. You are right of course and sometimes I ask myself the same question, but I try not to dwell, the cost is far too high to contemplate but the idea of failure is impossible to consider"

They continued to walk down the road, and eventually they reached the large steel bridge which carried the main road to Paris and the Belgium border over the Riviere Un.

"Right Madeleine, we get over this bridge and you think there is a track that leads to a footbridge over the Riviere Reese and to the watermill?"

"I don't think Peter, I know, my father and I used that path after church on a Sunday. We used to go fishing in the eastern bank of the Riviere Reese. It was far safer than the steep western bank, the fishing was great fun. It's only a track, you can't get a vehicle down it, so we shouldn't see any patrols"

"Sounds good to me, come on, let's get across this bridge whilst the light holds, I don't fancy falling into that river, especially in the dark!"

There seemed to be little or no traffic of concern in the area, a couple of farm vehicles and a man on a bicycle, otherwise the coast was clear. They moved across the bridge with some rapidity, quickly racing the other side, if they had been caught on that steel monster, there would have been nowhere to run, nowhere to hide.

Once they reached the other side, they quickly slid down the embankment, away from the level of the road and hidden from any passing patrols. It was completely silent, no traffic, no voices, it felt safe, or at least as safe as it could be deep in occupied France.

"Right Peter, it shouldn't be more that a five-minute walk until we find the track, once we start along it, we should be away from any German patrols or troops"

"Good, cross that bridge and we can hide out in the old water mill, with a bit of luck there will be a few old tins of food from my last visit, if they haven't been taken?"

"Also Peter, my parents farm is no more than a couple of hours walk, perhaps we could ask them for help, although I really don't want to"

"Let's leave your parents out of this, at least for the meantime, we can manage by ourselves"

They held each other closely, the adventure so far had been one of excitement mixed with terror and a feeling of complete disaster, but they were still alive, and Doctor Claude A Durand was getting closer every day. If they could just get to his location in the town called Chênes then they would be in with a chance of success, but that would be short lived, as Peter knew all too well, without the radio destroyed in the attack, they were stranded, with no hope of rescue.

"Let's do this one day at a time Madeleine, it's difficult to plan anything out here, every time you think you have it, something drops on you and your plan turns to dust. We need to concentrate on the here and now, let's just survive and move forward, one day at a time"

She looked up at him, he had a stoic but concerned look on his face, this was the worse of situation and the most difficult position he had ever been in. The chances of success where almost zero, the chance of being killed were much, much higher.

"Listen Madeleine, I shouldn't have asked you to do this, why couldn't I just say no to this stupid plan. When I was back in England, why did I even think it was a good idea to speak to you in the first place?

I could have done this by myself, I could have been shot at by my own side, found myself half-starved and chased by the Germans, laying filthy in a ditch. I shouldn't have come to you Madeleine, I am sorry"

"Wait a minute, as I remember it, it was me who said yes, I don't recall you holding a gun to my head, do you? The idea you put to me in Chateau Du Beck seemed a plausible one. No one would be looking for me, why would they, I could have travelled anonymously, no one would have been the slightest bit interested. I could get over to Chênes, find Durand and get him to come back and if he refused, shoot him, simple.

No Peter, it was me who changed the plan and demanded that you come with me, if I had been less selfish, there would have been no need for that radio in the back of the car, the border guards would have let me through sooner, I would have been driving that little car to Chênes by now, none of this would have happened"

He looked down at her face, streaked with mud, her hair dishevelled, that dress torn and the hem, it was his fault, and he knew it, now it was up to him to get them out of this dam awful mess.

They held each other again but as Peter closed his eyes and enjoyed the moment, he became aware of some movement, coming from behind them. In a flash he turned, drew his Browning 9mm and gazed into the darkness under the bridge.

"Who's there?", he said in French, "come out or I shoot"

There was a short pause before the reply came back in English, "sorry old chap, I couldn't help listening to your conversation, seemed rather nice hearing English out here. The name is Wing Commander Richard James. C.O. 694 Squadron. I got jumped by a couple of FW 190's, my navigator bought it and here I am"

Richard walked out of the gloom under the bridge, hands held high, his RAF uniform covered in grime.

Peter looked at the emerging RAF Officer with absolute shock, his mouth hanging open. He was around 5 foot 11 tall, average build, brown hair, several days light stubble around his face, he was dressed in RAF Flying gear with Wing Commanders insignia.

"What the hell are you doing out here, Wing Commander?"

"We were out on a search and destroy sweep, just about got the job done and on my way home. A couple of Focke-Wulf FW190's came from nowhere, shot out my starboard engine, killed my navigator and I had to crash land the old girl. That was three days ago and here I am"

Peter still couldn't comprehend what had just happened, he advanced to the RAF Officer to examine him more closely.

"What were you flying and what search and destroy sweep?"

"I was flying a De Havilland Mosquito old chap, and the last bit of action was shooting up a German guard post on the Belgium border. I should have been more careful, it was my fault, I should have been watching for the enemy not thinking about a pint in the pub"

Peter laughed, this guy had absolutely no idea what problems he had caused him, and he had been shot down thinking about a piss up with the chaps in the local pub.

"Listen Wing Commander, I have absolutely no idea who you are, although your story checks out, I was at the Belgian border post when you attacked. Any ID on you?"

"Certainly"

He handed over his ID documents and showed Peter his dog tags.

"And what about you old chap, what the hell are you doing out her, dressed in workman's clothes with a beautiful girl on your arm, sorry madam, we haven't been introduced"

"This is my, erm………..wife, Madeleine, we are on our way to Chênes to meet a friend, you are more than welcome to tag along for a while"

"Good afternoon Madeleine, pleased to meet you, even though your husband doesn't seem that sure as to who you actually are. As for you sir, I don't recall your name and that accent, it most certainly is English?"

"Sorry, my name, it's Louis Dubois, and yes, my wife Madeleine Dubois, I am French but spent many years in England before returning here just before the war broke out. Most people think I am English, but I am most certainly French. Why haven't you turned yourself in to the authorities, they will take care of you?"

"Not looking forward to spending the rest of the war in jail old chap, much rather get back to Blighty and carry on the fight.

I am sure I have seen you somewhere before though, my squadron was based at RAF Burton wood for a while, did you work there for the RAF or something like that?"

"Not sure what you mean, I have been here since 1939, never worked for your RAF"

"Sorry, I must be thinking of someone else old boy, anyway, any ideas of what I can do to stay out of the hands of the local security, how far from the coast are we?"

"You can tag along with us for a while, we will be staying at an old mill for a day or two, you are welcome to share what we might find there. As for the coast, if you could get a lift, perhaps two or three days, way too far to walk it"

"Very kind of you, the water mill sounds idyllic, let's go"

Madeleine and Peter laughed, "sounds idyllic", he clearly hasn't seen the place.

They soon found the old track, the one used by Madeleine and her father all those years ago. Very much overgrown now, but still familiar to her, the memories came rushing back of better times, safer times before the war ruined everything for everyone.

"Right, this is it, we follow this old track to the footbridge and the mill is on the other side, should take more than an hour at most"

They fought their way down the overgrown path, at times it was almost impossible, clawing brambles and nettles wrapped themselves around their arms and legs. On more than one occasion someone tripped and fell but they pushed on and just as the sun began to fade, they reached the footbridge.

The old bridge looked very rotten and rickety, covered in green algae and weeds of all kinds, but they had to chance it, it was their only way forward. One at a time they gingerly moved across the bridge, finally making it to the other side, the last one to cross was Richard, which gave Madeleine a chance to speak to Peter.

"Why didn't you tell him who you really were Peter, he is one of your own, you can trust him?"

"We really don't know anything of the sort, we can't be sure he is that pilot from the RAF, the truth is, we don't know anything about him at all. Also, if he is captured, he could spill the beans about us, at the minute all he can say to the Germans is "I met this married couple of their way to Chênes, that's enough for now"

"Then we treat him with respect but suspicion Peter, until we know any better, which I am sure will follow shortly"

"That's the plan Madeleine and we stick to it and yes, I don't suppose it will take very long to properly ascertain his identity, don't forget I am a serving RAF officer as well. I know how we think, the traditions, everything, it won't take long to figure him out"

Eventually and some great relief, they made it to the old watermill, it was by now dark, so they slowly made their way inside and lacking any light or candles, they found a reasonably dry spot and went to sleep for the night.

Peter woke sometime around dawn, it took a second or two to comprehend exactly what had woken him, it was the rain beating down outside. The storm had made the air smell sweet and refreshing, there was a damp atmosphere down in the cellar.

He sat up, he and Madeleine had slept on a pile of old newspapers and rags in one corner of the concrete and stone cellar underneath the watermill. It was difficult to see exactly where Richard James was, somewhere in the far corner of the basement. The large wooden shutters that lead to the ground outside were closed, so he was in the basement somewhere.

The rain was beating down outside, and water ran in small rivulets down the dirty and dusty walls, pooling on the dirt floor, before disappearing into the ground. It was cold and damp, Peter shivered as he looked about him. He wanted to look outside but lifting up the heavy wooden doors would not be a pleasant task and one best left until the rain had ceased.

He pushed himself, rather stiffly upright, "if I remember rightly, there is a box of candles on a shelf, near to the staircase leading up to the door to the old mill"

He stumbled across the cellar in the half-light, eventually finding the shelf and sure enough, a large box of candles and right next to them, a box of matches. He used several matches, all damp and useless before he got one to strike. The cellar might have been dry and dusty but at least it kept the matches in some sort of useable state.

The whole place lit up, not a bright light but a subtle, flickering hue, penetrating to most corners. He walked about, Richard James stirred in the corner, wrapped up in some old sacking and straw. It was probably the first night's sleep he had since the crash.

Something caught his eye, something flickering in the corner, near to where Madeleine was still sleeping. He walked over and bent down, it was a Zippo lighter, he picked it up, just about readable in the dim candlelight it read, 'Sergeant Carlo Franchetti, USAAF'.

"Well, Carlo, you are still here, I will take this back to England and make sure your family get it back. Maybe if I can track down Ginger, he could drop it off for me"

His mumblings woke up Madeleine, she spun around and eyes still sleepy, looked at Peter.

"Sorry, what did you say, is someone here?"

Peter laughed, "go back to sleep, I am going to look around, see if there is anything to eat"

It was sometime later that Madeleine and Richard had properly woken, Peter had amassed a small collection of tins, some with labels and some not. He placed them on the dusty floor in between the group.

"Right, here I have, three tins of peaches, one large tin of something with no label, two small tins of herring and four bottles of red wine. I suggest the peaches for breakfast, tinned herring never appeals at this time in the morning"

The feast also came with one very rusty tin opener, all provided by the Resistance group when Peter was last here.

"Right, I have been collecting the rainwater from outside, so we can have a drink, perhaps even a quick wash. For once I am really pleased it was absolutely throwing it down, the tins are full to the brim. Don't eat all the peaches at once, save some for me, and let's see who can guess what's in the big tin?"

The rest of the morning went well, the sun came out and the air warmed, at least they had full stomachs and a chance to bathe in the river, including cleaning their filthy clothes. This improved their mood considerably, washing away the grime of the last few days made them feel more civilised and somewhat refreshed.

"Right you two", Peter said with all the authority he could muster, "we can't stay here, we need to get moving. It's stopped raining so might I suggest we move up the road, towards the old pumping station. We could then carry on and try and make the disused slaughterhouse, there may be something there that could prove very useful indeed"

Madeleine and Richard looked at each other, "something very useful"?

Peter was just about to explain what he meant by that statement when the faint sound of conversation came drifting in from outside. It was clear that it was some distance off yet, but it was certainly coming closer. Immediately the two men drew their pistols and all three ran up the cellar steps and into the ruins of the old mill.

The ruins of the old water mill were just as Peter remembered them, apart from the numerous bullet holes, acquired when he was last here. Fortunately, the ruinous state of the building made a perfect place to hide and observe what was coming.

"Richard, get behind the old front door, keep low and don't do anything until I tell you. Madeleine, with me, we will get by that old window, we can see who is coming from there"

They took up their places, hearts pounding, adrenalin racing through their veins. They could hardly control their breathing, Peter tried to inhale more slowly, his panting was drowning out the voices coming down the track. They strained every sense to try and see who was coming but they were still some distance off, but one thing was certain, whilst they were speaking French, someone had a German accent.

Madeleine whispered in a voice so low, that Peter could hardly make out what she was saying.

"Peter, they must be soldiers, but there is a woman's voice in there and she is speaking French, what's going on?"

"I can only guess they have come here for a bit of privacy, it's not a good thing for a French girl to be seen with a German soldier"

"You might be right but what are we going to do?"

"Let's just wait and see what happens, we don't want to start shooting, especially if there are civilians involved"

The voices came closer and closer, to their absolute horror, it became clear that there were at least four different people, two German men, one German woman and a French girl.

Peter stared down at the ground and shook his head, "why does this shit happen to me, why can't just one thing on one day go to plan, why do people have to die because I am here?"

He looked up again, just as four people emerged from the overgrown trackway. They were right, there were two German men, one in a private's uniform and the other in civilian clothes. There were also two women, one in a German sergeant's uniform and the other in simple civilian clothes. It was clear that the two men were not local, they were very tall, had blonde hair cut very short.

To Peters absolute horror he recognised the German woman, she was Lena's boss, the one that threatened to tear Peters balls off if he harmed Lena but also got them back together again.

"Oh shit", he whispered, "I don't believe this"

"What Peter, we just shoot them and move on, what's the problem?"

"I know that sergeant, it's a long story but I owe her a favour or two, she doesn't deserve to die, not like this"

"She is a German Peter, she shouldn't be in my country, of course she deserves to die"

The four stopped and looked about them furtively, they held hands, the man in the uniform with the French girl, the other cuddled closely with the female sergeant.

"I guess you are right but, ...

Before he could finish, there was the sudden sound of gunfire, several cracks as a firearm was discharged. The noise came from the doorway and without warning, into the area in front of the mill, ran Squadron Leader Richard James, pistol in hand, firing at the group of people.

There were five or even six shots, the two men immediately fell to the ground accompanied with a spray of red mist. The French girl limped slowly back into the woods and the sergeant stood there with her hands in the air, clearly shocked and disorientated by what had just happened.

"No, no Richard, you bloody fool"

Peter and Madeleine jumped to their feet and followed Richard James out of the old building.

One of the German men started to slowly scramble to his feet, reaching behind him, perhaps to draw a weapon. Without hesitation Peter shot again, hitting him twice, he fell back to the ground like a lifeless rag doll, blood pouring out onto the wet ground. Richard ran over to the other German and kicked him a couple of times, he didn't move.

"Madeleine, you get after that French girl, bring her back here, don't lose her"

Madeleine ran after the young girl, disappearing into the undergrowth.

The whole scene suddenly calmed, Peter could hear his heart pounding as he surveyed the two dead men and pools of bright red blood splattered across the brown earth. His hands were shaking, he quickly looked back at the German sergeant, she was still standing, mouth open, hands in the air. He could hear Richard, standing behind him, loading his gun.

"Richard, stop bloody shooting, stand still man and get a grip"

"But they are the enemy, we need to kill them before they kill us"

Richard eyes flared, sweat pouring down his face, he was clearly high on adrenalin, he could explode into a feast of killing again at any moment.

"Richard, just put the gun away and go and sit back down in the mill, I can handle this, go, go now"

Like an obedient child, he pushed his revolver back into his blue RAF tunic pocket and turned and walked back to the mill. Peter spun back to face the female sergeant who was still standing, like a statue, with her hands in the air.

She stared intensely at Peter before she spoke, "we have met before, but last time it involved Lena and you were French. I must admit to being very confused, I assume by your language that you are a British Agent?"

"You assume correctly, I don't suppose there is any point in hiding that truth after what you have just witnessed"

She smiled, rather nervously, "it wouldn't do any good to say anything else, what was your name, Louis I think, I don't recall your second name though?"

"It was Louis Dubois, and I am sorry you had to go through this, we weren't planning an ambush, things do have a habit of turning to shit around here"

She laughed, "so what should I call you then and what the hell happened to Lena?"

"Just call me Louis, it's easier that way, as for Lena, sorry, I have absolutely no idea, I assumed she had been posted away somewhere?"

"Come on Louis, you know exactly what happened to her, was she a double Agent, Wagnor thought so, perhaps turned by you. You have no idea of the anger than man created once you two disappeared, you could hear him yelling all over the old manor house. The thought of someone getting the better of him, he couldn't stand that, he will never live it down. He had his security chief posted to the far-off edge of the eastern front, some shit place that's not even on the map, pour guy, he will be dead for certain"

"I didn't plan to have anything to do with Wagnor, things just happened that way, he was stupid enough to play my game and I got away with it"

"Yes, but you and Lena were an item right, did you turn her into a double Agent or was she just a good opportunity to get information from us. Did you just use her and leave her dead in a ditch when she couldn't help you anymore?"

"Nothing of the sort, we had a thing, you know that, but I didn't do anything to her, I have no idea where she is. She did talk about running off to Spain, maybe someone should check the border there"

"Well, I guess Louis, that won't be me, I can't see you letting me go, even if I promise not to tell Wagnor"

She laughed out loud, she didn't show any outward signs of fear, but he could tell that she was very frightened indeed.

"Thanks to my friend, I now have a very difficult situation to deal with, if you had only gone somewhere else for your intimate pleasures, if only Richard had done as he was told, but no. Sorry about your friends, I wish it could have been different"

"Don't worry about them Louis, it was just a passing affair, a bit of pleasure, nothing serious, a bit like you and Lena hey. Now, can I put my arms down, they are aching?"

"Ok, well turn around, I need to make sure you aren't armed"

He had just about finished rubbing her down when Madeleine came back from the woods, trailing a very frightened young French girl behind her. She was bleeding from a wound in her side and was struggling to walk. Her pretty dress was covered in blood, but Peter guessed that not all of it was hers.

"Right Madeleine, sit her down right there, and you sergeant, sit next to her, either of you move and I will shoot"

"Call me Mia, not sergeant, my name is Mia"

Peter turned toward the mill and shouted, "Richard, get out here and guard these two, don't shoot them unless they try to run, do you understand me?"

Richard had clearly calmed down since the start of the incident, he strolled out with a casual confidence, the adrenalin rush had clearly faded away.

"Sorry about that old chap, kind of got carried away, it was a reaction to loosing my Navigator Bob Swanbourne, we were very close you know"

"OK, point taken but try to keep these two alive, please!!"

Peter and Madeleine returned to the mill, out of earshot of Richard and the two women.

"What condition is she in Madeleine, is it bad?"

"I have to say Peter, I have seen worse, but the bullet has gone right through her side, I fear she will bleed out if we don't get her treated soon. She is just a young French woman from Saint Aderald, she has been working at the manor house, in the kitchens. In truth, she had done nothing wrong and now she is going to die. What about that German woman, what are we going to do with her?"

"Well thanks to trigger happy Richard, I don't really know. We could tie her up and leave her by the road, someone will find her, probably a passing German patrol. A member of the local resistance might shoot her and leave her in the woods, or just let her go, you choose"

"Not really a choice to be honest, but we need to get help for that French girl before it's too late"

"Just how do you propose to do that, call for a doctor?"

"Well, I might have an idea. Not far from here lives Sister Beverley Jane, she is a Roman Catholic Nun who has chosen to live in the community and tend to the sick. She eventually became the district nurse around here, in fact she delivered me, so you could say I have known her all my life!

It's about an hour's walk, perhaps two, I could get her to come and tend to the French girl's wounds, she's not interested in politics, the war, nationality or anything else, just helping the sick. She wouldn't say anything I am sure, it's worth a try"

Peter walked around rubbing his chin, thinking about what to do next, whatever they did was going to be risky, but they had to do something. Eventually he turned to Madeleine, still rubbing his chin and with a palpable air of worry in his voice.

"OK, get off, see if she will come over, we can't just leave that poor girl to die"

Madeleine left the mill, walked past the German women and knelt down by the side of the French girl. She was laying in the foetal position, shivering and slowly bleeding out onto the ground. It was clear that she wouldn't last the night without some expert care.

"Don't worry, I am going to get help, just try to stay calm, I will be back soon"

Peter watched as Madeleine disappeared off down the track, if she couldn't convince Sister Beverley Jane to come, they would have another casualty on their hands. With a certain amount of irritation, he turned to Richard.

"Right, since most of the bloody mess is your doing, you can help me move this girl into the old mill. We can put her on some straw, keep her comfortable until this sister arrives, in the meantime, we will tie up and hide Mia in the basement. There is no need to involve sister Beverley any more than she needs to be"

Together they took Mia down into the basement, tied and gagged her and made the young French girl, by the name of Adele, comfortable on some straw and old packing cases. It wasn't much of a hospital bed, but it was all they had.

"I am very worried about her Richard, I am no Doctor, but she looks bad and how much blood has she lost, she can't go on like this?"

"I can't argue with that Peter, but I have seen some terrible sites with returning aircrew, some of them managed to survive, perhaps she can to"

It seemed like hours later before they finally heard the noise of an approaching vehicle. The track that vehicles approached the mill on was somewhat wider than the foot path through the woods, so they could easily see what was coming. The vehicle was a very old and very rusty Citroen van, belching black smoke and coughing wildly. The best thing of all though, was that Madeleine was sitting in the front seat.

It eventually came to a stop at the front of the mill, screeching breaks and clouds of smoke. Madeleine jumped out of the old van and from the other side, another woman came towards Peter. She was dressed in simple working clothes, a sweater and jeans, with brown boots. She was quite tall for a woman from these parts, Peter guessed that she was possibly not local. She had fair skin, shoulder length brown hair and carried herself with a confident and eloquent but purposeful demeanour.

"This is Sister Beverley Jane, she has agreed to help and do what she can"

Peter stared for a moment, "sorry Sister, I kind of expected a Sister to be dressed, well a little differently"

She stared at Peter for quite some time, he wasn't quite sure of her reaction, she seemed somewhat cross, perhaps a little annoyed at his presumptions.

"We don't all dress in Nun's habits you know, that's a bit of a preconception on the part of society. It's something I get used to but perhaps it's time people educated themselves, I am not here to dress up, I am here to save lives you know! Now, where is this young girl, the sooner we treat her the better, if you haven't killed her already"

She roughly pushed past Peter and Richard and on into the mill, Peter looked over at Madeleine, she had a great big smile on her face. It was clear that Sister Beverley Jane was not someone to be taken lightly. She was in charge when it came to medical matters and that was the end of any discussion she might have.

"I like confident woman Peter, don't you?"

He laughed as he turned to enter the mill, "I am quite used to confident women Madeleine, and that's a good job really as Sister Beverley seems to be on a different level"

By the time they had entered, Sister Beverley was already kneeling at the side of Adele, examining her wound and generally assessing her condition. It was clear from her calm demeanour that she was confident in her own skills and would never allow any patient to detect the slightest amount of concern.

She turned to Peter, "Go to my van and fetch my medical bag, it's behind the front seat, go on, do it now"

Taken aback somewhat, Peter turned and went outside to fetch the bag like an obedient schoolboy, "no doubt who is in charge here", he thought to himself, with a reluctant smile on his face.

Once he returned, Sister Beverley began to work on Adele, she didn't say anything other than ordering the two men outside. It was some considerable time before she joined them outside and addressed Peter and Richard. She had a concerned look on her face, it betrayed her fears as to the health of Adele.

"Right, I have managed to control the bleeding and stich up the wound in her side. She was very lucky that the bullet passed straight through without hitting anything of any consequence. However, she had lost an awful lot of blood and the risk of infection is very high. So, the next few days will be critical, to be honest, if she pulls through, I will be very surprised"

"Ok, thank you very much Sister Beverley, so what do we do next, we have to move on, we have a job to do?"

"I thought you were going to say that, so the best thing for her is care and patience, I intend to take her home with me, that's the best place for her. Things will certainly get more demanding before they get any better. I will ask around and try to find out where she lives, has she any family close by. I will make some excuse about a hunting accident, and that she would be better with me for a few days"

"We owe you a lot Sister Beverley, I hope you can be discreet about what you have seen here? As I mentioned, we have a job to do and it needs to be done, no matter the cost. If the SS get to know where we are then we will die for certain and the whole outcome of the war will be lost"

"Listen Louis, or whatever your name really is. I am not the slightest bit interested in why you are here, or what uniform you wear. I guess from your accent you are not French and the fact that your friend is wearing an RAF uniform kind of confirms that.
I don't do sides, I don't do politics and I most certainly don't do war, so don't worry, I won't be saying anything to anyone, it's no business of mine. If you have a need to complete your job here, then go forward, I will not be interfering in any way at all.

What I will ask is that you take your war and your killing away from here, far away. The needless taking of lives is repugnant to me, it is a waist of humanity and for no reason I can see which is so important. Down the track, near the sharp bend is a large black car, I guess it belonged to this girl and whomever brought her here? Take that car and leave, I assume she came with a German soldier or perhaps even an officer? Anyway, they will be looking for their own shortly, and I don't want any more shooting around here, do I make myself clear? Take the car and yourselves and leave and don't come back, if I am asked, I will say I found Adele laying at the side of the road, nothing more than that, now go"

"Thank you sister Beverley, I owe you a huge debt of gratitude, and so does Adele"

"Don't thank me, just help me get her into my van and then leave. You bring with you death and destruction, no matter what your 'job', or who you represent, your kind will always leave a trail of misery wherever you have been, and people like me are left to clear it up"

With that, she turned and returned to Adele, leaving Peter and Richard outside.

"Well, that told you Peter, these locals are a bit fierce aren't they"

"To be honest Richard, she has a point, what the hell are we doing here, shooting up the place, dead bodies everywhere, it's not some wild west movie, this is real life and death. What the hell does that young girl in there have to do with any of this, other than we managed to shoot her? Sister Beverley is right, let's just load her into the van and get away from here and soon as we can"

"But we are here, me by a twist of fate, you because you want to be, I assume you have a job to do, and they are our enemy, they started this bloody war, not us"

"Adele is not our enemy, and I don't want to be here, I am here because my boss ordered me! Do you think I am happy to abandon my wife and child for months on end, risking everything for some spurious wonder weapon and some French scientist that doesn't want to be found?

Have you any concept whatsoever of how many people have died because of me and the crazy, stupid plans I come up with. No Richard you don't, you are not there at night when I wake up thinking about the decisions I have made. If only I had done things differently then those ten people would not have died, or that father of three would be going home tonight, or the SS would not have rounded up half a dozen locals and shot them.

All of these things are real Richard, and I must live with them, they occurred because of me, if I wasn't here playing at secret agents, those people would still be alive. To be honest Rischard, I ask myself daily, what the hell am I doing here, and the answer is always the same, I don't fucking know!"

Wing Commander Richard James stared right back at Peter, he could see a tear in his eyes, and most of all, a sense of absolute despair. He wanted to talk about the cost to his own life and that of his family, about Bob Swanbourne and his wife and children. The sacrifices of the young men who had been shot to pieces or burnt to death as they plunged to earth in their burning aircraft. They were all making sacrifices, everyone, but now was not the time. He simply turned and followed Sister Beverley back into the mill and prepared to help her with young Adele.

Chapter 7.
The Journey.
May 1943.

The old Citroen van pulled away up the drive, leaving the place quiet and strangely at piece once again. It was late in the afternoon, once the German soldiers were found to be absent from their mess, the chances of search parties being sent out were ever present. Of course, they may have been booked out for 24 hours, but they couldn't take the chance, it was not impossible that they had already been missed.

The evening was warm and in direct contrast to the rain of the early morning, the evening sun warmed them, delicate red and yellow hues filled the early summer sky. Darkness was only minutes away, a decision had to be made now as to what they were going to do.

"Right", Richard James announced, "so what the hell do we do next, and let's not forget that bloody sergeant still tied up in the basement?"

"Yes, well I have a plan, and this is what we are going to do. Madeleine and I are going to take that car, drive to our target, get him or kill him and return here. In the meantime, you will guard our prisoner. Once we return, we can dump her somewhere, way out of the way, so it will take her hours to raise the alarm. Once we do that, we will drive over the border and get the second radio, call for extraction and we are gone, simple"

"Why the hell am I guarding her?"

"One, because I said so and secondly, you are dressed in an RAF uniform, not an easy thing to explain to a German patrol, don't you think?"

"I see your point old chap, what if they come looking for her?"

"There is that chance, but we will be back in 24 hours, 48 tops and then we are gone"

"Why don't we just shoot her, she is the enemy, there is no reason whatsoever why we can't"

"Except she hasn't done anything wrong, she didn't even have a gun, she is our prisoner, and the Geneva Convention says that we just can't go around shooting prisoners. No, we just dump her, out in the countryside three or four hours away from anywhere, we will be long gone by the time she summons help"

"Look Peter I still don't like this, she is our enemy, and I am certain she would kill the both of us given half a chance. However, you have a point, but let me make myself clear. If a German patrol comes anywhere near me, I will shoot her and run, don't doubt me on that score"

"OK but let's keep as low a profile as we can, I will go and talk to her, explain what will happen if she tries to run"

Peter descended into the gloomy basement, it only added to his ever-darkening mood. He didn't entirely trust Richard, not that he would do anything to deliberately risk their lives, but he was unpredictable, especially after the death of his friend in the crash. What else could he do with him, he certainly couldn't take him with them? This wasn't the greatest of plans and it was vulnerable on all sides to risk, but he couldn't come up with anything else, it would simply have to do.

Mia was sitting on one of the old wooden chairs, it looked very dusty and rather unsafe. She still had the ropes tying her hands behind her back and her ankles together, and with a gag pushed into her mouth. Peter pulled out the gag, stepped back a little and looked directly at the sergeant. She was certainly very subdued, not the ebullient woman he first met at the manor house some time ago.

"So, are you going to shoot me or just leave me here to die?"

"Neither as it happens, providing you do as you are asked then we will release you once we are finished here, you have my word on that. We need another few hours to complete our task, once done we will release you in a remote area, nothing more than that"

"And when I raise the alarm, what then?"

"We will be far from here, so it won't really be of any concern to us"

"Let me ask you Louis, did you ever figure out what Lena really was?"

"What she was, what do you mean?"

"Well that she was working for Wagnor"

"Sorry Mia, I don't know wat you mean, yes he was the commanding officer at the manor so she would be working for him?"

She started to laugh, gently at first but then increasingly louder.

"You really didn't figure that one out did you. When I say that she was working for Wagnor, I mean she was his special project, she was working directly for him. Ok, not at first, she was what she appeared to be, a young army recruit working in France, nothing more than that.

I was screwing his security chief at the manor house, we got drunk most nights and he couldn't help spilling the beans on what was going on. Wagnor never really trusted you, it was all a bit too convenient. However, he thought you were worth perusing, goodness knows what information you might have provided.

Anyway, when Oberleutnant Otto Fischer was killed, he really began to doubt you and the relationship you had with Lena, did you really set Fischer up, did you get the information from Lena?

Anyway, he set about interrogating her, she didn't actually tell Wagnor anything, but he wasn't convinced. In the end he gave her a choice, spy and report back on you and he wouldn't send her to the eastern front, she was more than happy to oblige, and I don't blame her. Things progressed between you two, but she never really got any useable information, but she stayed with it.

Anyway, as time passed by, Wagnor figured that if he was right and you were some kind of British Agent, you would eventually go back to England. If Lena could somehow convince you to take her with you, it would be a fantastic opportunity to insert a German Agent into your back yard.

So, he gave Lena a promotion and a real chance to impress her father and to make her whole family proud. She was happy to oblige, Lena was a real clever woman you know, she was not that shy impressionable young girl that she often portrayed. I think she really took you in, you bought the whole vulnerable young girl character, you were had.

I asked you where she was, I guessed you wouldn't tell me, but I wonder if she did succeed in her mission, did you actually take her back to England with you, I wonder?"

It was now Peters turn to stand open mouthed, he couldn't believe what he was hearing, if Mia was telling the truth, then he was complicit in aiding the enemy and lying about her true nationality and vouching for her. Goodness knows what she was now up to, was she playing the innocent girl character once more, enticing the security guards at the RAF base to let her go into town or worse, walk around the base. He would have to sort this mess out when he returned but heaven knows what damage Lena would do before he was able to stop her. He felt a huge surge of anger, not just at Lena but at himself for getting drawn in, how could he have been so gullible, so bloody stupid?

"Interesting story Mia, thank you for the information about Lena, but nothing changes here for me. So, when I am gone, if you create any kind of problem, this man here in the RAF uniform will shoot you, if you try to run away, he will shoot you, if you call out, he will shoot you, no questions asked. We will be back in a few hours so stay put and things will work out just fine. I will lock you in here, it's a concrete basement, with heavy doors to the surface. I will lock them and pile large stones on them, you won't be able to get out, so don't try, do you understand me?"

"I will obey, I can wait as long as you want, I need to make sure my report to Wagnor is clear, Lena succeeded"

Peter shook his head, turned and left the basement, he was so angry that he could have happily shot Mia where she sat on that old stool.

The black Citroen Sport 4 sedan was parked, just where Sister Beverly had said, around 200 yards up the track on a sharp left-hand bend. It was by now, completely dark and approaching 10pm. It was not ideal setting off at this time of night but the sooner they reached their goal and returned to the mill, the better.

Fortunately, they keys were still inside, and the tank was half full of petrol. Madeleine and Peter slid inside and readied themselves for the journey to Chênes and the prison where Claude A Durand worked. Neither of them dared to think they might succeed, they had got this far, but the rest of the journey would be the most difficult and dangerous.

"I must admit Peter, it would be very tempting to drop into the Bar Le Chat and have a glass of wine with Laurent, but I guess the SS will be watching them and that's a shame I do miss them"

Peter didn't reply, he just fixed his gaze straight ahead and drove the car down the track and into the inky blackness of the French night.

"You have been very quiet this evening Peter, is something troubling you?"

"Nothing wrong, it's been a long day and we will have a few more before we have finished. I am tired, not physically but mentally, I am sick of the fear and the uncertainty and about the games we have to play, and the deceptions played by others.

I just want to settle down and do a normal job, I want to be away from all of this, I want the war to be someone else's problem. I dream about the beyondness of things, what I really want but what I can't have.

"That's not like you Peter, despite what we do, you have always been positive, determined to succeed"

"I know Madeleine but maybe I have reached the limit or perhaps I have finally understood about what I am destined not to have"

There was a long silence as they drove through the darkness, it enveloped them in a blanket of anonymity, protected them from the outside world, at least for the meantime. They drove past the water pumping station and on towards the crossroads, near to Laurent's illegal still. The car throbbed and the heater pumped warm air into the cabin. Occasionally they hit a small pothole but otherwise, the journey was quite ordinary, much to their relief.

"Peter, I know you have your doubts, this is not your country, it's not even your war but it's what you were destined to do. It's fate, the same with me, I would rather help on my parents' farm but no, I am in the stolen car, driving to find a French scientist in a town I hardly know. We were destined to do this and given the circumstances, I couldn't think of anyone better to do it with"

He didn't respond, he hardly heard what was said, the fact that destiny had a part to play didn't make anything easier. He was a pilot, he lived and died because of his training, his judgement and skill, not because of fate. They drove on into the night, with nothing more being said, passed the disused slaughterhouse and continuing towards their destination.

Eventually they reached the outskirts of Chênes, it was not like Saint Aderald, this area had seen some bitter fighting in the first world war and much of the town had been destroyed by shelling. The town itself was now divided into two main parts, the old town which still held onto its medieval charm and the new town, which was far more modern, and featureless. Both parts occupied a relatively high and commanding position on a ridge, which explained the reason why all sides wanted to possess it in 1916.

Since then, the new town had been rebuilt but without the same character that many of the local towns still possessed. There was however still a strong community spirit and a distrust of strangers, that included anyone not from this part of France. The two main employers in the area were the large vineyard on the north of the town and the prison located to the west. Despite the war, it was a busy place, a thriving weekly market provided somewhere to meet people, talk about the state of things and buy and sell. As the approached the edge of the town, Madeleine decided it was time to break the silence. Speaking softly in her French language, she turned to Peter.

"You never really explained to me about the man you did take back to England. He turned out to be an imposter, but how did he know so much about the real Durand?"

"That's a really good question, to be honest I don't know. The general feeling is, he must have been a friend or perhaps an ex-colleague of Claude A Durand, otherwise how did he know so much? I guess Durand will be able to answer that question when we manage to see him"

"So, what happens if we can't get to see the real Durand. What happens if he simply refuses to speak to us? He might just call the local German security police and hand us in. Why would he want to help us anyway, if he wanted to continue his work, then surely he would have stayed in England in the first place?"

"I agree with you Madeleine, he knows just how important he is, and that the SS will be looking for him. If they get their hands on him, they will make him help them, or torture the information out of him, he must know this?

So why hasn't he returned to England, even if he doesn't want to continue his work, at least he will be safe there? He could live in obscurity, away from the Gestapo or the SS, in a small English village where no one knows his real name!

But, if he doesn't want to return, my orders are clear, "you bring him back or shoot him", in either case, the enemy cannot be allowed to get their hands on his work"

"Nice and simple then Peter, but nothing ever seems to go to plan around here"

"That is my main fear Madeleine, nothing ever does, and this will end up being no exception!"

Chapter 8.
Chênes.
June 1ˢᵗ, 1943.

The next morning dawned bright and clear and from the very first light the birds were about and singing. Apart from a few wispy light clouds, the sky was a deep azure blue and from their elevated viewpoint, the blue seemed to stretch on forever in all directions. This was complemented by the gently rolling French countryside, dotted with the occasional wooded area and farm building and the confluence of two rivers. In the distance, Peter could see a bright red tractor ploughing a nearby vineyard, it was an idyllic scene and one that contrasted with their mission and the job now at hand.

They had parked up during the night at the back of the water pumping station, it was no longer in use and conveniently out of the way, so not somewhere where they might have been easily found. Sleeping in the confines of the car was not ideal but at least it served a purpose and hopefully they might be on their way back to the old mill before night fall.

"I hate sleeping in cars Madeleine, it's bloody uncomfortable and you wake up feeling filthy and unkept"

Madeleine laughed, "when did you start to worry about your appearance, you have spent the last several months laying in ditches and sleeping in freezing cold cottages in the middle of nowhere. We need to find somewhere for a coffee and something for breakfast. We could even wash our faces in their toilets if we are quick, come on, let's go"

Peter looked over the front seat to where Madeleine had been sleeping in the back. She had a natural beauty, not one that needed makeup or fancy clothes, she was still lovely, despite their rather dishevelled appearance. He smiled as he looked down at her, she was a little sleepy, rubbing her eyes and stretching the stiffness from her bones.

"What are you looking at Peter Parker, I have spent the night bent double, in the middle of nowhere, in the back of a stolen car, I am not meant to look at my best"

He laughed at her grumpiness, "you look just fine Madeleine"

She looked at him and frowned, "just get the engine started, I am hungry, thirsty, dirty and rather grouchy, so let's get going"

He started the engine a carefully drove their Citroen down the rough track and back toward the main road. Eventually they reached the road and were immediately greeted with two signs, 'old Chênes' or 'new Chênes'.

"Right grumpy, which one, you choose, I have no idea where the prison is, so have a guess"

"Ok Peter, I think the prison will be in the old part of Chênes, I can imagine the dark stone dungeons, so let's go to the old town, there is bound to be a bar there"

"Ok, sounds logical, let's go and look for breakfast"

Further on they crossed a rather impressive stone bridge which straddled a fast flowing and intimidating river. It looked angry and swollen despite the dry spring, it's depths and fast flow promised doom to anyone who ventured in.

He followed the left turn, signed posted 'old Chênes' and within ten minutes they found themselves on the outskirt of a charming old French town. The cobbled streets where narrow and full of appeal, they twisted and turned as they lead up towards the oldest part of town. At times, they were claustrophobic and intimidating to drive through, the car just about able to squeeze through the tight and enclosed network, they could sense the history of people, names forgotten. It felt as if the old buildings were reaching out to them, wanting to embrace the travellers, tell them of times long ago. Eventually, they emerged into a large square, it was exhilarating to pass from the tight confines into the bright sunlight of the early morning.

"I am glad that drive is over and that we don't have a larger car, let's go and find a café Peter"

Madeleine jumped out, still with a frown on her face, she gazed about her, the sun was warming which helped her disposition. Limestone buildings surrounded the square, some two stories high but many three or even four. The whole place had a busy but calm and relaxing feel, there were several shops, two bars, and water pump in the middle. People flowed into and out of the cobbled centre, always passing the time of day with a friend or neighbour, chatting about recent events, sharing gossip about the illicit affairs of the locals.

There was a constant hum of humanity, occasional laughter and a dog barking somewhere in the distance. This was the first place of life and reality that they had been since leaving Chateau Du Beck in Belgium. She smiled and her dark mood began to lift, at least a little, it felt good to be part of the human race again.

"Right Peter Parker, you need to feed me and buy me coffee, so where are we going?"

"Well, there seem to be two options but that one there has tables outside and a rather nice smell of fresh croissants, so let's go"

They marched with purpose across the square but as soon as they entered the café, the whole place seemed to stop, everybody looked at these two strangers as they walked in. Most customers returned to what they were doing, one or two followed Peter and Madeleine as they made their way to the bar.

A very smartly dressed barman in a white apron and dark trousers greeted them, with a warm smile.

"Good morning and what can I get for you, our croissants are fresh this morning, we have chocolate, marmalade, apple and crema. Our coffee is the best in the region, and we can prepare breakfast with a baguet, eggs and even a little cured ham"

Madeleine replied immediately, "yes please all of that and can I use your washrooms"

The barman smiled, "of course madam, just over to the right, breakfast will be just a few minutes, outside in the square would be the best place to enjoy it"

Madeleine wasn't listening, she had already left for the washrooms, leaving Peter to organise the breakfast and coffees.

Eventually, both of them cleaned and tidied up, sat down in front of the bar with coffees and fresh croissants and a serving of breakfast. The day was glorious, people strolled back and forwards, no one was rushing, life was here in this moment. It was strange however, in the middle of France that today, war seemed to be a million miles away!

"So, Peter what next, we have to find the Durand guy and put our proposition to him"

"Actually, I have another idea, there is Jacques Forelle, I have never met him, but he does work in the jail. Laurent knows him, he used to be the local police in Saint Aderald, Laurent says he is a patriot and can be trusted, in between being drunk that is. If we can find him then we can get some more information about Durand, where he lives, where he drinks, so we can plan our approach. The last thing we want is for him to do a runner before we have chance to explain fully what we want"

"So how do we find this Jacques Forelle?"

"We ask in the bar, if he is a big drinker like Laurent says, they are bound to know him in there"

They finished their breakfast, it was the first proper food they had eaten in days, it certainly made Madeleine feel a whole lot better. They stood up, stretched their aching backs, and walked back into the bar, the same smartly dressed barman watched them approach.

"I hope you enjoyed your breakfast, is there anything else I can help you with?"

"Yes", Peter said in a friendly and quiet tone, "I am looking for a friend of mine, Jacques Forelle, works in the prison, used to be a policeman in Saint Aderald"

"Ah, Jacques Forelle, we know him. If you wait until tonight, you might find him in here, or any of the other bars in town. If he comes in here, he usually sits over there by the fire. He doesn't always make an appearance, I get the feeling he enjoys a drink at home, no need to drive then is there?"

"Oh, thank you but I was hoping to catch him before he had a drink or two, if you get what I mean"

The barman laughed and winked at Peter, "I do sir, in that case, you need to head out of town towards the coastal road. You turn right at the Post Office. About twenty minutes up the coast road, just before a small bridge is a turning onto a track. Follow the track, through the woods and eventually you will get to his house. It's an old farmhouse so it's well out of the way, don't give up, you will get there eventually"

"That's very kind of you, we will pay him a visit this afternoon"

"If I see him first, who should I say was asking?"

"Oh, just say we are friends of Laurent from the Bar Le Chat in Saint Aderald"

"Will do sir"

Peter paid the bill and they left, "what makes you think he will be there Peter, he most likely is at work, maybe we should ask where the Jail is?"

"No, I don't think so, I get the idea this place is gossip central, I guarantee you that within 30 minutes, everyone within ten miles of here will know exactly what has just happened. I don't want anyone knowing that we really need to find the Jail and Durand, not until we are ready. Don't forget what my orders are, find him and if he doesn't want to come back, kill him"

The car slipped between the narrow streets, the journey was no less stressful second time around. Eventually, things started to open up a little as they moved downhill, into the wealthier part of the old town. Finally, at a main T junction, they reached the post office, a large and impressive building, with a queue of people outside. They turned right as directed by the barman and proceeded up the coastal road.

It was a pleasant journey, the day had become warmer and warmer, melting their early morning resentment at sleeping in the car. The road was twisty, but the sights were impressive, the hillsides carpeted with vineyards almost as far as the eye could see. Peter almost missed the right hand turn just before the bridge but with firm use of the breaks, they stopped just in time.

They turned right down the track, it had an enclosed and somewhat relaxed feeling, the ever-present sense of nature producing a soothing balm. The track itself was well maintained, generally level with the occasional pothole in the gravel and stone surface.

"The views down towards the river are spectacular Peter, I can see why they chose this place, it's wonderful"

"It's certainly out of the way and that woodland in front of us just enhances the remoteness of the place"

The woods leading up to the house were thick, oaks and beach trees hanging over the track like guardians, observing every visitor who approached. The bright warm sun of the early June day and their initial impressions quickly disappeared, giving way to a foreboding shadowy gloom, with portents of ill and menace.

Without speaking, the two travellers watched as the track turned sharply to the right, still covered by the forest, the occasional spear of bright sunlight thrusting down to the ferns and brambles of the under growth. On and on the track continued, turning left and right, seemingly never ending. Just as they began to wonder if the barman had sent them on a wild goose chase, the darkness opened up, like the curtains on a stage as the performance began.

In front of them was the old farmhouse, it was a very impressive building, three stories high, several large windows, all with shutters, decorated the front facade. A large barn was set a few yards to the left, four steps lead up to the veranda and the double front doors.

"Wow, Peter, what does this guy do, this place is something very special"

"You are right, let's hope someone is home, if not, we wait"

They drew up on the gravel pathway in front of the house. They both exited the car at the same time, surveying the magnificence of the house and the woodlands. There was a damp but sweet smell in the air, and a silence as the trees muffled all but the local sounds of nature. This place had a certain power and presence about it, perhaps it was the gently rustling forest or the house with its size and splendour.

Peter lead the way up the steps onto the veranda, "well I suppose I better knock"

He lifted the large brass knocker in the shape of a lion's head and knocked twice on the heavy oak door. There was no response, so he knocked again, this time a little harder. There was still no response, he knocked for a third time but still to no avail.

"Looks like we have drawn a blank, there is no one in, I should have guessed by the time of day, let's have a walk around, someone will tun up eventually"

Just as they were turning to walk away there came a voice from somewhere beyond the door, a woman's voice, "just wait a second please"

After a few more minutes, there was a noise of locks being undone and eventually, the catch opening, as the door finally swung inwards. In the doorway stood a woman, in her forties, dressed informally in a brown woollen sweater, a green cotton skirt, and strangely, she wasn't wearing any shoes. She had long auburn hair and dark brown eyes, rather tall, perhaps almost as tall as Peter. She was slim and classically attractive, with fine features, the kind of person who always looked good at any time of the day.

She did however look somewhat flustered, as if she had been interrupted, unexpectedly shaken from what she had been doing. She shook her head and with her fingers drew her hair back over her shoulders. Brushing herself down she looked at Peter, then at Madeleine and finally back at Peter again.

"Yes, can I help?"

"Sorry to intrude", Peter said, "but we are looking for an old friend and we have been told he lives here, Jacques Forelle?"

"Erm yes, I am Mrs Forelle, I am afraid that Jacques is at work, he should be home around six this evening, it would be better is you called back then. Who should I say was looking for him?"

"We are friends from way back, when he was a Police officer in Saint Aderald, we are friends of Laurent from the Bar Le Chat"

"Right, I will tell him, it's best if you come back later, I am cleaning at the moment, so you can't come in"

"That's ok Mrs Forelle, we didn't mean to intrude, we will call by again this evening"

Without another word, she slammed the oak door closed, threw the bolts back into position leaving Madeleine and Peter standing on the veranda. Without saying anything, they both turned and walked back to the car, opened the doors and got inside.

"That was a bit odd Madeleine, I didn't expect to be invited in, but she just slammed the door in our faces"

Madeleine started to giggle then laugh out loud, "oh Peter, sometimes you are so naive"

"Why, what have I missed?"

She laughed again, "right, she is a very attractive and clearly quite a sophisticated woman, but she was dressed in an old brown sweater and a green skirt, a green skirt Peter! She looked like she had been dragged through a hedge backwards, she had no shoes on and no bra, and she slammed the door in our faces, what do you think was going on"

"Erm, sorry, she was cleaning?"

"Peter, start the car and let's drive away and I will explain"

They began the drive, back through the dark forest of might oak and beach before immerging back into the bright sunshine of a June afternoon.

"Right Madeleine, what on earth are you talking about?"

"She had a man in there, we interrupted her and him, she threw on whatever clothes came to hand and in panic that perhaps this was her husband returning from work opened the door. So, she ended up running downstairs with no shoes on, no underwear and in complete dread"

"Oh, I see, I wonder who that was then?"

"Goodness only knows, it could be anyone from the local population, let's call back this evening and talk to Jacques Forelle"

Actually Madeleine, I wonder if we should go and find out, I do like knowing things about people, especially those who I might need in the future"

"Oh right, so we just pop back and ask her?"

"No, we go and hide in the forest, no one will see us. We drive back, park the car on one of those tracks and sit in the woods for a while.

Shouldn't be difficult to spot who it is, and given the shock that we just gave her, I guess that won't be too long before they leave"

"But what if we are seen Peter?"

"We won't be, let's turn around, we might not have a lot of time"

He quickly spun the car around and headed back into the forest, kicking up a whirl of grey dust as they sped off back the way they came. It didn't take more than five minutes to find a hiding place for the car, just off one of the tracks in a glade, dark and hidden.

Moving quickly through the woodland they found a place where they could easily observe the comings and more importantly outgoings from the old farmhouse. Their hiding place was at the junction of two tracks a few hundred yards from the house itself.

"Right, let's settle down and see who appears, I bet it won't take long"

"It better not Peter these dam mosquitos are becoming a nuisance"

They were sat in the undergrowth for what seemed like an age, the mosquitoes buzzed about their heads, occasionally biting, forever tormenting them. Peters prediction of a quick exit was not even close, it seemed like hours before the heard a heavy wooden door close and a car engine start.

Madeleine leant over to whisper in Peters ear, "I didn't see a car when we went to the house?"

"Must have been parked around the back, there is certainly plenty of space, you could hide a whole tank squadron around here"

"I still don't see the reasoning behind this, it's bound to be some local, we won't have a clue who it is, what use is that going to be?"

"You are right of course but at least we can pretend to Mrs Forelle that we do know who it is, she won't know any different. If for any reason we need her help or some information from her, that info on her lover might prove useful, even if it's just a bluff.

Don't forget her husband holds the key to Doctor Claude A Durand, where he lives, how we get to see him, who he actually is, if her husband doesn't want to play, maybe Mrs Forelle could bring some pressure to bear"

"I guess it might help, I don't suppose it will do any harm"

"Correct, now heads up, here he comes"

The whining of a gearbox and gentle hum of an engine came closer, they both crouched as low as possible, keeping their eyes locked on the track leading from the house. Closer and closer the car came, it was almost upon them now, Mrs Forelle might come to regret her indiscretions before this mission had come to an end, only time and fete will tell.

They caught their first glimpse of a vehicle, it was black, rather grand, an impressive set of chrome headlights and radiator glistened in the evening sunshine. Closer, it was almost upon them, Peter could just about make out the shape of the driver, he was alone. Mrs Forelle had said her goodbyes, no doubt happy that she had remained undiscovered.

It was just about at the turn, "keep still don't move, we must remain hidden for this to work".

The car was no more than a few yards away now, it made the left hand turn on its way out of the forest and off towards the main road. Just as it glided past where they were crouched in the thick carpet of ferns and young saplings, Peter managed to identify the driver. As he did so, the shock made his head throb and his blood run cold, he gasped in absolute incredulity, almost falling over.

Madeleine spun her head around to face Peter, his whole visage was a pale grey, the blood had visibly drained from his face. His eyes were wide open, pupils were large black circles in his blue eyes. He turned to face Madeleine, his mouth wide open.

"Peter who is it, who was that man?"

"Madeleine, I don't believe it, it can't be him, it can't"

"Can't be who Peter, I have never seen him before, who was it?"

"No, how the hell did this happen, how did they meet, bloody hell, if he knows who she is, then we have a massive problem, he is only one step from Claude A Durand! Madeleine, the war, victory, we have to do something about this soon, very soon"

"Peter, for goodness sakes, answer me, who is it, who was that man?"

Chapter 9.
The Old Watermill.
June 2nd, 1943.

Wing commander Richard James ran through the woods surrounding the old water mill, his head was pounding, he could hardly breath. He turned left then right, perhaps he could hear something, maybe not. The whole world seemed to be whirling around in front of him and there was nothing he could do to stop it.

"How the hell did she escape, bloody hell, I need to find her quick"

His prisoner, sergeant Mia had somehow managed to get away from the concrete basement of the water mill. If she should find help then he would be lost, the German forces could arrive at any moment. Not only that, but if they questioned him about Peter and Madeleine, they might be able to force out of him when they might return.

"I had one job to do, and I blew it, she bloody tricked me, conditioned me into thinking she would not do a runner. How dam stupid am I, what was I thinking?"

He had no idea when she had escaped, she had lulled him into a false sense of security. The last time he checked her was over three hours ago, she could be anywhere by now.

He stopped running and bent over, hands on his knees, he tried to stop himself from hyperventilating. He stared down at the green grass, what a mess, if only he had done his job, followed the instructions Peter had given him.

"Right, stop running around like a startled rabbit and think. She has gone, she could be miles away by now, she might be on her way back with half a dozen soldiers, guns loaded. I won't be able to find her, of that I am sure, so I must try and evade whatever she sets loose.

So, when they come to find me, I need to be somewhere else, can't go far, not on foot and wearing an RAF uniform. I need somewhere to hide, I need to be able to contact the other two, tell them to stay away, or they will be caught"

He wracked his brains to try and come up with some kind of plan but to no avail. He was totally alone, beyond anything he knew, there was no one and nothing he could call on to help him.

He eventually left the track and started wandering through the woods and finally came upon the access road to the mill. He could see the tyre tracks in the mud that had been left when Peter and Madeleine had driven away in the car.

"Bloody idiot, I have really screwed this up. We might all die because of my stupidity…….."

Before he could finish talking to himself, he heard the faint noise of a vehicle approaching.

"Shit, this is it, they have come to get me"

The vehicle came closer and closer, down the access track, towards the old mill. He dived into the thicket and young trees to his left in an attempt to hide. He knew this was largely useless as they would probably have dogs and would find him in seconds.

Closer and closer, he could hear it engine popping, occasionally back firing. He gazed up the track and noticed a grey-white smoke trail coming ever closer.

"I know who that vehicle belongs to, it couldn't be anyone else, it's Sister Beverley Jane, I am certain, well to be honest, I hope!"

Despite the clawing brambles and nettles, he readied himself to jump out and stop Sister Beverley, if it was indeed her. The vehicle came closer and closer, followed by the plume of oily smoke and rattling engine.

"It must be her, here we go"

He jumped out in front of the old van, causing it to screech to a stop and slide slightly from left to right. It was indeed the good Sister, Richard dashed around to the driver's door, Sister Beverly wound down the window.

She had a rather perplexed and perhaps a somewhat irritated look on her face. She glared at Richard as he approached the side of the vehicle, shaking her head as he did so.

"Clearly you want to get run over, I assume?"

"Sorry Sister, but I need some help, you see I have lost the prisoner and the Germans will be here at any moment and then I am doomed. Also........"

"Stop, stop, stop, what the heck are you talking about, what prisoner?"

"The German woman, we were holding her in the basement, but she has escaped and it's my fault. No doubt she will summon help and then I will end up in custody. Also, my two companions, when they come back to pick me up, they will be caught as well"

"Sorry young man, I am still not fully understanding you, can I assume the German woman was part of the group of people that the French girl belonged to?"

"Yes Sister, we got involved in a dust up with them, that was my fault, I shouldn't have fired first"

"This is getting more and more complicated, can we just skip that bit and let me concentrate on what I do know, before the Germans or anyone else turns up and jumps out at me"

"Certainly, Sister but you need to get me out of here and soon"

"Look, can we start again. I came to tell you about the French girl, she is back with her parents. I told them she was involved in a hunting accident. I said I found her by the side of the road, a stray bullet must have caught her, good job I had been passing. She won't tell her parents about the relationship with the German soldier, so I think that will be fine. She will be back on her feet in a few weeks, no real harm done hey"

"That good news Sister Beverley but you need to get me out of here"

"Right, can we get something absolutely straight. I don't care what uniform you are wearing or which language you speak, I don't take sides, I am here to help the sick, no matter where they come from.

To that end, I can't take sides or do anything that doesn't involve my main calling in life, which is helping the sick. If you want a lift, I could do that because you are in need but hiding you away would jeopardise what I do, it means me taking side, can't you see that?"

"Sister, please I am in need, if the Germans get me, I am done for and so are my friends. Can't you see that we are the good guys here, not the local SS?"

"Oh, I fully understand what you are saying but the truth still remains, I cannot take sides. You think you are the good guys, but I am sure that the local occupying forces think they are the good guys in the same way!

Don't you see that I am here to help anyone who calls upon me, it's God's work that I do, not the work of the RAF, the German army, the SS or anyone else for that matter"

"So, you are not going to help me then?"

"I will give you a lift because I am going home but I am afraid I won't do any more than that"

Richard looked despairingly at Sister Beverley Jane, he couldn't think of what else to say. He was desperate to get away, at least she would help with that.

"Ok, ok, get me out of here before the local SS hove into view"

He swung around to the other side of the rusty old van and jumped in. The van was somewhat smelly, the seats thread bear, with metal frames poking through, they were very uncomfortable but at least he was getting away from the old mill. Sister Beverley turned the old van around and headed back to the main road. Richard was half expecting to see an SS vehicle come the other way at any moment, he was constantly turning his head, peering into the distance, trying to see if anything was approaching.

To his great relief, they managed to get to the main road without being stopped. Sister

Beverley turned right and amongst considerable complaint from the old van's engine, moved off in the direction of her house.

"I hope you understand me, Mr RAF but I don't have any choice"

"The name is James, Wing Commander Richard James. No quite frankly, I don't understand you. You could be helping people who would always do you harm as and when they choose to. If they win this war, then people like you will come to regret losing the freedoms you used to take for granted. Of course, it will be too late by then but don't say I didn't warn you Sister"

"I understand what you are saying Wing Commander but it's Gods and my life's work and I can not deviate from my oath to help others, no matter which side they represent"

The rest of the journey was conducted in complete silence, Richard James felt frustrated and understood little of what Sister Beverley was saying. He had lost many friends and colleagues, including Bob Swanbourne in this war, what she was saying simply didn't make any sense to him.

It fell to him to write those letters to families telling of how bravely your son or husband had died. Those anonymous correspondences that would drop through a letter box and change someone's life and not for the better. The worst part about it was he hardly knew any of them, if at all. They had died in a blazing cockpit, somewhere over occupied Europe, and for what exactly, so someone else could take their place, just another potential anonymous letter to write.

The problem was, he didn't see an end to any of this, the war had been raging for four years and nothing much had changed, except the people actually fighting in it. They had changed, they had become broken and cold, inhuman, a waisted life, perhaps even a pointless death.

Maybe Sister Beverley was right, just do what you do and don't ask any questions, don't take sides, don't have a favourite, just live your life. Perhaps that was the answer, the trouble was, the other side didn't see it that way, so you had to fight. The paradox was of course, he was doing what he thought was moral and justified, just the same as Sister Beverley, but who was doing the right thing?

It wasn't too long before they reached a driveway to a house on the left, "this is my place, sorry Wing Commander but this is where we go our separate ways. If you continue up the road, you will come to a footpath on your left. This will take you across country and away from the old mill"

"Thank you, Sister, please can I ask you one last favour. I have no food or water, I haven't even got any civilian clothes, please can you help. I will be away from your home in a few minutes but please, I need a little assistance"

She turned to look at Richard and thought for a moment.

"Ok, I have some bread and cheese, you are welcome to that, I could help with a couple of empty wine bottles, you could fill them with water, they will last you. I don't have any clothes to spare, unless you want my old Nun's habits?"

They both smiled, "thank you Sister Beverley at least the food and water that will be most welcome, but not the habits of course. For what it's worth, I greatly admire your strength of purpose and values, maybe we all need to have the same ideals, it might help, perhaps"

Sister Beverley crunched the van back into gear and turned up her drive, her house was some distance away, a rather modest affair, single story, white clapboards with a large vegetable patch to the front. The track leading up to the house was dusty and covered in potholes, some deeper that others but the whole place had a calm and dignified air about it.

Eventually, they arrived at the front of the house, the old van spluttering and coughing to an undignified stop.

"Right Wing Commander, follow me, the kitchen is around the back, I will sort you out some food and water and then you can be on your way"

"Thank you, Sister, I very much appreciate it, I will leave immediately"

He followed Sister Beverley around to the back of the house and that's where the whole situation changed. As they rounded the corner of the house, they were met by four German soldiers, one of them holding a large and very aggressive German Shepard on a lead. They all stopped and stared, it was clear that none of them expected this situation to happen. Before anyone could react, the dog started to bark manically, pulling at the lead, bearing its vicious looking teeth.

The older of the four soldiers stepped forward holding a Luger pistol in front of him.

"Ah, I assume you are the missing RAF pilot, the one who shot our comrades, put your hands above your head and kneel on the ground"

As he was saying this, the other three unshouldered their rifles and loaded a bullet into the chamber with a sharp 'click, click'.

"May I ask the lady who she is?"

"I am Sister Beverley Jane, I was simply providing this man with some food and water before he went on his way. This would be the same humanity I would offer anyone who asked, including yourselves"

"I have heard of you Sister Beverley and the charitable works you undertake. Unfortunately, this man is a serving RAF Officer, and he is guilty of murder and as far as I can see, you are helping him, possibly to escape"

At this point Richard James spoke out, even risking reprisals for doing so.

"Listen, she is nothing to do with any of this, she gave me a lift and said she would give me some food before I went on my way, she is totally innocent"

"Well, we will let Hauptman Wagnor decide that, so far as I can see she was helping him but that will all come out in the interrogation, now, come with me"

The four soldiers marched Sister Beverley and Richard James to a track a little north of the house where was parked a military lorry. They searched them, removed Richard's gun and tied their hands behind their backs, forcing them up into the back of the lorry. Two of the guards jumped into the back with them, including the dog handler.

"Sister Beverley, I am so sorry, I didn't mean for this to happen"

"Richard, it was my decision, I offered help, don't blame yourself, it all part of the great plan, don't worry"

She smiled at Richard which to be honest, just made the situation worse. He looked down at the floor of the lorry, he didn't have to courage to look her in the eyes. He would probably end up being shot for what he had done and so would she, and she just smiled at him.

The lorry rocked from side to side as it made its way to the manor house and their appointment with Hauptman Wagnor. The journey went on for some considerable time, bouncing from side to side, turning left and then right. They occasionally came to a stop, sometimes the engine would be switched off and the soldiers left the cab. They could hear talking outside, but Richards German was woefully lacking so he had no real idea what they were talking about. On one occasion, the dog handler with his dog exited the lorry before returning some moments later.

Richard looked across at Sister Beverley, "it would seem that they are having some trouble with the engine Richard, perhaps we will be walking to our destination before the day is out"

Again they stopped, this time there was a smell of burning oil, it would seem that this was the end of their transport, as for their location, neither Sister Beverley nor Richard James had the slightest clue. The rear tarpaulin opened once more, and the older soldier peered in.

"Out, you need to get out, we walk from here, the truck is broken, do you understand?"

They jumped, rather awkwardly down from the back of the truck, the bright sunlight stung their eyes, causing them to squint against the glare. They were parked on a normal looking road, there was a bridge to their left with a large river flowing under. A wood was at their backs and open farmland in front. To the side of the road was a sign, 'rail station', it pointed out towards the bridge.

"Right, I will untie your hands and we will walk to the manor house. One false move and you will be shot, do I make myself clear?"

He untied their hands and pushed them forward, without another word they started to move off down the road towards their destination. They had taken no more than ten steps when a crack, crack rang out from somewhere behind them. Again, another crack and a whizzing sound as a bullet passed right by Richard's head. The bullet passed so close to him that he felt the heat and the pressure as it flew by.

"Get down Sister Beverley, in the ditch, get down"

She didn't need to be asked twice, she dived into the ditch, followed by Richard. He landed right on top of her, excusing himself for doing so. Several more rounds went off, followed by an explosion and then another burst from a machine gun.

Richard peered out above the top of the ditch, the lorry was now ablaze, two of the German soldiers lay in a large pool of blood just in front of where the truck was parked. There were three other bodies, dressed in workman's clothes, two laying in the field opposite and one in the middle of the road. Two bullets hit the road just in front of him, the shards of tarmac and some dust flew in his direction. The dust made him cough and blinded him momentarily. He felt a hand grip his ankle, it was Sister Beverley, she was dragging him back down into the ditch.

"Get down Richard, it's the local Resistance, they are attacking, they won't know about us, they will shoot anything that moves, you must stay down until they tell us otherwise"

Richards tried to look at Sister Beverley, but his eyesight had been compromised by the dust, he blinked repeatedly and tried to rub the irritation away. Meanwhile, the fighting continued. A scream rang out, a deep bloodcurdling scream, despite Richard experiences as a pilot, this noise chilled him to the bone, he wanted to put his hands up over his ears, block out the agony of this other human being.

More shooting, bullets flying over the ditch, thudding into the earth behind them.

"Sister, we need to get out of this, we need to move away down the ditch and try and put some distance between us and this kill zone"

She didn't hesitate, turning to her right she started to crawl away as fast as she could. Richard followed, he wanted to look around, but he dared not, just in case someone was just about to put a bullet in the back of his head.

"Keep going Sister, we might get away unnoticed, just keep going"

The sound of the fighting reduced a little, but it still seemed very close by. However, the intensity had slowed somewhat, instead of the continuous firing, it was more sporadic. Eventually, it stopped altogether, the piece of the French countryside returned, Richard even noticed a lark flying overhead.

"Sister, I am going to have a look, try and see what's going on, who the hell is doing all the fighting"

As slowly as he could, he peered over the rim of the ditch, they had moved further away from the fighting than he had realised, but they were not so far away that they could make a run for it. The German lorry was by now fully ablaze, the tyres popping and making a screeching sound as they burned. The tarpaulin back cover was burning and pieces of it drifted away into the sky, issuing black dense smoke as they did so.

There didn't seem any sign of movement, he could still see the two dead soldiers laying in the pool of blood but no one else.

"What can you see Richard, what's happening?"

Before he had a chance to reply, he heard the familiar, click, click sound of a rifle cocking behind him. "Bloody schoolboy error Richard' as he chastised himself, "check who is behind you first"

He dared not turn around, if it was a German soldier they were done for, if it was the local Resistance then they might have a chance for survival. Before he had a chance to face whomever it was with the rifle, Sister Beverley Jane started to speak.

"Ah Pierre, I thought this would have something to do with you, how the heck did you know the Germans had us?"

"We didn't Sister, well not at first, we followed the truck out of the manor house, the plan was to hijack it, kill the Germans and steal the truck. We followed them waiting for a quiet place, well out of the way before we made our move. Eventually, we ended up all the way out at your place, we wondered what they were up to? We thought we would hang back until we had a better idea, might be useful intelligence perhaps?

Then we saw you and the RAF man get captured and loaded up, so we thought we would wait and pounce at the right place, somewhere where the gunfire couldn't be heard. As luck would have it, the truck began to break down, so why try and stop it, just wait until it stops itself.

Anyway, Sister Beverley here we are, and more than happy to rescue a woman of the cloth, I hope your God will reward us for that, we could do with some salvation? Who is your friend the RAF man, what is he called?"

"My name is Richard James, Wing Commander Richard James RAF. Who may I ask are you?"

The man standing in front of Richard was a very tall, slightly built man of about thirty years, perhaps a little younger. He had slicked back dark brown hair and a few days' worth of stubble growing on his tanned face. He was dressed in a blue cotton shirt, and dirty blue jeans with strong looking brown leather boots.

"My name is Pierre, I am the leader of the local Resistance. I would not normally tell a stranger this but since you and Sister Beverley are clearly friends, I feel confident that you will keep this information secret and if you don't, I will kill you anyway.

Over there, by the dead Germans is Monique, she is my lieutenant and the strongest fighter in all of France. Standing with her is Marcel, they are cousins, and he is a genius at making explosives and planting bombs. Unfortunately, we have lost two brave fighters in today's attack, but we are still happy with our days work.

We have killed the four Germans, unfortunately we did not manage to take the truck but there are plenty more like that. What is your story RAF, why are you here?"

Richard looked about at the scene of total destruction, the two people Pierre spoke about stood, rifles slung over their shoulders, laughing and joking by the burning truck. The woman was in her early forties, she had long auburn hair and was dressed in clothes similar to Pierre. She looked self assured, and confident, she had an air of strength and mental toughness, Richard could clearly see why Pierre thought she was the best fighter in all of France.

The other man, Marcel, was far more diminutive in height but stocky in build, again dressed in workman's clothes. His expression was one of aggression, perhaps borne of the current situation, only time would tell.

"I was shot down by a couple of FW 190's, didn't see them coming, I can't believe they got the better of me, stupid error. Worse of it is that my navigator bought it, I had to leave him in the bloody field, I hope they buried him properly?"

Pierre just stared back into the ditch at Richard, "you can't trust the local SS, maybe they did, maybe not. We have lost two brave fighters today, we will bury them with the greatest of honour, they are heroes of France. We have loaded them into the back of our van, we must leave here soon, the SS will no doubt have seen the smoke and will send out a patrol, you must come"

They all crammed into the silver van, similar to, but in much better condition than Sister Beverley's. They sped off at a rather alarming rate across the local countryside, to where, Richard knew not. They raced over bumps, turned many corners, almost turning the van onto its roof.

With them in the back of the van were Marcel, and sadly the bodies of the two dead Resistance fighters, they were covered with a dirty grey sheet. Despite the sadness of the situation, Sister Beverley and Marcel chatted away as if they were old friends, laughing and joking. It became evident to him that this was just part of life out here, death stalked them every day. He felt much the same about his life as a pilot, the difference was, his dead comrades never came back, and so he rarely if ever had the chance to say goodbye!

Richard tapped her on the arm, "you obviously know these people"

"I know them very well, I have helped them on more than one occasion, it's God's work you know"

"I thought you didn't get involved or take sides"

"These people are in need, and they fight for what they think is right, I help them, that's not taking sides, is it?"

She winked at Richard and smiled, it was clear to him that Sister Beverley Jane was not as impartial as she first made out to be.

"Then why did you tell me all that stuff about being impartial, not helping anyone unless they had a medical need, treating everyone the same, not taking sides?"

"Well, I had to be sure who I was dealing with Richard. If you had continued on your journey and had been captured by the Germans, which would have been certain, then I would have just been a Catholic Sister who helped anyone, no real news to the local SS"

"So, you are not that person then?"

"It depends on what questions you are asking. I am a woman who works in the community, I will help anyone in medical need, I am a qualified nurse and midwife. I am a Sister in a Catholic Order who has taken a vow to help others, live a life of chastity and poverty. I am not a member of the French Resistance, but there is nothing that says I can't help them out, well help them out quite a lot, is there?"

She smiled again, tapping Richard on his leg, "don't worry, you are with friends, you are safe now"

'Where are they taking us?"

"They said to a disused slaughterhouse to the north of Saint Aderald, we should be safe there, at least for the meantime. The reason the Germans were out searching was three of their comrades were missing, two men and a woman, they didn't return to the manor house when expected. Well, I guess we know the reason for that, don't we Richard!

We need to keep a low profile for a while, we could return to my place I guess but we don't know why they appeared there, maybe they think I was up to something, perhaps it was just bad luck on our part. However, if they were looking for something specific at my house, or someone, they will be back, of that I am certain"

Chapter 10.
The bar in Chênes.
June 2nd, 1943.

It was very early in the morning back in the bar in Chênes, despite the hour, the place was very busy indeed. Several men pushed wooden carts past the café, they were laden with various produce, some with local vegetables, some fruit, others had clothes, leather belts, one old rather worn-out cart contained several pairs of second-hand shoes.

"It must be market day", announced Peter, it's going to get busy around here, that's good cover for us. We also need to get this job done, we can't leave Richard James any longer, we really need to get back there today or tomorrow at the latest"

"And let me add, that there is no way, Peter Parker, that we are spending a third night sleeping in that dam car either. You are right Peter, a busy market day is perfect cover, people going about their business not really caring about anyone else.

Also, about the man who we saw yesterday, are you sure Peter, are you sure it was him at Jacques Forelle's house in the woods?"

"Oh yes, I am absolutely certain, it was Hauptman Karl Wagnor, the Officer in charge of the local German SS at the manor house, near to Saint Aderald. He must be having an affair with the wife of Jacques Forelle, this makes the whole operation 100% more dangerous, if he sees us, we are dead for certain"

"Does he know that Jacques Forelle works with Doctor Claude A Durand, does he know what information we have, that Doctor Durand is the French scientist that everyone wants to get their hands on?"

No, if Wagnor even slightly suspected who the Chief Warden of the local jail really was, he would send twenty heavily armed men to grab him. He could then spend the next week torturing the information out of him.

We, on the other hand, have to slowly get close to Doctor Durand, we have no choice. If we spook him, he could just run, and we have no chance of stopping him. We need to be careful, need to use some diplomacy and stealth. He has to be persuaded to come back to England with us, there is no way we can make him.

I don't think Wagnor has any idea who Doctor Claude A Durand really is, the trouble is, Wagnor is very close, one wrong word from the wife of Jacques Forelle might give him a clue, or if he sees us in this area, he might well start putting one and one together. The Germans have been on the hunt for Durand for months and months,

Wagnor is only too aware of how important this man really is"

"I assume that Doctor Durand is not using his real name?"

"I don't doubt it, but I have a very accurate description of him, a patch hiding a completely white eye, and Jacques Forelle made mention of such a man to Laurent from the Bar le Chat, and that he was the boss at the local prison, there can't be many men like that around here"

"So, what the hell do we do next, chance a visit to Jacques Forelle's house and hope that Wagnor doesn't turn up?"

"I can't see any other way out of this. If we go knocking on the prison gates and ask to see the Chief Warden, I don't think that will do any good at all. We need Jacques Forelle to get us in with Durand, perhaps tell us where he lives, corner him.

We go this morning, we try and see Jacques Forelle, if he is not there, then ask his wife when he will be back. We can't wait until he makes an appearance here at this or any other bar, we need to sort this today"

"Then let's go Peter, no time like the present"

Chapter 11.
The office of SS head, Hauptman Karl Wagnor
The manor house, near Saint Aderald.
June 2nd, 1943.

There was a knock on the door of Hauptman Karl Wagnor, he ignored it, hardly looking up from his paperwork. The knock came again, this time a little firmer.

"Come in but it better be very important"

The door slowly opened, a tall slim man in an immaculate SS lieutenants uniform entered. He had a shock of light blonde hair, deep blue eyes and a very pock marked face. He marched in very formally, stood to attention and waited for Wagnor to look up.

"What is it Schneider, I am very busy?"

Lieutenant Schneider, the new head of the security office, drew himself up into a rigid frame, looking directly over Wagnor's head.

"Sir, we have a report from Berlin, from the Security Service, they have been contacted by an operative in England. The operative gave the correct code name and it's one that was issued by yourself sir"

Wagnor looked up, with a rather puzzled look on his face. He reached for his silver cigarette case on his desk, taking one plain cigarette out, slowly putting it between his lips and lighting it. The red glow appeared as did the first whisps of smoke, after inhaling, he blew it upwards towards the ceiling.

"That's interesting Schneider, I wasn't expecting any contact from my operative over there so soon. It was supposed to be more of an undercover mission, report anything significant, if not, kill the British agent she went over there with"

"How did the operative contact Berlin Hauptman Wagnor, did you issue a radio?"

"No, she was issued several coded letters, addressed to a business in Paris, obviously run by our own Security Service. I am surprised the British let the letter through, they are becoming arrogant and complacent Schneider, typical British overconfidence"

"Well, it worked sir, I have the report here, should I read it?"

"Go ahead Schneider, be my guest"

"Yes sir, it reads,

Am at large in England.

Many airfields in this location, will report on significant movements.

British agent, code name Louis Dubois, real name Peter Parker is back in France, believed your location.

Reason for Parkers return unknown.

I will kill Parker when he returns to England if you are unable in France"

"That's it sir, that's the end of the communication"

"Interesting, I am surprised he is back here, whatever he is risking his life for must be very, very important"

Wagnor pushed back into his leather chair, swinging it around to view out of the large bay window. He drew several more times on his cigarette before speaking again.

"So, what the hell are you up to Louis, or should I say Peter Parker, what has brought you back here so soon? There are many important things to be going on with, this is war, so why here? I know you, some of my staff know you, one false move and you will be dead, it's a suicide mission surely? What is that important Mr Parker, what makes you risk certain death with such alacrity?"

He slowly spun his large leather chair back to face Schneider, looking slowly up into his eyes with a large beaming smile on his face.

"As you know, I have had a rather pleasant afternoon Schneider away from here, erm how can I say, entertaining, yes, very entertaining, you might even say fun. So, in order to keep my mood happy, what have you got in that dark little office of yours that might unlock this conundrum?

Why would a British agent risk his life by returning, so soon after escaping, especially since I know him so well, it doesn't make sense, what is so important?"

Schneider thought for a while, looking left and right, attempting to bring some resolution to the issue.

"It's difficult to say sir, troop movements, there is a large army base not far from here, we are not far from the Belgium border, perhaps that has something to do with it? Maybe the British think we are up to something that we are not, but all of that could be taken care of with local informants and reconnaissance flights by the RAF. I apologise Hauptman Wagnor, but I am at a loss to offer any reasoned explanation!"

"No. it's something far more important than that kind of day-to-day thing, they would use the local Resistance fighters to report back on troop movements. No, there must be something else, we are missing something here Schneider, why is he back?"

"Nothing in particular comes to mind sir. There is the plan to expand the railway in order to get troops to the coast more quickly, in case of invasion but that's only a plan at this time. There was some talk about a new airbase next to the army base, there has been several Allied aircraft shot down around here, perhaps he is evacuating downed airmen?"

"No, no Schneider, none of that is important enough to bring him back here. I need you to do three things and do them quickly. Firstly, find out where he is, I don't care what you do or who you torture but find out. Secondly, find out why he is here, there is something we are overlooking, I am sure of it. Thirdly, if Berlin get any more communications from my agent, they must get that communication to us directly, no delays, do I make myself clear?"

"Yes sir, perfectly clear, I need to know the name of your agent sir, so I can expedite your orders with Berlin"

"Yes, good point, her code name is 'Little Bird', her real name is Lena, Lena Webber"

Chapter 12.
Jacques Forelle's house
June 2nd, 1943.

The evening had started to draw in, it wasn't particularly warm, perhaps there was a suggestion of rain in the next few hours. They had decided to wait until later in the day, the chances of coming across Wagnor would therefore be considerably reduced.

They had parked on the main coastal road, just over the bridge after the turning to the home of Mr and Mrs Jacques Forelle. The darkness wasn't helping them see anything, but they were waiting for him to return from work. It was only a guess of course but this time of day seemed normal for the locals to travel home.

"What happens if he doesn't appear Peter, do we just go and knock on the door again?"

"Well, he must arrive at some point, he can't stay away for ever, even if he has a few beers on his way home"

They both sat back and waited, one or two cars passed by a tractor and several men on bicycles but there was no sign of Jacques Forelle. Late evening had by now turned into night, and it was very dark indeed where they were parked by the river.

The first spits of rain dropped onto the windscreen of the car, there was a slight pitter patter on the metal roof as the rain began to increase in intensity. With the rain came a drop in temperature, it was becoming markedly cooler in the car, sending shivers through their bodies.

"Peter, I can't take this much longer, why don't we go and knock on his door, try to find out where he is. If not, I am sure we can go back to town and search the local bars, he is bound to show up sooner or later"

Peter began to tap the steering wheel of the car, "right, let's go and knock on his door, see what his wife has to say"

"I won't argue with that plan Peter"

Peter started the car and gently eased it into gear, cautiously driving over the bridge and turning left down the track towards the house. It seemed a wholly different place at night, the dark overhanging trees had now been enveloped by the night. The only visible things were those illuminated by the headlights of the car. It was a criss crossed picture of low hanging branches and the undergrowth, without any colour other than the slight yellow light cast by the headlights of the car.

It seemed to take a whole lot longer to reach the house in the darkness, maybe Peter had been driving slowly, maybe the night had changed the perception of time. Eventually though, they reached the house, just as the rain turned into a heavy deluge, hammering on the metal body and glass screens of their car.

"That rain is going to soak us Peter, maybe we wait a while before getting out?"

"Not a bad idea Madeleine but I am not sure anyone is in, the place is in complete darkness. I wonder if we had missed them both, perhaps they are in town somewhere?"

"I think we should try before we leave, I am cold tired and very hungry, let's not totally waist the day"

Without speaking, Peter through his door open, jumped out of the car and ran towards the house, turning his collar up as he ran. It took only a few seconds for him to reach the veranda and rest bite from the heavy rain. Madeleine watched him brush down his coat, turn his collar back down and knock firmly on the door.

She could just about make out what was happening in the dim lights of the car. As he knocked for the second time on the door, it appeared to gently swing open. At first, she thought someone had answered but Peter just turned and beckoned her towards him.

As she exited the car, he shouted something at her, penetrating the cold, wet darkness of the night.

"The torch, get the torch from the boot"

Without questioning him, she moved quickly round the back of the car, opened the boot and fished around in the darkness for the torch. Eventually, she hit upon a cold, hard cylindrical object, she instinctively grabbed it and turned to runt through the rain, towards the house.

"I have the torch Peter, why do you need it, is the power out?"

"No, there doesn't seem to be anyone in, and the door was left unlocked, I am sure it just my suspicious mind, but something doesn't seem quite right"

Madeleine looked up at Peter, she was even more cold and shivery than she was in the car, but those sensations quickly seemed to disappear. All she could sense was her heart beating and weakness in her knees. There was an odd silence to the house, it was impossible to explain it, but it felt dangerous, evil and dead!

"Well, they went to town and forgot to close the door properly, don't tell me you haven't done that"

He looked down at her as he switched the flashlight on, illuminating down the long hallway, "sorry Peter but I can't say I have"

They both peered into the long stream of light, Peter moved the beam from left to right but other than the normality of a French home with its pictures, wooden floor and patterned wallpaper, there was nothing amiss.

"Right, stay behind me and keep your eyes open, there is something amiss here, it just doesn't feel right"

The light from the torch lead the way, like a figure of safety projecting into the inky blackness. They moved from room to room, but nothing seemed wrong, the furniture, ornaments all seemed to be in an orderly and well-kept manner.

"Right, we need to go upstairs, this place has something to tell us, I am sure"

"Peter, this is someone else's house, we can't just go wandering around"

"You are right but why leave the door open, surely in this remote location and in the middle of a war, you would certainly check that you had closed it behind you"

"I don't like it Peter, what happens if they come back?"

"We will deal with that if and when it happens"

Slowly and carefully, they made their way upstairs. The stairway was wide and made of the local yellow limestone and felt solid and purposeful underfoot. Eventually, with the torchlight leading the way they reached the first floor. Peter scanned the beam about, again there didn't seem to be anything out of place, all ordered and neat.

"Right let's start with the bedroom at the front, stay close to me"

The pair made their way into the bedroom, the door was wide open, inviting them inside but as soon as they entered Peter stopped. There was a smell, one that he was familiar with, one that he had encountered many times before. A smell of war, a smell of death, one that he often dreamt about, a smell that he would always carry around in his memory.

"Wait wait, stay here Madeleine, don't come any further in, just wait here"

"Peter, what is it, why can't I come with you?"

"Just wait here, I will explain in a minute"

He disappeared into the bedroom, leaving Madeleine standing on the landing, just outside the door. Peter went into the bedroom, taking the light with him, she felt very vulnerable and scared standing alone in the darkness. The fear of the night, something about to take her gripped her mind, she shook with anxiety, she wanted to run.

"Peter, I am scared, I am coming in, I don't want to wait out here, I can't see a thing"

Without any further hesitation, she made her way slowly into the bedroom. There was a smell, Peter was right, but she couldn't remember what that smell was. She searched her memories, she had encountered it before, but where, and then the sudden realisation hit her, that smell, it was of spilt blood!

She rounded the door and entered the room to see Peter standing by a man, tied to a chair, his throat cut, red blood staining his bare chest. A gaping tear in his throat producing a grotesque grin, it was dark red, sharp, and deep. She gasped and stepped back, the black gaping wound went most of the way through, almost decapitating him, making his head lean unnaturally to one side.

"Peter, oh, what the hell has happened here?"

"Well, I guess this is Jacques Forelle and someone has enjoyed themselves at his great expense. This happened some time ago, this blood had dried, turn the light on Madeleine, whoever did this is long gone"

With trembling hands, she switched on the light, for a second it blinded her, causing her to blink. Slowly she turned back to the dead man sitting in the chair. The full horror now unfolded in front of her.

He was sitting in a wooden chair facing the end of the bed. He had been stripped to the waist, his wrists tied to the arms of the chair and his ankles to its front legs. It was clear from the indentations and the disturbed bedding that whoever had tortured him, had been sitting on the end of the bed.

The blood had sprayed everywhere in the room, almost every surface had splatters on it. There were other injuries, cuts to his face and chest, bruising around his eyes and swollen nose. Both his ears had been cut off, this man had been tortured, not just murdered.

"Whoever has done this Madeleine certainly enjoyed themselves. This was an act of pleasure not need, it must have taken hours to do this, I can't begin to imagine what hell he must have gone through"

"Why do this Peter, what possible reason would they have to inflict such pain?"

"Well, there are two reasons that occur, one, they simply enjoy doing this kind of thing and two, they wanted some information from him"

"What kind of information?"

Peter spun his head around to face Madeleine, the look of sheer shock on his was obvious.

"What Peter, what is it?"

"If this is Jacques Forelle, and I have no reason to believe otherwise, then someone might have been trying to get the same information out of him as we need!"

"You mean the SS at the manor house Peter?"

"I do, but why would they torture him, it doesn't make sense, why would they think he knows

Claude A Durand. The only reason I know is because Laurent from the Bar Le Chat said Jacques Forelle had mentioned a man with a patch and an eye as white as snow, and that he was his boss at the jail. Otherwise, I would still have no idea of where or in fact who Durand was.

Unless Wagnor had overheard that conversation, he would know nothing about Jacques Forelle's connection to Durand and in any case, why sneak around, as I said before, he would send the whole local SS to get Durand at the jail"

"Well perhaps we are jumping to conclusions, this might be nothing to do with Durand or Wagnor, it's a local lunatic at large committing terrible crimes. Just because there is a war on doesn't mean the psychopaths and the criminals have all gone away"

"I hope you are right Madeleine, of course this does land us with a major problem, this man here is our only connection to our target"

Madeleine didn't seem to be listening, she was looking around the room with a puzzled look on her face.

"What's wrong Madeleine?"

"Where is his wife Peter, she must be here somewhere?"

He looked straight at her, "I hadn't thought of that, we must look for her, she may still be alive"

They searched the rest of the house but to no avail, every room was intact, everything in its place with no signs of further torture or murder.

"Right, the house is clear, let's have a look outside, we might find what we are looking for there?"

Very slowly they moved outside, the light from the torch was beginning to fade, it wouldn't be long before it stopped working altogether. There was nothing amiss at the front of the large and imposing house, just their parked car. They moved to the left of the house and pushed into the darkness and into the rain.

The deluge that first greeted them as they arrived had now slowed to a constant drizzle, blowing about the night. The touch illuminated the fine drops, like a million small fireflies drifting about in the breeze. The path lead them around the back and a few feet further along was a small barn, perhaps large enough for a couple of cars or a tractor and some machinery.

"I have a bad feeling about this Peter, I am not sure I want to find out what is in there"

"I know exactly how you feel but we have to have a look, there is no point in just walking away now and let's remember, whoever killed Jacques Forelle might still be here"

Very carefully they approached the double doors of the barn. They were several feet high and about the same wide. There was a large bolt holding the two doors together but no lock.

Peter pulled the large bolt across, as carefully as he could.

"Well, if it's locked from the outside, the chances are, no one is inside"

Very carefully, he opened the right-hand door, as Madeleine shone the torch inside. The sight that greeted them made them both step backwards in horror, making them gasp for breath. About ten feet inside the barn was Mrs Forelle, hanging a foot or so from the ground. She was suspended by her wrists from a large beam somewhere up in the darkness in the apex of the building. She was completely naked and covered in blood.

She had her throat cut, just like her husband and the blood had run all the way down her naked body, forming a now dried pool on the dirt floor. As they approached, it became obvious that she had also been mutilated, cuts all over her body, some small, some large and gaping open.

Madeleine, stopped, turned, and wheeping ran out of the barn, Peter took one last look at the dead woman and followed her back to the car. He slammed the door as he settled back into the driver's seat, Madeleine was still very upset, he reached out and held her hand.

Chocking back the tears, Madeleine spoke first, "who would do such a thing Peter, who?"

"I don't know, for all I know this might not be the first such incident in the area, maybe this killer has been committing these crimes for a while, we need to report this to the local Police. Also, we have now lost our one and only contact with Doctor Durand. We now need to formulate a plan, we will just have to try and find him ourselves and hope he doesn't do a runner"

"Do you think it's a good idea just to walk into the local Police station, what happens if they arrest us for these crimes?"

"I must admit that you have a very good point, perhaps we just walk away from this, they are dead, there is no helping them now"

Madeleine turned quickly to Peter, "we can't Peter, we must do the right thing by them, we can't just let them rot, we have to tell the authorities"

Peter Parker didn't seem to be listening, he was tapping with the fingers of his right hand on the top of the steering wheel. He nodded his head a couple of times before turning back to Madeleine.

"Who do you think did this Madeleine, go on, have a guess?"

"I have absolutely no idea, it could have been anyone from around here. The main coast road is only a minute or two up the track, they could have come from anywhere, that's why we have to tell the Police"

"No, just think, who did we see here the other day"

She put her head down and ran her fingers through her hair.

"There was that Wagnor from the SS at Saint Aderald, but I don't know him, would he do such things?"

"Oh yes, I wouldn't put this kind of thing past him, and he was here, we know that much. Maybe he came back this morning, found Jacques Forelle still at home and decided to have some fun, maybe Mrs Forelle came back later, who knows? An afternoon of fun, that's exactly what that lunatic would enjoy.

I don't think it's connected to our mission, I certainly hope not, but it has certainly screwed things up. Also, if we go marching into the local Police station and report this, who knows what might happen. If they arrest us, Wagnor might get to know about it and then we are dead for certain, no we must play this very carefully indeed.

I hear what you are saying Madeleine and you are right, but the consequences of us reporting this are something I don't really want to contemplate. Yes, we have lost a major lead, but we are still at large, we have a little money, a functioning car and no one knows we are here. Let's just stay like that, I am sure someone will report this in due course, we have to simply accept that"

Chapter 13.
The Disused Slaughter House.
June 3rd, 1943.

They day broke dull and grey, there was just the suggestion of further rain. The ground was already very muddy from the inclement weather yesterday. The local Resistance had left them with a rifle and several rounds of ammunition, "not much", Richard thought but it was better than nothing.

Richard and Sister Beverley had spent the night huddled around a small fire in a sheltered part of the old building. It wasn't the best but at least it was protected from the wind and the rain and with the fire burning and the few supplies left by Pierre, Monique and Marcel, it had been a reasonable place to hide out.

Richard had been out most of the morning searching for anything that might prove useful, eventually he returned, with a huge smile on his face.

"You will never guess what I have found"

"Go on, you will have to tell me"

"It's an old Triumph motorcycle, it was parked around the back of the building, they keys are still in the ignition"

"Sorry Richard are you sure, you don't normally find Triumph motorcycles parked at the back of old buildings, that simply doesn't happen. Have you been drinking some old wine you found in a ditch out there?"

"I am telling the truth Sister Beverley, come and see"

Rather stiffly she stood up, brushed the grey dust from her clothes, and in an attempt to drive the cold from her bones, had one more warm by the fire, and followed Richard out of the building. He led her around the back of the ruins and sure enough, parked in a concrete shed was an old Triumph motorcycle. It was covered in dust, but it did have the keys still in the ignition.

"Who would leave such a thing here, that doesn't seem to make any sense Richard?"

"Well, the only thing I can think of is that someone was in a hurry to leave this place, maybe even France, they might have met some friends here and then they all left together. One thing is for certain, they didn't come back"

"Will it start, it looks very old and dusty?"

"Leave it to me Sister Beverley, I am a whiz with these things, Richard James will get this going, I can assure you of that. I have been playing with Triumphs since I was a little boy, my dad had three of the things you know"

Leaving Richard to revive the Triumph, she started to walk away from the building, stretch her legs and see if indeed there was anything of use around here. The ground all around was heavily overgrown, brambles and young trees abounded, breaking the concrete, creating cracks for the winter weather to open even further.

It wasn't that long ago since people worked here, a bustling busy place, but now it was a sad dilapidated shell. The ghosts of former employees and the sad end of all the animals who passed this way, hung around like smoke from a distant fire.

She looked into the east, the sun was trying to break through the grey murk but with little success, she breathed a deep sigh.

"This war asks too much of people, it creates and extreme disturbance in the flow of life. People die before they should, babies never get to know their parents, lovers aren't able to fulfil their desires, all because some lunatic decided that he should be in charge"

She heard the approach of footsteps from behind, turning, she saw Richard approaching, hands covered in oil, and a streak or two of black gunk on his face.

"Talking to yourself Sister Beverley, it's the first sign of madness you know"

She laughed, "me mad, I don't think so, there are a lot of people out there who are though. Sometimes I think it would help, maybe an amount of insanity would act like a filter on the things we have to endure"

Richard looked at Sister Beverley with a frown on his face, she had always seemed so strong and enduring, a woman with an inner strength and power, someone who would never, ever give in.

"I guess this is all getting to you Sister, you have lost your home, you are on the run, goodness knows what will happen next. I think about my wife, she will have had the dreaded telegram, 'missing in action, presumed dead'. Also, there is Bob Swanbourne, his wife will still be hoping he is just missing, little does she know. I think you must plough on, it's not easy though. I can't remember all those young faces that have served with me, sometimes a face pops into my mind, but often I can't even remember his name. Is that wrong Sister, all those young men and I can't even remember their names?"

"No, not at all, like I said, this war asks too much of us, people die, often alone, and no-one knows their names, it's just a fact of war.

Anyway, as for me, I have taken vows of chastity and poverty, I have nothing to lose materialistically, it's just a house and a few items of clothing. It's the imposition of this war, how it changes the direction of normality. It sickens me but as you suggest, we just get on with it"

"We will fix this I am sure, there will be an end to it all, there has to be. Eventually there will come a day when I don't have to write another letter to a mother telling her that her son died heroically, when in actual fact I have no idea what happened to him, he just didn't come back, and is probably lying dead in a field somewhere"

Sister Beverley sighed, "I know what you mean Richard, and it can't come soon enough. However, talking about fixing, have you got the bike running yet?"

"I have Sister and it runs like a dream, come and see. I don't think there is much petrol in it but it's worth a shot, let's go for a ride"

She laughed out loud, it was the first time she had done so for some considerable time, perhaps even months. The enthusiasm of Richard was somewhat infectious and the absurdity of being so pleased at getting an old motorcycle running in the middle of all this madness was irrational. However, it seemed to brighten the day and just for a moment, the war seemed to be someone else's problem.

"Richard James, are you actually suggesting we go for a pleasant ride through the countryside in the middle of all this?"

"I am Sister and why not, can't say I have ever had a Roman Catholic Sister on the back of my bike before but hey, there is always a first time. Also, with God watching over the both of us, what could possibly go wrong?"

"Richard, I can assure you that plenty could go wrong, these things a very dangerous you know?"

"Nah, jump on, it will be fine, in any case if the Germans spot us, they will never catch us"

She laughed again, "well get it started then, the Resistance people said they would be back after dark, so we have some time to fill"

"Great, let's go"

The Triumph coughed and spluttered as Richard kicked down hard many times on the starting lever. Eventually it fired, great plumes of grey smoke spluttered out of the back accompanied by several backfires but eventually, it settled down and ran smoothly.

"Right Sister come on, let's go"

Sister Beverley gingery threw her leg over the back of the bike and wrapped her arms around Richard's waist. She held on so tightly that he could hardly breathe, but he clicked it into first gear and slowly headed towards the main road. Once there he turned right onto the smoother tarmac, he quickly accelerated until they were thundering across the French countryside.

Sister Beverley shouted into his ear, "this is very exciting and tremendously terrifying at the same time. You are obviously well practiced in riding such a beast"

"Never been on one before Sister Beverly, well not more than twenty times, but it is fun. Where should we go, where does this road take us?"

She laughed again, the absurdity of an RAF officer and a Roman Catholic Sister racing along on a Triumph motorcycle seemed so bizarre, it had to be funny. Fortunately, Pierre had left Richard with a jacket and some corduroy trousers, so at least he wasn't so conspicuous as he had been in his RAF uniform.

"I think this road takes us to Chênes, we should enter a forest soon, especially at this speed, we could ride to an old bridge and then turn around and come back"

"Then let's ride on Sister, this is great fun"

They thundered on, into a dark forest with a deep green canopy, even in the grey afternoon light, it shone like an emerald cloud above them. The road was still wet and slick, but they didn't care, the danger of crashing, in comparison to their overall situation, seemed trivial and perhaps even exhilarating.

She wanted to scream, faster, faster but the words wouldn't come forth, her mouth was completely dry and devoid of any meaningful action. She held on, the wind tearing at her, turning her hands into ice, her ears and cheeks ached with the cold, her nose was completely numb. Sister Beverley could feel her heart pounding, she was certain that any moment now, it would burst but she didn't care.

The road twisted right and then left and right again, Richard kept the pressure on though, there was no slowing, it felt as if they were running from the devil himself. On and on they went but eventually, the bike began to fail, it coughed, faltered and then came back to life gain, before once more failing.

"Sister, we have a problem, I need to stop and try and find out what is happening"

Richard guided the sickened motorcycle to a stop, at the gates of an old military hospital. The huge iron gates were rusted and the sandstone building, whilst in a good state of repair, was beginning to show signs of losing a long battle with abandonment and nature.

They both dismounted from the bike, Richard undid the petrol cap and whilst moving the machine from side to side, peered inside.

"Ups, we appear to be out of petrol Sister, looks like we walk back unless you have a better idea?"

"As a matter of fact, I do, right up this road on the right is a petrol station, I know the man who owns it, in fact I delivered his baby granddaughter in Saint Aderald last year. I wonder if he might help, I am sure he will, has no love for the occupying forces, he was somewhat of a hero in the first war. Let's go and talk to him, see if he can spare us a little petrol"

Chapter 14.
The bar in Chênes.
June 3rd, 1943.

"Right then, that's agreed, we must go back, get Richard from the old watermill before something happens to him. Or before he decides to declare war on the whole German army, by himself! We bring him back here, drop a note under the door of the local Police about the murders and then go off and look for Durand, simple!"

"I don't see any other way out of it Peter, it's not a plan really, we still don't know where the man is or how we can get in contact with him. Sure, we can ask the guy behind the bar, and I am sure he would help but we risk Durand running before we can get close to him, we need an introduction from someone he trusts"

"You are right, but first let's go, we need to rescue Richard, that's if that German Sergeant hasn't killed him by now, she is a formidable woman I am sure"

They finished their lunch, paid the barman and got into the car. Very carefully, Peter guided the vehicle out of the old town, down the cobbled streets and off onto the main road towards Saint Aderald. It was a grey afternoon but at least it was dry, the overcast summed up their mood, after the events of yesterday, the reality of what they were doing and the people they were dealing with had been brought back into focus.

"What are you going to do after this Peter, you know, when the war is over, it will end, one day?"

"You sound very optimistic Madeleine, I must admit being somewhat less so. I wonder if this war will just become normal, life as it is, for ever more"

"No, no Peter, you mustn't think like that, because of what we and others are doing and dyeing for, it will end, it has to"

"Let's hope so"

"You didn't answer my question, what will you do once it's over?"

"I guess I will return to Susan and the baby, settle down, get a job selling cars for a living, nice and safe with no one trying to kill me"

She looked over at Peter, he stared straight ahead, he didn't seem to have any real emotion on his face, he didn't seem to be registering what he was actually saying.

"So, if you crave normality, why did you come back this time or the last time, why didn't you just fade away into the background. Get a desk job, hide away when the German bombs fell, stay out of the war?"

"I was promised a desk job, some safety and regularity, but I was ordered back, I had to come.

If I had said no, someone else would have had to do it. I am sick of people dying because of me, so I had no choice"

"Had to Peter, or wanted to? I am not so sure, I wonder if this is what you really do want, you need this danger, the pumping adrenalin. You living an ordinary life Peter, not certain about that?"

He didn't look away from the road, never even acknowledged what she had just said, she wondered why, what was he thinking, what would he really end up doing?

The road quickly opened up, the car sped along, making short work of the bumpy French road, back towards Saint Aderald. They crossed the first bridge, passing the pumping station on their left and then crossed the second bridge and entered the woodland covered part of the main road.

It wasn't long before the road opened out to farmland both left and right. The vista rolled on for miles, a classic French view, it could have been a perfect scene, if only in another time.

The grey sky that had persisted since the days dawn had begun to break and some welcome late afternoon sun started to make an appearance. It shone directly into their eyes as they headed down the road towards Saint Aderald. There was no real traffic on the road, a couple of tractors and a furniture removal van. As they sped past the filling station, Peter noticed a Triumph motorcycle with two people being pushed into the petrol pump area.

"Hey, did you see that bike Madeleine, I was given one just like that on my last visit, I had to leave it at the disused slaughterhouse, I bet someone has found it by now"

"Peter, I am sure the woman next to that bike was Sister Beverley, what would she be doing here?"

They looked at each other, just a swift glance but a knowing look, they both spoke at the same time.

"That was Sister Beverley!!!!"

Peter pushed hard down on the brakes, changing gear swiftly, he spun the Citroen around in the road and drove back to the petrol station. It only took a moment or two to reach the forecourt and sure enough, standing there as bold as brass was Sister Beverley Jane and Squadron Leader Richard James.

Peter pulled the car up next to the bike, Richard was standing next to the Triumph and Sister Beverley was chatting to a slightly oily man some feet away. It seemed a perfectly normal scene, a ride out on a sunny afternoon, they had run out of fuel, nothing strange about that, except for the circumstances. Given the situation, it was an odd and somewhat obscure shot of reality into an otherwise ordinary sight.

Peter opened the driver's door and jumped out, "what the hell are you two doing here?"

Richard looked slightly sheepish, "well hello Peter, fancy meeting you here old chap! It's a bit of a story I must admit, where do I begin?"

Chapter 15.
The office of SS head, Hauptman Karl Wagnor
The manor house, near Saint Aderald.
June 4th, 1943.

There was a knock on Karl Wagnor's door, no reply a second knock, this time a little firmer.

"Come in"

Lieutenant Schneider, the head of security walked rather stiffly into the room. He came to a stop at the edge of Wagnor's desk and snapped quickly to attention.

"Yes, Schneider, what can I do for you?"

"Sir, it's about the information you requested as the possible reason for the return of the British Agent. I have been speaking to the Security Service in Berlin and they have come up with two possible reasons"

Wagnor stopped what he was doing, put his pen down on his desk and looked up at Schneider. He rubbed his face and then took a deep breath whilst massaging the back of his neck.

"Right Lieutenant, what did they have to say?"

"As I said sir, they had two suggestions. The first was, he has been sent back to carry out a very high-profile job. They think it could be an assassination, may be even you sir"

Wagnor screwed up his face, "no, not buying that one, why would the British want me dead, I am not that important to risk the life of an Agent, and there is no one else around here worth the trouble. Sorry Lieutenant, you are going to have to try harder than that"

"Right sir, the second reason is concerning a French scientist by the name of Claude A

Durand. I have no information on him, and Berlin would not fill me in, they just said it was above my level and not to ask any question. They did however say that you would know what it was concerning.

It is possible that the British Agent knows the whereabouts of this French scientist and he is here to take him back to England. I was informed by Berlin that finding this man is one of the highest priorities of the third Reich"

"Well, it was the highest priorities of the third Reich Lieutenant, all the areas in this part of France had their orders to find this scientist, no matter what the cost, the victory over the allies depended on it, he is that important.

We threw everything we had and more at trying to find him but after turning every single stone and searching everywhere, we decided that he wasn't around here, or possibly even dead. He was evidently in some other part of the world, but certainly not in my area, not even close to it"

"Sir, may I ask why he was so important, what secrets did he hold?"

"Berlin told you Lieutenant that information was restricted to those above your level, well I have some news for you, it was restricted to those above my level also. I tried my best to find out exactly what this man had been up to but to no avail. Whatever it was, was something huge, probably beyond my comprehension, but I do know this much. The powers in Berlin really, really, really wanted this man, they were prepared to go to any lengths to get him, expend any number of resources. The pressure on me to find him was immense, I was really glad when we finally decided he wasn't anywhere near here, and to be honest, I am glad about that, given the force from above"

"So, what are your orders sir?"

"I have to say that Berlin don't seem to have provided us with any creditable theory as to why this British Agent would risk almost certain death in coming back here, so soon after leaving. It's either a reason of rank arrogance and stupidity or it's something that's beyond whatever ideas we have, something so important that it simply must be done, irrespective of cost or loss of life.

Perhaps we should consider the French scientist notion, maybe he has come back to this area? We need to treat it with at least some credibility Lieutenant. If this is true then we must find Peter Parker, we must find him before he snatches the scientist from under our noses. The British obviously rank success of this mission above any price no matter how high, perhaps we should do the same.

Get onto the army base nearby and tell them to send me one hundred men, transport, dogs and anything else they might think useful. Draw up a search plan, we need a strategy, find Parker, keep him under surveillance until he finds Doctor Claude A Durand, if that's why he is here. Then and only then will we pounce and bag the both of them, we don't want to do that until we have the good Doctor in our sights, or he will be off into the sunset"

"So, you just want me to keep the British Agent under surveillance, not bring him in for questioning?"

"We don't do anything until we know he has Durand, or whatever he is looking for. Unfortunately, we don't know what the scientist looks like, we need to play that by ear, but I think we will know when it happens. I must stress this Lieutenant Schneider, if the Doctor and or the British Agent escape me, you will go to England and get them back. When you return, I will shoot you myself, and then the rest of your family, that's not a threat by the way, that's a solemn promise"

"Understood sir, I will get onto it straight away"

Schneider turned and marched briskly out of Wagnor's office, closing the door quietly behind him. Wagnor slowly spun around in his leather chair to face out of the large bay windows. He sighed again and rubbed his chin.

"So, Mr Parker, what exactly are you up to I wonder, is it really the French scientist you are after, do you know where he is, have you managed to contact him? Perhaps it's not that at all, maybe there is something else you seek, something we know nothing about, yet?"

It was some considerable time before he returned to his work, if it was the French scientist, this could mark a turning point in the war. For whoever managed to bag this particular prize might at that point, gain the victory and the war would be won.

Lieutenant Schneider's phone began to ring, he reached over to answer it but missed it altogether, he wasn't looking, he was too involved in the request paperwork to the commander of the army base.

"They are never going to give me one hundred men, I will be lucky if I get twenty, try explaining that to Wagnor, well, all I can do is my best. The trouble is, Wagnor is a lunatic at not one to listen to excuses, if this doesn't go well, this could be the end of me and a trip to the eastern front beckons, and I don't fancy that at all"

The phone rang for a second time, after signing the request form, he eventually looked up. Snatching at the annoying distraction he answered.

"Lieutenant Schneider"

"Sir, it's Private Schultz on the reception desk, I have a phone call from Corporal Schmitt, he is with the Private who is the last survivor from the cowedly Resistance ambush on our truck a couple of days ago. Apparently, the Private has regained consciousness and Corporal Schmitt has some information for you"

"Right, put him through"

"Sir, it's Corporal Schmitt at the military hospital, the last survivor regained consciousness and I have questioned him. After some time, our brave colleague managed to give me some information about the attack and murder of our comrades. As suspected, it was the local Resistance, but our patrol had previously detained a British RAF pilot, he was being hidden and assisted by that Nun, they found them whilst looking for our female Sergeant, who is still missing"

"Sister, Corporal Schmitt, she is a Sister"

"Pardon sir?"

"She is a Sister, a Nun spends all her time locked in a Nunnery, a Sister lives in the community"

"Sorry, a Sister, well the survivor says they detained them and were bringing them back to the manor house for questioning. He thinks that the Resistance must have followed them and attacked, this may be because the Sister was one of their own. Anyway, they both escaped but he doesn't recall in which direction or if they had a vehicle"

"Right, thank you Corporal Schmitt, I will report to Wagnor and get that Sister added on to the local Resistance file. Interesting news about the RAF pilot, I will look into that. I know there was an aircraft shot down a few days ago but it was thought the pilot had been killed, apparently, he lay near to the burning aircraft. I hope the Private recovers soon, he is a brave soldier indeed.

Anyway, I need to request some help from the local army base, this will help my case, perhaps I will get what Wagnor wants now, report back here Corporal Schmitt once the survivor has given a full statement"

"Yes sir"

Lieutenant Schneider put the handset back on the receiver, he had a smile on his face for the first time today.

"Well, that would make an interesting line in the local newspaper, 'Catholic Sister part of a murdering local resistance cell'. If nothing else, it will help Wagnor get the resources he wants and keep him off my back"

Chapter 16.
MI5 HQ, Blenheim Palace Oxfordshire.
June 5th, 1943.

Major Walker picked up the black phone that sat on the plane wooden table in front of him, in interrogation room 4. It was a few seconds before anyone answered at the other end.

"Bring the girl in Thompson, I am in interrogation room 4 thank you"

He replaced the tatty black handset, leant back in the rather uncomfortable wooded chair and waited. The room was dark and threatening, it's plain grey concrete walls and floor reflected a dim and depressing light from the one single bulb hanging from the middle of the ceiling. There was a smell of damp and dust, it felt like an abandoned place, somewhere you wouldn't want to dwell, a place of devils and demons.

Several minutes past before there was a knock on the door.

"Enter"

A man dressed in a British military uniform brought a young woman into the room. She had a sweet and delicate form, she seemed a lot younger than her years, a pretty woman, one desperately out of place down here. Her hands were cuffed behind her back, her hair was somewhat dishevelled, and she seemed a little grubby and unwashed.

"Sit down my dear, I am a very busy man, so I will make this quick and easy to understand. You are a German spy, you will be taken to court and found guilty. From there you will be taken to the tower and hung by the neck until you are dead. Before I set those particular events into motion, do you have anything to say?"

She just sat on the wooden chair on the other side of the desk and looked straight ahead and said nothing.

Major Walker opened the small file he had on the desk and spent a few seconds scanning through the documents contained therein.

"Right, you were found on the perimeter of RAF Blackstone and arrested by the local RAF Police. You don't have any papers and insist that you are a Swiss national, but the Swiss embassy deny all knowledge of you.

Drawings and notes were found about your person detailing aircraft types and movements, all written in German. A communication was intercepted, with your fingerprints on it, which was sent to a postal box in Paris. We know that this is a drop box for German agents and have been monitoring it for some months now.

The code in that letter, amongst other things, talked about a British Agent by the name of

Louis Dubois, with a real name of Peter Parker. You said he had returned to France and that you would kill him when he returned to England. We are a little puzzled about this, who is this Louis Dubois, why has he returned to France and why will you kill him?"

She said nothing, just continued to gaze straight ahead without any emotion at all.

"Let me make you an offer my dear, if you answer my questions, I will see what I can do about your appointment with the hangman. Trust me, it's not a nice way to die and I can make sure you spend the rest of the war in a more comfortable place and of course alive. You will be able to return to your family when the war is over, and pretend none of this happened, now what do you say?"

She looked sarcastically over at Major Walker, raised one of her eyebrows and laughed.

"Peter Parker is one of your own spies, why don't you know this, just check your files you incompetent fools. Yes, I will kill him when he gets back, or at least I was going to before your RAF boys arrested me. Did they tell you they felt my breasts after they put the handcuffs on me, they said they would let me go if I fucked them, did they tell you that?

As for the reason he returned to France, well you clearly know as much as me, that's absolutely nothing. How the hell do you expect to win this war, you are bumbling fools, take me to see the hangman, I don't fear him, you or anyone else"

Major Walker stared at her for a minute of two, before taking a deep breath before he replied.

"Look, I really don't care if you live or die, I will still go home tonight, I will see my kids, kiss my wife, take the dog for a walk. I just thought I might be able to help you out, you know, do you a favour, make sure you live long enough to see your family again.

You do have a family don't you, a mother a father, they will be so worried about you, they don't want to find that you died alone, in a far-off place, now do they?

Now all I want is an answer to a few simple questions. How did you get into the country, who was your contact here, what is your real name and what is this about Peter Parker, how does he fit into this?"

She looked at Major Walker, looked down at the floor and then back up again.

"I am not your double agent, I am proud of being German, proud to serve the fatherland, if I am condemned to die, then so be it. A thousand brave men and women died today in this war, why should I be an exception.

I will be just another casualty, just another telegram sent to a grieving family, another name on my local list of heroes.

As for my name, I am happy to give that, at least you can tell my family that I am dead, my name is Lena Webber, I am a Private in the German army. Peter Parker brought me back here, we were taken to an RAF base, I don't know what it was called. He left and returned to France, and I don't know why but he did.

I said I will kill him when he returned, not because he is British, not because he is a spy, but because he took advantage of me. He entered into a relationship with me, with the express purpose of getting information from me, not because he loved me or even cared for me, but just to get what he wanted.

So, you have all your answers, please tell my father I died well, I couldn't stand the thought that he thinks that I didn't do my duty"

There was a long silence before either of them spoke, finally Major Walker broke the hush.

"Well, you certainly seemed determined to die Lena, which is a shame for such a young person. I would normally suggest that you will have plenty of time for that once you have lived your life, but in your case, I am not so sure.

There is another way of course, you could come and work for us, become a double agent.

That way you get to live a long life and perhaps do some good, instead of surrendering to the hangman in the tower of London"

Lena looked directly into his eyes, "thank you for the offer but no, I am not a traitor or a double agent, I have tried my best and failed, you have me here, I am at your mercy"

"Nice words Lena and I accept your decision but please take a little time to reconsider. You would be working for the right side in all of this, your parents would never get to know and most importantly of all, you get to live.

We would never ask you to do anything that would risk the lives of your friends and family, we just need a little help, some extra information"

She laughed, "that's not far removed from what Peter Parker wanted, just a little bit of information. No, I have made my decision, I will die, and my parents will be proud"

She didn't say another word despite Major Walker's attempts to persuade her. He left the room, closing the half rotten door behind him, the guard turned to look at him as he left.

"Any luck with this one sir?"

"No, just another squandered life, take her back to her cell, I will get the court onto it in the morning, shame really, we could have used her. Oh well, I guess the hangman will have another job on in the next few days"

Chapter 17.
Hotel Paris,
New Chênes.
June 5th, 1943.

Sister Beverley, Richard, Peter and Madeleine all sat around a table outside the very impressive Hotel Paris in new Chênes.

The afternoon had turned out rather well, given the weather of the last few days. The grey clouds had disappeared, and the warm June sun was bathing everyone in a bright golden glow.

The Hotel sat on one side of a large square, in the newer part of Chênes, it had a more modern look than the square in old Chênes where Peter and Madeleine had eaten their breakfast over the last couple of days. None the less, the buildings looked traditional having been crafted out of the local yellow sandstone by craftsmen of unlimited skills. It had a wide and imposing façade, extending up four stories with many bay windows, some with balconies. There was a large covered area to the front, with canopies, tables, and chairs. It was a very popular spot with people of all ages, especially when the sun was shining.

It was a very busy place, much more so than where Peter and Madeleine had spent the last few days. There were many shops and offices bounded the large square, people moved from place to place, chatting to friends, laughing occasionally, disagreeing but always moving.

There was a flower seller on the opposite side of the square, an older woman with grey hair, dressed in black. She was extremely busy, her wooden cart was full of multiple-coloured blooms, all looking resplendent in the summer sun.

There was a young boy selling newspapers, another man sharpening knives and tools, several women pushing prams, it was a scene of total normality in a time of absolute insanity.

A very smart looking waiter came from the front of the hotel with a tray of coffees and brandy for the four sat at the table. He was immaculately dressed, black trousers, shiny black shoes, and a white shirt with a bowtie.

"Just let me fully understand this Sister Beverley, you know the man who owns this place, in fact he was your lover, at the same time as being married to his first wife. Is that really the behaviour of a Sister?"

"Listen to me Peter Parker, I am a woman, I have needs, in any case, this all happened before I took my vows. I had a life you know, I did enjoy the more physical side of things, in fact it was very pleasurable indeed. I am sure you and Madeleine enjoy your private times together, don't tell me you don't because it's obvious you do"

Madeleine coughed as she sipped at her coffee, Richard James spun around to look at Peter.

"I didn't know you two were an item Peter, you lucky so and so"

"Erm, I think we will change the topic thank you and for your information Richard James, we are not an item, understood?"

Richard looked at Madeleine, she was gazing across the town square, he might have detected a sense of disappointment on her face at what Peter had just said.

Peter turned to face Sister Beverley, a flash went through his mind, perhaps this was the answer to their problem.

"Wait a minute, how long has the owner of this hotel, your ex-lover, been living in Chênes?"

"You mean Didier, all of his life I think, he was the Mayor four or five years ago, just before the beginning of the war, why?"

"I need to see him Sister Beverley, I need to ask a couple of questions, can you set something up?"

"Yes of course, I will go and find him now, I am sure he will help. He is not a member of the local Resistance, but he often helps out with finance, places to hide and other things, he can be trusted"

Sister Beverley got up and disappeared into the hotel, leaving the other three to enjoy their coffee.

"What questions do you what to ask him Peter old boy, what could he know that you want to find out about? Oh, perhaps a good restaurant, somewhere where the dancing girls are perfect?"

"I will tell you Richard once this is sorted out, for the mean time I just need to ask you to be patient. You are an English RAF officer here in France, with no papers and dressed in civilian clothes. If the Germans catch you, they will certainly shoot you as a spy, once they have interrogated you, so I can't take the risk you might give anything away. Oh, and it's nothing to do with dancing girls, I can assure you"

"Understood old chap, not a problem"

A few minutes later Sister Beverley returned, "right, come with me, Didier is more than happy to see us, he is in his office"

They walked through the lobby of the hotel, a rather opulent place with dark wood and shiny brass everywhere, it all seemed a little out of place for a small French rural town. Beverley took them to one side of the large reception desk and into a long corridor, at one end there was a light oak door.

She knocked once, the reply came from inside, "enter"

Beverley opened the door, the office was large and light with classic, heavy wooden furniture. Some expensive looking paintings adorned the walls and a huge chandelier hung from a central rose.

Standing with his back to the window was a rather tall and elegant looking gentleman in his fifties. He was slightly tanned with salt and pepper hair, which was a little longer than was the norm and a slight grey stubble showing through.

"Come in everyone, grab a seat around the coffee table, I have ordered some wine and a little food. It's so nice to see you again Beverley, and your friends, what can I do for you, all you need to do is ask"

"Didier, my friends are Peter, Richard and Madeleine, they are fighting the occupation, they are risking their lives for us and our country, they need your help"

"Well in that case, I can assure you of my absolute assistance, all you need to do is ask"

"That's very kind of you Didier, before we go any further, I need to ask a large favour. My friend Richard has no papers, clothing, in fact nothing at all. I assume you have already guessed his true identity?"

"I assume he is an RAF airman who was shot down?"

"Am I that obvious?"

The whole group laughed at Richard, he looked aghast and rather boyish and very embarrassed.

"I am afraid you do Richard, you are more than welcome to stay here for a while though. I am sure we can find some work for you, behind the scenes of course, may be in the kitchen. I will talk to some of my contacts, the acquisition of identification papers shouldn't be a problem. The Germans have changed the format recently, it might be a good idea for all of you to get the new documents.

You are all welcome to stay here for as long as you like, we are a little short on customers anyway, as you can imagine. That's not a huge problem as I have, well, several other businesses, some not that legitimate if you understand, but all rather profitable. Tines are difficult you know but one has to manage, and in my case, I seem to be managing very well thank you. Is there anything else I can help you with?"

"There is Didier, but I must ask Richard and Beverley to leave the room, what I need to talk about is highly sensitive and if they hear what I have to say, it puts them at extreme risk with the SS should they be captured"

Without question, Sister Beverley and Richard got up and returned to their coffee and brandy at the front of the hotel.

Didier got up from the table and walked over to his desk. He opened an onyx cigarette case, gently took a French cigarette put it to his lips and using an American Zippo lighter he had in his pocket, lit it. It produced a bright red glow on its tip and gentle whirls of grey smoke. He perched himself on the edge of his desk, blew a couple of smoke rings into the air and then addressed Peter directly.

"OK Peter, what is it that is so sensitive? This doesn't sound good, I suspect something to do with the local SS, the resistance perhaps?"

"Firstly, Didier, has there been any reports of a double murder recently?"

"Funny you should say that, the local Police chief was in here yesterday evening. There was a murder of Jacques Forelle and his wife, terrible thing, what a scene. Apparently, there was a note under the station door, that was a bit odd, but they are looking for the perpetrators, what do you know about it?"

"I am certain the person who did this was Karl Wagnor, the SS chief at the manor house near to Saint Aderald. He was having an affair with Forelle's wife, myself and Madeleine saw him leaving the house the day before. There is no doubt that this man is more than capable of this kind of thing, it was him. Please feel free to tell the Police but the very best of luck bringing Wagnor to justice.

The next thing I need to know is, well, very sensitive indeed. Do you know the Director of the local jail?"

"Yes I do, he comes in here a couple of times a month, always by himself, he has dinner, a bottle of the local red, good payer and tipper too. His name is Antione, he has a patch over his eye, quiet guy, always nicely dressed"

"Didier, I need to talk to him, but it needs to be carefully controlled. You see, he might not want to talk to me and there is a risk him running. If he does, I might never see him again and that would be very serious indeed, I can't let that happen!"

"I guess this guy is very important indeed?"

"More than you could imagine, do you know where he lives?"

"I don't but I could try and find out, give me a day or so, perhaps he will turn up here in the meantime"

"Thank you Didier, thank you very much"

Didier and Peter finished their drinks and re-joined Sister Beverley, Madeleine and Richard and sat down for a very welcome lunch of local wine and food. The afternoon was glorious, and things had moved forward, at least a little.

Chênes, the Hotel Paris.
Three days later - June 8th, 1943.
It was by far and away the warmest day of the year so far, Madeleine and Peter were enjoying an iced tea outside the hotel Paris. The scene was again busy, late afternoon seemed to bring with it an increase in activity, especially amongst the shops around the square.

The last few days had proved a pleasant distraction from their mission and the war in general. They had new documents, as supplied by Didier, some clean clothes, again courtesy of Didier and had slept in clean comfortable beds in the hotel Paris.

Most importantly of all, Didier had found out where Doctor Claude A Durand was now living, or as he was now known, 'Antione'. He lived alone in an old fishing lodge on the other side of the river from new Chênes, well out of the way. Didier couldn't understand why anyone would want to live so far away from civilization in such a remote location, but Peter knew all too well why 'Antione' had chosen such a spot.

It had been decided that Richard and Sister Beverly should stay behind in the hotel. There seemed to have been a large increase in

German activity over the last few days, so it would be safer for them and the whole mission if they stayed hidden, well out of sight. Another valuable piece of information Didier had been able to provide was what time Durand finished work each day and travelled back to his home by the river.

"Goodness knows how he finds all this stuff out Madeleine, but I guess we shouldn't complain. He told me that he leaves the jail every day at 5pm sharp, not a minute before or after. He then drives back home to the fishing lodge, which takes him approximately 45 minutes. There is only one way in and out, so it shouldn't be too difficult to corner the good Doctor and explain to him what he needs to do"

"So, what happens is he just flat refuses to come with us, do we shoot him on the spot or try again on another day?"

"Good question, I sometimes wish I had the resolve of Laurent of Philipe, I know what they would do if he refused to cooperate. Still, I think we just see what happens, once he understands that we know about him, he might be a little more compliant. Especially if I tell him that the Germans are just about to swoop and cart him off to SS headquarters in Berlin. I don't think that particular option will appeal to him, it certainly wouldn't to me"

"Let's hope that works Peter, let's hope he doesn't pull a gun out and shoot the pair of us on the spot!"

"Good point let's stay sharp, we don't want a blood bath, we have witnessed one of those not so far away from here. Right, let's get to the car, I fancy getting across the river and waiting in one of the passing bays in the forest, we can wait for his car to go past and then we follow him home. Apparently, according to Didier, it's the same Citroen as ours but silver in colour, shouldn't be that hard to spot"

They finished their iced teas and started off towards their Citroen, which was parked around the back of the hotel. The car was boiling hot inside, they wound the windows down but that didn't help but the increased airflow was very welcome. The journey out of new Chênes and across the river was conducted in complete silence. The tension was palpable, this was now the highpoint of their mission, the whole reason why he had returned to France. If this failed, the war might be lost, it was all down to them, the feeling of responsibility was almost unbearable.

Eventually, they entered the forest and found a suitable spot to wait for Durand's car to flash by. It was five fifteen, the Doctor would not pass them for another thirty minutes or so, so they had time to think carefully about their next step.

"Peter, can I ask you a question?"

"Yes of course"

"When we were talking outside the hotel a few days ago, when we first arrived, Sister Beverley said that she thought we were an item. Your told Richard that we certainly weren't.

I know our relationship has changed, it was once more physical, in the past, but now we seem more like friends. I guess I am asking, do you still have any feelings for me, you know, like they used to be, or has that all now faded away?"

The silence seemed to go for on ever, Peter just kept looking straight ahead, it was if he hadn't heard a word, but he obviously had.

"I know what you are saying Madeleine and it was somewhat insensitive of me, you know, what I said the other day. I just reacted to a situation, I didn't think, I am really sorry.

Yes, I still have feelings for you, I always will, that will never change. You wanted to know if our relationship has altered, I guess it has but that doesn't mean I think any less of you. I have a wife and child at home, but of course I did the last time we were together.

We have been through hell together and I am sure it's not over yet, I owe you my life. You wanted to know if it's ever going to be like it used to be, I guess by that, you mean when we were lovers? Who knows, I keep thinking about my life back in England but maybe I won't live long enough to see that, maybe I should live more for the present?

To be honest Madeleine, I don't know what to think sometimes, life is short, love is rare, do I still need and want you? I dare not think like that, I must protect myself, too many people have died in this bloody war, some of them I have called my friends. I must focus on what I have to do, not on anyone else, that way I can't blame myself when someone else dies because of me.

Let me ask you the same question, do you still have the feelings you once had for me?"

She smiled, those dimples appeared on her face again, she looked down at her feet before looking back at Peter, she was obviously blushing.

"I do Peter, I always have, and I always will, I wish we could be together, in a proper relationship but I realise that can't be, so I live in hope. Maybe one day things will change, in the meantime, let's just get on with the war. I understand that one day you will return to your home and I will never see you again, I guess that just the way things were meant to be, what a shame"

He reached out and took hold of her hand, he squeezed it gently, it felt warm and soft in his hand.

"Tomorrow is another day Madeleine, who knows what the dawn brings, or which plan fate has in mind for us. Not that long ago I was flying Spitfire's, happy as Larry, chasing the Luftwaffe all over the skies of Kent.

Now look, am sitting in a car, somewhere in France, waiting for some mad scientist who holds the secret to the destruction of the whole world. The SS want to kill me, Karl Wagnor has murdered two local people, who we found. I have a downed RAF pilot and a Catholic Sister in tow, both of whom are being hunted by the local German security forces.

Best of all though, I am holding the hand of the most beautiful woman in France. What does tomorrow hold, what kind of relationship will I be in, will I still be alive? Well Madeleine to answer your question, I have absolutely no idea"

She smiled and squeezed his hand in return, she looked to her right, out across the woods, perhaps there was hope for her after all.

No sooner the conversation had finished than a silver Citroen car flashed passed.

"That's it Peter, that's the car"

He started the car and gently pulled out behind.

"We need to be careful, we don't want to spook him, I have never followed anyone before. At least we know where he lives, let's just let him move ahead and we will slowly make our way to his home"

The silver car moved quickly away and out of site, they followed, it took just a few moments to find the turn to the fishing lodge and their meeting with Doctor Claude A Durand.

The track was surprisingly well maintained, reasonably wide with clear views down to the river. Peter dropped the car into a low gear and they carefully made their way towards their target, Doctor Claude A Durand.

"It seems beautiful Peter, look down there at the river, how wonderful but I don't know why it seems oddly sinister?"

"I know what you mean, it's because of the potential of the man who lives at the end of this track. If he has come up with a weapon that might end the world as we know it, can we trust him not to use it for the greater good. What happens if he takes the side of the Nazis, what happens if he unleashes the weapon on us, that's why I feel very frightened and nervous about the potential of all of this"

The slow journey down the track continued in complete silence. As if to enhance their ill feelings, grey clouds began to gather, blotting out the warm summer sun. By the time they reached the end of the track, a fine drizzle had started to blow in the wind, forming tiny rivulets on the windscreen of the car.

Eventually, they came upon the house of Claude A Durant, the man whom Peter had been chasing for all these months. He thought he had him once, only to find out that the man he was taking back to Britain was an imposter. He had died in an air crash, Peter wondered what the fate of the real Doctor would be.

He stopped the car a few feet from the silver Citroen parked in front of the fishing lodge. It was a modest single-story building, covered in white stucco, a red tiled roof and bright blue shutters, open at the two front windows. The front door was painted in the same vivid blue and had four steps leading up from the gravel path.

"Wait in the car, I hope this will be a simple in and out, but I get the feeling it isn't going to be. If anyone goes to the trouble of hiding out down here, they certainly don't want to be found, under any circumstances"

"Just to be clear Peter, if he flatly refuses to come with you, what are you going to do?"

"I have no choice Madeleine, my orders are clear, he comes with me, or he dies. There is no circumstance where I can leave him alive, eventually the Germans will find him and that will be then end for the Allies. He has one choice and that's to come with me"

"Just be careful Peter, as you said, this man has taken extraordinary steps to stay hidden, I am sure he will back that up with force if necessary"

Peter slowly and quietly opened the car door and checking that his browning 9mm was locked and loaded, he proceeded to carefully walk towards the front door, pushing the gun into the rear of his belt. He swallowed, scanning the two windows for any activity and movement from the front door. He continued up the four steps, reached out with his right hand, it was trembling slightly, he had to force himself but eventually he knocked.

He could hear a noise from somewhere inside the house but there was no answer at the door. He knocked again, this time a little harder, this seemed to produce a response as he could now hear someone was walking down the hall.

A moment later, the front door opened and there stood a man, in his late middle age, very tall, distinctive and with a patch over one eye.

"Yes, can I help you?"

"Yes sir, I wonder if I can come in, I knew a friend of yours, he has sadly been killed, I need to pass on my condolences"

"You can do that from where you are standing, who is this friend anyway?"

"I think I would prefer to come in sir, it's not that easy speaking about what happened"

"I can assure you I won't be distressed by anything you have to say and that there is no one here who can hear either, apart from that woman in the car. Anyway, you haven't told me his name, and all this comes as somewhat of a surprise, as I can't actually recall having any friends?"

"Yes, he was killed in an air crash, horrible story"

Peter reached for the gun in the back of his belt, his story wasn't working, this could turn nasty at any moment. He decided to be direct, tell Durand that he knew about him and why he was here. Perhaps that might shock him enough to make him think, perhaps start to listen.

"Ok, I need to speak to you, I hoped we could do this inside, but it seems not. You are Doctor Claude A Durand, there is no way you can deny it, I know who you are"

The man in the doorway laughed, "who the hell is, what's his name, Durant did you say?

"Durand sir and yes that's you, I have spoken to someone who you used to work with, so there is no point in denying it, it's you. I have been trying to talk to you for months now, and I have finally managed to track you down"

"Sorry, I have absolutely no idea what you are talking about, my name is Antione, I am the Chief of the local prison"

"I know what you are sir, but your name isn't Antione, unless that's the 'A' in the middle of Claude A Durand is Antione?"

"Sorry, but I am rather busy, so I must ask you and your wife to leave"

With that, he slammed the door in Peters face, leaving him standing on the doorstep wondering what to do next. He quickly spun around to the car where Madeleine was sitting.

"Quick, get over here, watch his car, if he comes out of the front door, shoot him"

He immediately turned to his right and started to run around the back of the house, just in case Claude tried to exit from the rear. It was just moments before he rounded the back corner, there was no sign of the Doctor, he had either escaped or was still in the house.

"Doctor, listen", Peter shouted, "I just need to talk, I know about the Simurgh project, I know exactly what it can do. Before the SS find you and believe me, they will, I need to give you an option, a chance to live, even if you don't want to complete your work"

He waited for a response but there was none coming.

"Doctor Durand, it's important that we talk, if I have found you, be assured that those lunatics in the SS will, you can be certain of that. When they do, there won't be any options, they will torture you until you give them everything that they want, I promise you that much, and when they finally kill you, you will thank them for releasing you from the pain."

There was still nothing, "I can't leave this place Doctor Durand without speaking to you. We can to this in a civil manner, out here in the garden, or I can come in there and that won't be anything like as polite, it will most probably end up in one of us dying, do you really want that?"

There was the sound of two bolts being drawn back and the creaking of rusty hinges as the blue door gradually unlocked. The door at the back of the house slowly opened and out came Durand with a Luger pistol in his hand.

"Just because I am not pointing this at you right now, doesn't mean I won't shoot you. Now, you seem to know my name, could I please ask for yours, at least I would like to know who I am speaking to, before I kill you that is!"

"My name is Louis Dubois, I have come from Britain and the scientific community there, to ask you to return with me. You must know all too well the consequences of the information you have and it falling into the hands of the Nazis. You have to come with me Doctor, we could be back in a few days and you would be safe, even if you don't want to continue with your work, you have my assurances"

"Well Louis, if that's your real name, which I doubt, you see I don't have to do anything. I am comfortable here and as you suggest, I do know the consequences of the Nazis getting their hands on me. To be honest, I have taken precautions should that eventuality arise. You see Louis, I don't actually trust anyone, no matter what side they represent. I am certain that whoever gets their hands on my work will use it for their own ends, and those ends will not be peaceful. The monster I created is too dangerous to be let out of its cage, to do so would be utter madness. I have absolutely no intention of doing that, no matter which side you represent!

So, I do not intend going anywhere, so shoot me if you want, I no longer care. I am sick of the hiding, false names, sleepless nights wondering if that noise in the darkness was someone coming to get me. One question though before you do, how on earth did you find me?"

"It's a long story Doctor, it began with and imposter who said he was you, but the truth was, he was a colleague of yours I guess, he is now dead. It's been a prolonged job on my part and all I want is to return to Britain and live the rest of my life with my family, in relative safety. I have cheated death and ducked away from danger on numerous occasions, like the proverbial cat, I will soon run out of my nine lives"

"Imposter Louis, how did that happen, I would imagine there are not too many men with a patch over their eye purporting to be a scientist?"

"I didn't know at that time of your exact description Doctor, much to my disgrace. I kind of fell for a cognac salesman and his story, he said he was you. It all seemed very plausible at the time and perhaps in my hurry to be out of France and back with my family, I believed him"

"Oh, you don't mean Claude Allen do you, that old rascal? No, I can see why he deceived you, he certainly had a silver tongue, he was able to spin the very best of stories. He was my main assistant in England and here in France during the early days. He knew all the main concepts of the project but none of the details. How is the old dog, I owe him a drink or two?"

"I am afraid he died in an air crash on the way back to Britain, I was lucky to get away with my own life. It was only later that I found out that he wasn't actually you"

"That's a shame I rather liked Claude, you know he stole my briefcase, it took me ages to work out what had happened to it. My father bought it me when I graduated from university, it had my initials on it C.A.D. I don't suppose you saw it did you?"

"As a matter of fact I did, it was those letters on the case that sent me off on a wild goose chase. I am afraid it was also lost in the air crash, sorry about that"

Doctor Durand looked down at the ground, "it was the only thing I had left from my parents, dam you Claude!"

"Now Doctor, please, can I ask you to return to Britain with me?"

"No, I am afraid this is where I stay and there is nothing you can do to persuade me otherwise"

With that, he turned, went back into the house and closed the door behind him. There was a complete and eery silence about the place, even the sound of the river had faded into the background. It seemed that the Doctor had made up his mind, there was no way Peter could force him back to Britain, so it seemed that only one possibility now remained.

He turned to walk back to the front of the house and Madeline when the rear door opened once more. This time Claude A Durand had left his pistol behind, he was looking somewhat dejected, but he looked directly at Peter.

"You better come and bring your wife or whatever she is with you, we need to talk and have a glass of wine"

"Thank you Doctor, we will be with you in a second"

He ran around to the front of the house and summoned Madeleine, she joined him at the rear of the bungalow. They carefully walked inside, acutely aware that this could be a trap, carefully surveying every detail as they slowly entered.

Claude A Durand was sitting at a small square table with four chairs, in the middle of the kitchen. It had certainly seen better days, as had the kitchen in general. It was neat and tidy and appeared very clean. A wood burning range, a small sink and a couple of cabinets, one with glass doors displaying a number of decorated plates completed the scene.

"Come in you two, I am in no mood for violence, here have a glass of red, it's rather nice, I buy it from a local in the town"

He poured a glass for each of them from a clear glass bottle with no label. The sound of the wine spilling into the glasses felt very familiar and helped to settle the situation.

He pushed a glass towards Peter and Madeleine and gestured for them to sit at the remaining chairs.

"Now, Louis Dubois, what is the name of your wife, or perhaps girlfriend?"

"She is my wife, and her name is Madeleine, she is part of what I am doing and knows as much as I do, so please speak freely"

"Welcome to my humble home Madeleine, I hope you enjoy the wine. Now Louis, how much do you know about my work, about project Simurgh?"

"Well Doctor, apart from the historical material, I know it's a weapon that's more than capable of winning the war or losing if the enemy gets their hands on it. I know that my masters are desperate to get you back to Britain and have ordered me to prevent the Nazis from getting their hands on you and your knowledge, no matter the cost"

"Well, I understand what you are saying Louis, I come with you or die, simple really. To be honest, ever since I constructed Simurgh, I kind if guessed something like this might happen.

I had made a monster and I knew that one day someone would want to use it. That's one of the reasons I came back to France, not really to fight for my country but to get away from those lunatics who would use Simurgh, and they will

Louis, no matter what they tell you. Once they do, be they British, American or German, the world will be very different for those generations who follow, if it survives at all. You see Louis, there are some things that cannot be freed, cannot be used, no matter what circumstances prevail at the time"

He sat back in his chair and took several mouthfuls of his wine, emptying the glass completely. He reached forward for the bottle and re charged his glass, this gave Peter his chance to ask a question.

"So why is Simurgh so dangerous Doctor, I don't know any of the details, what is it that makes it so perilous?"

He laughed gently before answering the question, taking another large mouthful of wine before he did so.

"Louis, it would take me several days to explain exactly what project Simurgh is, but if you don't mind the simple version, I am more than happy to help"

"Please go-ahead Doctor, simple is good, especially to me"

"Simurgh is a gas, a very clever gas that destroys all living things. It's clever because it can, well for want of a better word, take care of itself. It will replicate its matrix and persist for, well for ever if left unchecked.

The original idea was to produce a chemical weapon, as they had in the first world war, a gas that could be sprayed from aircraft, or fired from shells. The problem with that, is we have advanced in protective clothing and gas masks. Most of those older weapons would not be particularly effective, so we had to develop something better.

Well, things advanced over time and of course money really helps, and the Allies were very liberal with their money, especially once it became obvious what Hitler was doing in Germany in the 1930's.

Anyway, I had the best facilities, the most intelligent scientists and all the money in the world. I guess I became complacent about all of this, for a scientist to get absolutely everything they want is unheard of. When I say complacent, I mean I wasn't thinking about the consequences of what I was doing, you see people like me have a duty to understand what our work will ultimately be used for, but I didn't.

I lost all sight of the end game and just threw myself into my work, we crossed frontiers in science that no one thought possible. We were working around the clock, seven days a week, it was relentless. Developments came weekly, sometimes daily, new improved variants, better effectiveness, enhanced deadliness, we were drunk on our success.

Eventually we developed T65/49, the ultimate and most advanced Simurgh, the end was now here. We had a gas that could be sprayed from aircraft, shot from a gun, even thrown in a grenade. It would not degrade over time, it would stick to any surface it came into contact with, it would kill, without prejudice, any living thing it touched.

There will never be any type of equipment that will protect you. Any kind of natural or manmade clothing would be burnt away in a few seconds and worse of all, in the right circumstances, it will actually replicate itself.

The only people who would have the antidote would be the Allies, so why not use it, so long as you have the antidote, what would be the harm? The harm Louise would be to the people, the children, plants and animals, everything out there that this weapon touched, it would all be burnt away and to what end? Why gain victory over a black and burnt earth, a seared rock, a lifeless void. All so the politicians and generals could claim victory, cover themselves in medals and hope that everyone would forgive them.

You see Louis, we had developed a weapon, like the Simurgh of legend, that would burn the world, destroy it many times over, we were the bringers of death. Of course, we scientists knew this thing wouldn't ever be used, it was just a scientific project, how stupid and naive were we, I can't believe we even thought like that!

Anyway, the powers that be now wanted the formulars, all of the details they had paid for, so they could weaponize T65/49, make the ultimate dooms day weapon. Of course, they said they will never use it, it's just a threat, why would we want to destroy the world?

The answer to that is simple, we have always used what we have, especially if things aren't going to plan. Worse of all, I never really thought they understood what Simurgh could actually do, they were just as drunk on their own power as we had become. The excitement in the meetings with the military and the politicians, the laughter at the thought of what they could do, the eagerness to get at the enemy, burn them black and turn their country to ashes. Louis I have never felt such fear, no terror, and it was all my fault.

So, I decided to hide that information, get rid of all of the Simurgh T65/49 we had made and disappear, somewhere where I could not bring about the end of the world. It was easy really, they had the result they wanted, I just had to make some excuses about tidying up and I would deliver everything in a few days.

We destroyed all the Simurgh, we dispersed ourselves as far away as we could and I hid the documentation in a bank vault, caught the next ferry to France and disappeared.

I thought that was the end of that, but here you are so that didn't work very well. The thing is though, I simply don't have the Simurgh project in my head, I am surprised anyone even thought like that. It's all safe and sound in a bank vault in England, not here in France. Even if the Nazis captured me and tortured me for days, I couldn't give them even ten percent of the details they would need. Even if they gave me the best labs and minds in Germany, it would take me years to replicate what we had. Without that documentation, Simurgh simply doesn't exist.

So, Louis and Madeleine, this is now your decision, are you going to become the purveyors of death, are you going to take me back, tell them where the documentation is hidden? I will leave that decision to you, it's your call but please bear in mind what the consequences will be for humanity and the world, and please remember, it will all be your fault!"

Chapter 18.
The office of Oberleutnant Karl Wagnor.
June 8th, 1943.

Lieutenant Schneider sat down at the conference table opposite Oberleutnant Karl Wagnor. The room was wood panelled, dark and somewhat oppressive with a slight odour of cigarette smoke. A tray with a pot of steaming coffee and two cups had been positioned in the middle of the table. The smell of the coffee reminded Lieutenant Schneider of his favourite café in Berlin, just before the war.

"Right Lieutenant, what's the progress with the extra troops and the search for the Sister, the RAF pilot and the British Agent, Louis Dubois?"

"We have been given sixty troops, the base commander said that he could not spare anymore and would not extend. I have deployed forty to the area around Saint Aderald, they are already searching for the persons you mentioned and the members of the local Resistance. I am certain that they will find everything we need very soon. They have already made some arrests, I will commence interrogation this morning.

I have deployed the rest to Chênes, there has been a report of a double murder of a prison manager and his wife. There may be some connection, but we need to find out more first. I have also received some information from an informant that some strangers have been seen in the area, two men and two women. The informant could not identify them, but they have been seen around Chênes for several days"

"Right Lieutenant Schneider, slight change in plan, I will head up all of the investigations here, get the man in charge of the forty troops to report to me, this morning. You will proceed immediately to Chênes, take Corporal Schmitt with you and base yourself in the Police station over there. Find out who these people are and bring them back here. Take charge of the twenty soldiers and use any means necessary, I don't care what you do or how you get them just bring them to me, do you understand?"

"Yes sir, I will start immediately"

Chapter 19.
The Police Station, Chênes.
June 9th, 1943.

Lieutenant Schneider and Corporal Schmitt made themselves at home in a large office on the first floor of the police station in Chênes. Up until their arrival, it had been the local Police Inspectors office, and he was none too pleased to be told to leave and take all his personal belongings with him. He was now sharing an office with his second in charge on the ground floor.

There was one large desk and many document cabinets in addition to an oblong conference table and six chairs. The large windows opened up over a square with many shops, a couple of street sellers and opposite, the impressive Hotel Paris.

"I think we will dine in the hotel this evening Schmitt, it looks rather nice over there, perhaps we could book ourselves in for a week, it would be easier than traveling back to the manor house each night. Wagnor did say 'base yourself in Chênes and I don't care what you do and to use any means necessary'. Well, it might be that he meant us to stay in that splendid hotel, eating their food, drinking their wine and enjoy being in France, even if it's just for a week or so"

"I am not sure that Oberleutnant Wagnor meant all of that sir, but I can say that we became confused about his orders, and I ended up walking over there and booked us in, for a week, with meals provided?"

"Yes Schmitt, orders can be very confusing, so we understand that Oberleutnant Wagnor wanted us to stay here, for one complete week, in that hotel?"

"That's what I understood sir, a full week, all meals and wine provided, in large suites"

"Yes, that's what he meant, so what are you waiting for Corporal Schmitt, can you not simply follow the orders of Oberleutnant Wagnor, so get over there and book us in"

The young Corporal Schmitt sprang to attention, and with a smile on his face, about turned and marched out of the office.

He had gone for no more than ten minutes when there was a knock on the door, "enter"

A rather tall and aggressive looking Sergeant Major entered the room, he marched over the desk at which Lieutenant Schneider was sitting and came to attention.

"Sir, I am Sargent Major Wolfs, I have twenty men at my command from the army base, I am reporting to you for further orders"

"At ease Sergeant, where are your men staying?"

"We have tents and three trucks, we have set up a camp near to the prison, my men are quite happy there sir"

"Excellent Sergeant, well I suggest that you and your men make yourselves at home in your camp, and I will see you here at 08:00 tomorrow morning"

"Yes sir"

Lieutenant Schneider smiled at the Sergeant marched smartly out of the office. This was going to be an interesting few weeks, he had plenty of help, a comfortable office and with a little luck, he would catch the people involved.

Best of all, Wagnor had given him complete control to do exactly as he pleased, and if he managed to catch the people in question, he would certainly do that. After all, Lieutenant Schneider had certainly enjoyed himself on the first time he was here, when he visited the brothel in the old town and spent much of his wages on Champaign and women.

That evening Lieutenant Schneider and Corporal Schmitt settled down outside the Hotel Paris for their evening meal. Schmitt had managed to book two very luxurious rooms with the provision of breakfast an evening meal for a whole week.

The evening was about as perfect as you would ever get, calm, sunny and warm. They sat back, still wearing their uniforms and enjoying the cummings and goings of the large square. There were fewer people about at this time in the evening, but the place still had an active and community feel.

"It reminds me of some of the squares in Berlin sir, makes me feel a little homesick"

"I know what you mean Schmitt, but we are here in France, and I am going to enjoy every single minute. We need some girls to entertain us and a bottle or two of the local wine, don't worry, you will soon forget Berlin"

"What about catching these people sir, who exactly are we looking for?"

"Right, most importantly of all, we are looking for a British Agent by the name of Louis Dubois, a downed RAF pilot and a catholic Sister by the name of Beverley Jane. The Sister is a member of the local Resistance and after I have interrogated her, I will have her shot, no wait, hung, yes, I will hang her myself. The pilot will be of little use, so I will have him disposed of in the nearest ditch, and of course there is the British Agent. This is where we need to be careful Schmitt, we don't know what he is up to, why he is here, it's not his first time you see. There are a couple of possibilities, Wagnor seems to think it's something to do with a French scientist. Once we capture him, I will interrogate him, I will find out exactly what he is up to before he dies"

"Sounds like a reasonable plan sir, when we find him should I begin a surveillance operation on him, try to find out what he is up to?"

"Possibly, but I would rather interrogate him for a few days, much more fun than following someone around for a week. I will see how I feel, I do fancy inflicting some pain, making someone's life an absolute misery, just before they die"

Schneider burst out into an uncontrolled laugh, his face turning red as he started to cough, his eyes sparkling with emotion as he thought of the agony and absolute misery that he could soon be inflicting.

"Oh yes Corporal Schmitt, I am going to like it here, I am going to like it a lot"

Upstairs in the Hotel Paris, Peter sat on the corner of the bed in Madeline's room. The room was somewhat larger than his and had a view over the square. The heavy drapes over the window and the thick carpet enhanced the luxury feel of the room, along with the classic French boudoir furniture.

She was still in the bathroom, he had been waiting for what seemed like an age and he was starting to feel very hungry.

"How long are you going to be in there, I said we would be at Doctor Durand's house by six, it almost five thirty, hurry up"

"Don't rush me, anyway you haven't told me what your final decision is going to be. It's been twenty-four hours since we were over there last, are you going to take him back or not?"

"I will tell him the same as the imposter last time I was here, it's not up to me, they are my orders, I have no choice. I will let the powers that be answer all the ethical questions, in any case if I don't take him back, they will send someone else out to get him. So, I can save someone else a job and take him or kill him myself, leaving him here, no matter what I think, isn't going to change anything"

"So, what if he says, I am not coming?"

"I don't think he will, we have found him, so what's to say that the SS won't. No matter what his worries are with the Simurgh project, it's better trying to deal with the British that the SS and the Gestapo"

"I am still not sure Peter, it wouldn't surprise me if when we get there, he has simply disappeared. Why didn't we just take him yesterday, if you were so worried about him running, why didn't we take him prisoner?"

"Good question, but what exactly where we supposed to do? Our only radio is hidden in a ditch in Belgium, our car is stolen from the local German Army. Richard in an RAF pilot who is on the run and I assume the SS now think that Sister Beverly Jane is a member of the French Resistance.

Oh yes and that lunatic Wagnor has murdered the only contact we have out here and his wife. So, unless you have a better take on things, I would say that we are well and truly screwed. That's why I didn't just grab him and run, we would need the local bus to get us all out of here and a cage to lock Durand up in, so he didn't escape!"

He could hear her laughing on the other side of the bathroom door.

"Can I assume Peter, that we will need one almighty plan to get us out of this mess?"

"You are right there, and I am not so sure such a plan exists, in fact I am certain that it doesn't, we need to get creative and very soon"

The door handle to the bathroom started to turn, the door opened and there stood Madeleine. She looked stunning, dressed in a simple blue dress, heels and with her hair hanging loosely around her shoulders. She reminded Peter of the first occasion that they had met, all that time ago in the old shack, just after the crash.

She smiled at him, her dimples and her sparkling eyes shone, in all the problems and dangers they had survived together, he had forgotten just how beautiful she was. Time seemed to stand still, she gracefully moved across the room, over to the dressing table, looking in the mirror to check that everything was in place, she had never looked so beautiful.

She flicked at her hair, checked her lipstick and then caught a glance of him looking at her in the mirror.

"What Peter, have you never seen a woman checking her makeup before? It's not being vein you know, it's our duty"

He chuckled, "I know but with everything that's been going on I kind of forgot"

"What, that I am a woman?"

"No, well yes, no, it's just you tend to concentrate on staying alive, trying to stay one step ahead, come up with the next plan, you know what I mean. It's not about normality it's about survival, isn't it?"

"I understand what you are trying to say, our whole time together has been abnormal. Fishing you out of a burning Spitfire, fighting the Germans, trying to find the traitor in the Resistance, just trying to stay alive.

Hell, have we ever done anything regular, I don't think we have, we have hidden down a well, been shot at in the forest, run off to Belgium, been strafed by the RAF and look at us now?

Normal, not sure I know what that means anymore, whatever it is, I would like a few days of normality to relax in, that would be just fine"

He stood up, walked over to where she was standing and took her gently by the shoulders. She was wearing a sweet-smelling perfume, her hair still smelt of the shampoo and he was reminded of her gentle and supple body.

"One day Madeleine you will have your wish and you will be able to spend the rest of your life just relaxing in consistency, I am sure"

She turned to face him, she was smiling, the shivers ran down her spine with the firm touch of his hands. She wanted nothing more than to give herself to him but thought better of it, well at least for now!

"I will hold you to that Peter Parker, maybe you will be there to help me out?"

He laughed, turned and moved away, he had to before he lost control and threw her down onto the bed and spent the rest of the evening making passionate love to her. He stopped by the door and turned, "where did you get that dress, it really suits you"

"Sister Beverley gave it to me, she said I had to wear it but to ask no questions as to where it came from, I guess it was something to do with Didier"

She turned to look out of the window, "so you like it Peter?"

Before he had time to answer, she stood back from the window, with a hasty movement, like a cat startled by the arrival of the local dog.

"Peter, there are two German SS soldiers down there having their evening meal, do you recognise them?"

He slowly moved towards the window, taking care not to attract any attention from below.

"No, I can't say I do, I wonder what they are doing here, it might be worth staying out of the way until we find out?"

"I wonder if the other two know they are here, it might be an idea to tell them, we don't want to be spotted, especially Sister Beverley, they will have her description I am sure"

They hurriedly gathered in Sister Beverley's room, Madeleine went to find Didier, perhaps he could shed some light on the issue. It was several minutes before Madeleine finally returned.

"Didier is on his way, he has gone to find out what he can"

The four paced around nervously in Sister Beverley's room, Didier eventually arrived, carefully opened the door and closed it warily behind him.

"Right everybody, I have some very bad news for you, you will need to change whatever plans you have. Gabriel, the chief of police has just called in for his evening drink before he goes home. He calls it his, 'my time', before he goes home to his family. Well, he is very angry indeed, in fact I have never seem him like this in all the years I have known him. He is normally a controlled and measured man, in everything he does.

Apparently, the two German SS men outside are here to look for some dangerous enemies of the state. I guess that's you four, I can't think of anyone else around here who is at least a little dangerous, apart from being drunk at the weekend.

Anyway, they have thrown him out of his office, and he is now slumming it on the ground floor with a 'load of smelly idiots', his words not mine. Can you imagine how he feels, the local Chief of Police, ordered out of his office, command of the local forces turned over to the SS? They wouldn't tell him any more than that, but I will bet it's you they want. I would suggest you stay upstairs in the hotel, you are safe here, at least until they go"

Peter was the first to speak, "thanks for the information Didier, however, myself and Madeleine have got to go out tonight, we have no choice. I am fully aware of the potential of the SS, and I am in no mood to tangle with them, but we have to continue with our mission"

"OK, give me your car keys and I will get the porter to bring your car around the back. Just give me a minute or two, at least you can stay out of sight, once you are away from the Hotel you should be fine"

Without another word, he turned and left, the four remaining were silent, no one could think of what to say next. Eventually Peter addressed the group, he ran his fingers through his blond hair several times before speaking.

"Right, we need to think fast and prepare to move away. Madeleine and I are going to see someone tonight, we will be back late. Don't go out, stay in your rooms, you should be safe there. As soon as we get back, we will get out of here, not sure where but we can't stay. I assume that Saint Aderald will be just as dangerous for us, so we might be travelling far from here, any questions?"

The room was completely silent, "right, we are off, don't panic, just stay put, see you later"

Madeleine and Peter left, making their way down the back stairs to the rear entrance of the hotel. At the same time, their stolen German army car arrived, they took possession from the porter and drove away from the hotel. Their journey out of town was done in complete silence, partly from the shock of the arrival of the SS soldiers and partly because of what now lay in front of them. Tonight would be the culmination of many weeks work on the part of Peter, the whole mission would now depend on the next few hours, as might the outcome of the whole war.

They drove south, out of the new town, past the turn for the brewery and over the bridge. They soon entered the large wood and turned right down the road, parallel to the river, eventually turning onto the track towards the fishing lodge.

"Do you think he will be here Peter, or will he have done a runner?"

"Part of me hopes he will have gone, it will save me and you a whole lot of trouble, but trouble, as you might have noticed, seems to follow me around. I think he will be there, what else is he going to do, he can come with us or wait until the SS find him, I know which I would prefer"

"Then what do we do, just drive back to Belgium, get the spare radio and ask for help?"

"Yep, I am afraid that's the plan, seems a bit inadequate doesn't it but I can't think of anything else, can you?"

"No but we can't just drive all the way back there for that radio, can we? We were nearly caught coming this way, we were strafed by the RAF, searched at the border, we won't get away with it again Peter, I am certain of that. It was a miracle that we got this far, in my experience, miracles don't happen twice!"

"The problem is Madeleine, I think you are absolutely right, but I don't see any other way, if you have a plan, now is the time to speak up?"

Before she could reply, the little cottage came into view, it was just as pretty as she remembered it, the evening sun shining, the whole place had an idyllic feel to it. One good piece of news was Doctor Durand's car was parked at the front of the cottage, at least it looked like he was still here.

"Right Madeleine, let's go and see what the good Doctor says"

They both exited the car, walking across the crunchy gravel towards the front door. Before they reached the steps, the front door opened and there stood Doctor Claude A Durand.

"Well, I didn't think you two were coming, all that fuss about taking me back to England and you reneged on the deal"

"No Doctor, we never let anyone down, the deal stands, come back with us and then you have the choice of what you want to do next"

"Come in you two, I have dinner ready, it's not much but there is plenty of wine and some local beer"

The meeting went better than either Madeleine or Peter expected, Durand seem to be happy with the move back to England. He had no family in France so there was nothing in particular keeping him in his native country.

"I have to ask the question Louis, how are we going to get back, I guess by aircraft?"

Peter laughed, "we were just talking about that on the way here. We do have a bit of a problem you see, the only radio we have is a bit of a journey from here. In fact, it's a lot of a journey if I am perfectly honest, and the chances of not getting caught are slim at best"

"So, what you are saying is, I stay here and get caught by the SS or come with you and get caught by the SS, seems like me and the SS have an appointment at some time in the near future!"

"I wouldn't be that pessimistic Doctor, but we do need to be very careful. We have no choice but to try, you must understand that, and the truth is, you will never be safe anywhere in France. If I can find you, by myself, the whole German army shouldn't have much of a problem at all!"

Durand started to laugh, louder and louder, perhaps it was the wine and beer, perhaps the partial release of stress in the situation but he couldn't stop laughing. Soon Madeleine and Peter had joined in, they topped up their glasses, tucked into the dinner and drank the night away. The power of the alcohol and the easy company set a hazy comfort over their worries and concerns, smoothing like a balm to their fears.

June 10th. Doctor Claude A Durand's house.

It was Madeleine who woke first, just after first light, she looked at the clock on the mantle, it gently ticked away. After forcing her eyes into focus, she managed to read the time, it was a little past eight in the morning. The waves of nausea and banging headache soon overwhelmed her as she curled up into a ball and pulled the blanket up over her head.

"Where the hell am I, I thought we went back to the hotel last night?"

She pushed the blanket back down again, she was prostrate on a large settee in the lounge of Doctor Claude A Durand's house. With blurry eyes, she looked around for Peter, he was half laying and half sitting in an old leather armchair in the corner of the room. The low table in front of her was covered in bottles of varying different colours, most without labels, but judging by the taste in her mouth, all had contained some form of alcohol.

"Oh, my head is going to explode, I need to wake Peter, try and find out what's happening next, that's if all last night's drinking hasn't killed him off"

With the room still turning slightly, she pulled her legs up and placed her feet on the floor. It was difficult to stand but she made the effort, bracing herself on the low table before standing completely upright. Moving gingerly, she made her way over to Peter and gently shook him awake.

"Peter, wake up, I can't remember anything about last night, what are we doing here still, shouldn't we be back in the hotel?"

He opened his eyes, one at a time and looked straight at her. His eyeballs were red, the sockets around his eyes puffy and dark. He took a deep breath and slowly pushed himself into an upright position, taking several deep breaths as he did so.

"What's the time Madeleine, I feel so ill? It was too late to travel back last night, and I was way too drunk to drive. The Doctor said he was going to wake me at dawn, well that plan didn't go so well did it!"

"It's past eight Peter, we need to get going, and find out where Durand is"

"I am hoping he is sleeping in his bed, I don't fancy chasing him around France feeling like I do"

"You go and check Peter, I will make some coffee"

He dragged himself up by the arms and pushed off the leather armchair and stood upright.

"Peter, you look worse than me, do you remember much about last night?"

"Not really, we had dinner came in here and got drunk, that's about the lot. I do remember saying goodnight to Durand and tucking you in. The next thing I remember was you waking me up"

Madeleine slowly made her way into the kitchen, grabbed the coffee pot filled it with water and coffee and put it on the stove. There was a box of matches next to the cooker, she lit the gas and looked around for some cups. Within a few minutes the pot began to gently boil, the aroma a fresh coffee made her feel a little better. She removed the percolating coffee pot and poured three very strong cups of coffee, sat at the table and waited for Peter and Durand.

Doctor Durand was the first to come through the door, he looked fresh and rejuvenated by his nights sleep. He had a smile on his face and a twinkle in his eyes, he appeared very happy indeed.

"Good morning my dear, did you sleep well. I did offer you my bed, but you refused, saying that you would rather sleep with Peter, I assume you had some fun?"

Madeleine looked up slowly at the bouncing Doctor, he was cutting a thick slice of bread from the loaf on the kitchen top.

"I think I went straight to sleep Doctor, I don't remember very much to be honest"

"Seems as if you two aren't heavy drinkers, not a bad thing of course. I slept like a baby, I do like a session on the red wine and cognac from time to time. Now, I am going to fry some bacon, would you like some?"

Madeleine got up and quickly made her way to the bathroom, the remainder of last nights food and drink was just about to make a re appearance.

June 10th. Mid morning the office of Lieutenant Schneider, the Police Station, Chênes.

There was a sharp knock on the door, Schneider, somewhat surprised by the sound, looked up from his paperwork.

He had been daydreaming, reminiscing about his last visit to Chênes and the call he made on the couple in the remote house in the woods, and how much he had enjoyed himself.

Wagnor had boasted to him about having an affair with the lady of the house, he thought she was Mrs Forelle, but he couldn't remember her first name. Worse of all though, she had threatened to expose Wagnor, tell everyone about his nasty little obsessions in the bedroom, the way he used to beat and humiliate her.

Also, she was pregnant, and it was certainly Wagnor's baby, no doubt about that. She was threatening to say he had raped her, got her pregnant. Oh yes, she was really gunning for his boss, she even had relatives in Germany, they would certainly make sure Wagnor's wife found out about his indiscretions and of course the pregnancy.

So, Wagnor had given him an order, "dispose of this slut, I don't want her spreading all kinds of rumours about me. If you see her husband, he is a manager at the local prison, his name is Jacques Forelle, get rid of him too. They are just local scum, and they don't deserve to live, especially if she is threatening me, do you understand Lieutenant Schneider, do you understand what it is I want you to do?"

That was all Schneider needed, with great relish, he called at the house, tortured Mrs Forelle before finally killing her, listening to her last rasping gasps as the blood trickled down her naked body. It was a wonderful experience for him, the kind of thing that gave him repeated pleasure in remembering. He eventually described fully what he had done to the man's wife before killing him also. The look on that man's face was a wonderful end to the day, to think he knew what had been done to his wife and what was going to follow for him. It had been fantastic, his best so far in this war and since joining the SS.

There was another knock on the door, this time a little firmer.

"Come"

Corporal Schmitt came smartly into the room, stood to attention and waited to be addressed.

"Yes Schmitt, what is it?"

"Sir, there is a man in reception, he says his name is Didier Allard, he is the owner of the Hotel Paris. He wants to see you, seemingly he has some important information about some enemies of the state?"

"Can't he give this information to you?"

"No sir, he will only speak to you"

"Very well, show him up here, I will talk to him"

The Corporal turned and marched out of the office, closing the door behind him. Lieutenant Schneider sat back in his leather office chair, and rubbed his pock marked face, his deep blue eyes shone with excitement, his thin frame squirmed in the chair.

"This might be a good day after all, I didn't expect any information this soon, I wonder what he wants in return?"

He could hear the creaking footsteps as they came up the wooden staircase and onto the top floor of the police station. His office was the only area up in the eaves of the building, apart from the small bathroom opposite. The staircase lead up to a small landing that split the two rooms, Schmitt turned and knocked on the office door.

"Come in"

Schmitt marched smartly in, followed by Didier Allard, the owner of the Hotel Paris.

"Ah, good morning Monsieur Allard, please come in and take a seat. Corporal, can we have two coffees, do you take cream and sugar Monsieur Allard?"

"Just cream thank you"

Schmitt turned and left, Lieutenant Schneider steered Allard to the oblong conference table.

"Please take a seat Monsieur Allard, whilst we are waiting for out coffee's, what is it that I can help you with?"

"I would like to do my duty Lieutenant, make sure that everyone is safe around here, ensure that you are able to do your jobs and run France in an efficient and profitable way, for both of us, if you get what I mean?"

"I am very pleased to hear that Monsieur Allard, I do enjoy working with the important people in the area, the men that have a future here in France"

"Good, well I will get down to business Lieutenant, you don't mind me talking about business, do you? You see, I do enjoy business, making deals, and of course money, after all, that's what life is about"

"No, no of course not, business makes us all richer, it's most important to the third Reich, please continue and speak freely"

"Well, since the beginning of the war, my business has suffered, as you can imagine Lieutenant. I need to boost my profits, ensure that I continue to live a comfortable life, I am sure you understand. One way I can do this, is to offer my better clients, such as yourself and your comrades, a luxurious stay in my magnificent Hotel.

I would relish the opportunity of hosting yourself and the senior members of staff here in my hotel. You could make it your officers mess, where the higher ranks live, for the duration of the war. I would of course give you the best rooms, excellent food and wine and provide girls for your entertainment.

The cost of this service would be at a reduced rate, not enjoyed by any other guest. I could even stretch to allowing yourself free access to my considerable wine cellar and provide entertainment whenever you required it, if you get my meaning Lieutenant?"

"Well Monsieur Allard, this sounds a very attractive business arrangement, but as you can imagine, we have reasonable quarters at the manor house near to Saint Aderald and trying to persuade my seniors to move here might not be easy"

"I have already thought of that Lieutenant, and I might have some information that will prove very useful. You see, I am at the heart of the community here and I know some things that could be of benefit to yourself and your superiors.

If I were to, for example, provide some information about enemies of the state, might you be able to persuade you senior officers to re locate here?"

"Well, if that information turned out to be useful, who knows, and as you are at the heart of the community, your continued support would certainly be invaluable"

"Well, this sounds very interesting Lieutenant, I think I would like to help you and the occupying forces by providing some very helpful information"

Before he had time to answer, there was a knock on the door. Corporal Schmitt entered with a tray with two coffees and a small plate of biscuits.

"Put them here on the table Schmitt"

The young Corporal did as he was ordered and left the room. Lieutenant Schneider poured two coffees, added cream for Allard and handed him the plate of biscuits.

"So, Monsieur Allard, what is this information you have about the enemies of the state?"

He took a sip from his coffee, sat back in his chair and watched Lieutenant Schneider resume his seat.

"I have recently become aware of four strange people staying at my hotel. As you can imagine, it is a large place with many guests, and I am not familiar with everyone staying there, but these four have come to my attention.

One is a Catholic Sister by the name of Beverley Jane, there is a man, I am not sure what he is, but he certainly isn't French, he speaks only English, he maybe a downed RAF pilot? Then there are the other two, he is called Louis Dubois and he has a girlfriend called Madeleine, I am not sure what they do but they seem very secretive, wanting to know information about people and where they live.

They are staying at my hotel, all you need to do is come across and arrest them"

It took every bit of control from Lieutenant Schneider not to give away his absolute delight at this information. In one foul swoop he had been handed exactly what he had been looking for, the precise mission Wagnor had given him was now within his grasp.

"Oh, now that sounds very interesting Monsieur Allard, they certainly are persons of note, let me pick them up, ask them a few questions. If this proves useful, I will certainly champion your idea with my boss and insist that we move out here to your hotel"

"That's sounds like a very reasonable idea and a profitable one as well Lieutenant Schneider"

"I will get back to you in a couple of days, once I have had a chat with these four people and my boss. I am sure we can come up with a very agreeable deal. Now, if you excuse me, I am rather busy Monsieur Allard, as are you I am sure"

They shook hands, Didier turned and left, leaving Lieutenant Schneider standing by the conference table with a huge smile on his face. He moved back to his desk and picked up the phone, pressed 4 and waited for an answer.

"Corporal Schmitt, can I help?"

"Get up here now Schmitt but before you do, get those useless soldiers up and running, I want them here in thirty minutes, fully equipped. Send that idiot Private to see the Sargent Major at the camp, no excuses, thirty minutes, do I make myself clear?"

"I am on it sir, thirty minutes"

June 10th. Mid afternoon, the house of Claude A Durand.

They and their stomachs had finally settled down somewhat, the addition of several cups of coffee and some bread and jam had helped. They sat around the kitchen table, looking rather grey and very tired, well except Doctor Durand who was still bright and annoyingly cheerful.

"Ok Peter, so what's the plan?"

"Right Doctor let's get back to the town, we need to pick up the other two and make our way to the border. The only radio we have, I buried in a ditch near to Chateau Du Beck in Belgium, just after I arrived. I did have another but that was destroyed at the border crossing on our way here. We do however have two cars, yours and mine but ours was stollen from the Germans, so perhaps we take yours and leave ours here.

They won't be looking for a silver car, that's going to help us on our journey, and we will need all the help we can get"

"Right, well I will pack a couple of things, including two pistols and a box of ammunition, I get the feeling we will need that. We should drain all the fuel into my car, that will be useful, I also have a couple of spare cans of petrol in the shed. How long before we get to Chateau Du Beck?"

"That depends on the German patrols and check points, I would imagine three days, perhaps longer, it's not going to be easy, and I still don't know what we are going to do with Richard James"

"I guess we just pray and do our best, I am looking forward to seeing England again, see some of my old friends. Of course, I actually believe that the Germans will kill me long before I get there, but what the hell, life was getting very boring indeed in that prison"

"Well, there is always hope Doctor, I am sure we will succeed"

"The only thing we will succeed in Peter is getting killed, of that I am certain"

They all got up and started to prepare for the first leg of the journey, back to pick up Beverley Jane and Richard from the Hotel Paris. Doctor Durand brought down the two pistols and ammunition and fetched the petrol from the shed, emptying it into his silver Citroen. Peter drained the fuel from the stolen German car, again putting it into the silver vehicle.

It wasn't long before they were ready to leave, Durand seemed a little reluctant at first, spending some considerable time simply looking at the cottage and walking down the bank of the river. It was a perfect afternoon, insects buzzing over the surface of the water, dicing with death from the hungry fish below, who were eying up a free snack.

"Having second thoughts Doctor?"

"No Madeleine, not really, I have spent many happy days here. I fished in the river, enjoyed the stress-free environment on a sunny afternoon. It was in such contrast to my old life, stuck in an airless lab, no feelings for a real existence or the humans who lived it. I was driven by my work, it all seems a bit pointless really, exactly what did I achieve, I will tell you, absolutely nothing of value, nothing at all.

I used to sit outside the Hotel Paris and look at the young couples, the mothers with children, people running an honest business, even the man selling stolen fuel coupons.

I felt a sense of jealousy, they had all built something real, something you could touch, experience. I on the other hand, had done nothing, I had no wife, no children, I didn't even have my own home. I never had the chance to say goodbye to my parents before they died, I was too busy with my work.

So, Madeleine, what did I achieve, what was my life all about, I really don't know is the honest answer. Living here though was pleasant, I got to enjoy nature, I could see how life passed from season to season, from year to year. All I actually achieved was the potential destruction of all of this, it wasn't worth it Madeleine, I wish I had never been so egotistic to think that it was all worth it, to think I was so important!"

The silver Citroen pulled away from the cottage, slowly crunching its way up the track towards the road. Doctor Durand was driving with Madeleine and Peter sat in the back. It was eerily quiet, it felt more like a funeral cortege than a move for freedom.

Eventually they reached the main road turned left towards the woods and on towards Chênes. As they almost exited the woods, the bridge by the brewery came into view but things were different. Durand slowed the car, there was a queue both sides of the bridge and German soldiers everywhere.

"Peter, there is a checkpoint on the bridge, I have never seen that before, what do you want me to do?"

"Stop here, before we leave the protection of the trees. Madeleine and I will jump out, we will wait here. You get to the Hotel and pick up Sister Beverley, I think you know what she looks like, ask the Hotel owner, and don't forget Richard, and get them back here, do you know another way, one that won't be checked by the Germans?"

"Yes, I do, I will come back via the water pumping station, there in an old bridge there, it's just wide enough to get a car over. There is no way they will know about that, I will come back via a track I know, it comes out by the closed Military Hospital. Stay here, I will pick you up and we can make our way to Saint Aderald, I shouldn't be more than an hour or so, just stay out of the way"

Durand slowed the car, Madeleine and Peter slid out, stumbling to the ground as they did so. Within a second, they were deep in the forest, safe in the dark cool coverage of the trees. It felt like they had embraced them, protecting them from detection. Durand pulled away, towards the bridge and an uncertain situation.

"What's that all about Peter?"

"I am inclined to think a routine check of documents and people, but I am not sure. There seemed to be a lot of soldiers there just for a document check, I wonder what they are up to, they may be looking for us?"

Durand slowed the car to a stop at the bridge and wound the window down. A tall and very young-looking soldier approached, he seemed angry, perhaps frustrated by this routine work.

"Documents, where are you going and why?"

"I am the Manager of the prison on the other side of town. I need to call into work for an hour or so, someone has escaped, is that who you are looking for?"

"No it not, where do you live?"

"Just on the other side of the river, not far from here. I have a small cottage, it's rather nice, do you know it?"

"No and I don't care about your pathetic home. Have you seen anyone suspicious around your house recently?"

"I haven't, I would report that to the Police if I had. I know the Head of the Police in Chênes, he is a personal friend of mine"

"Oh is he, well you come and tell us if you see anyone, not him, do you understand?"

"Certainly, I will do that straight away"

"Right, move on"

Durand pulled away from the checkpoint, trying not to rush or look suspicious in any way whatsoever. Inside was a different story, his heart was pounding and his mouth dry. This had been a close call and a lesson in why you should never become complacent.

It didn't take long to reach the square in the new part of Chênes. He didn't see any more military but there was an increased feeling of stress about the place. He pulled into the square and parked his car in front of the impressive Hotel Paris. There were several people sat outside enjoying a coffee and an afternoon snack. Prominent amongst them was Leo Monet, the Chief of Police for Chênes.

Durand exited the car and walked over to Monet's table, he seemed withdrawn in a dark mood, something Durand had not often seen.

"Good morning Leo, having a break?"

He looked up at Durand, he raised both eyebrows and almost smiled at his old friend before the frown returned to his face.

"Ah, Claude, I didn't see you pull up, on your way to work?"

"No, I just fancied a coffee"

"Please sit, have your coffee with me, I need someone to talk to, these Germans have driven me mad, do you know what they have done?"

Leo Monet summoned the waiter and ordered coffee and some snacks for himself and Durand. He gestured for Durand to sit down next to him, he was very insistent, so Durand accepted his invitation readily.

"Leo, I have a job to do so I can't be more than a few minutes. what's happened, I have not seen you liked this before?"

"It's those dam SS, they marched into my office, threw me out and now they are making arrests and setting up roadblocks without even talking to me. They even took two people from the Hotel this morning, I think the woman was Sister Beverley Jane from Saint Aderald, I don't know who the man was"

Doctor Durand's mouth fell open in shock when he heard this news, a rush of panic surged through his body. Sister Beverley was certainly one of the people he was supposed to get, he assumed the other was the RAF pilot Richard James. This turned the mission completely on its head, whatever Peter had in mind would now have to be changed, even if there was an alternative, which he doubted.

"What did they want them for Leo?"

"That's my point Claude, they don't even talk to me about what they are doing. Goodness knows, I mean Sister Beverley, what on earth would you want to arrest her for? They marched her and that other man across the square and straight into the Police station"

"Did you not think to ask, you are the Chief of Police?"

"I did, I followed the goons over to my Police station, yes 'my' Police station, and was promptly told to get out before I found myself in the cells. I tell you Claude, that Lieutenant in there is an absolute lunatic, who the hell does he think he is?"

The coffee arrived along with the snacks, Durand looked at the two small cups and the plate and wondered what to do next? He was certain that the two arrested people were the people he was supposed to pick up, he had to get back to Peter and Madeleine and give them the news.

"What will they do with them Leo?"

"I don't know, I suppose it depends on what they think they are, they could release them, throw them into your jail or shoot them, who knows? I don't envy them I must admit, if it's got anything to do with that lunatic, well if they didn't survive the night, I wouldn't be surprised. You looked shocked Claude, do you know them, are they friends of yours?"

"Now you sound like a Policeman again Leo. Thanks very much for the coffee but I must be off, time and tide wait for no man and neither does a mountain of paperwork on my desk"

He looked up at Durand as he stood, "If you need any help with anything Claude, all you need to do is ask, you know that don't you, absolutely anything? I am your friend, you know you can trust me, whatever the problem is!"

He looked down at Leo Monet, he had a very serious look on his face. They were good friends, he knew him very well. Did Monet want to say something else, had he already guessed what the issue with the arrested couple really was?

"Thank you Leo, I will bear that in mind, take care, I will catch up with you tomorrow"

"You know where I live and work Claude, I will be here at lunch time if you need me"

He got back into his car and drove back towards Madeleine and Peter, this time taking the diversion towards the water pumping station and the hidden bridge over the river. He was certain that the Germans would never find that bridge, he hoped he was right!

June 10th. Early evening the cells under the Police Station, Chênes.

Lieutenant Schneider walked around the single chair which had been placed in the middle of the dusty and dry concrete room under the Police station. Richard James sat motionless, hand tied behind his back and blindfolded.

His mouth was dry, he tried not to shake or show any signs of fear, but it was becoming increasingly difficult. To date his experiences in France had been somewhat of a jolly jape, a rather fun game but things had now become extremely serious indeed. In the next few moments, he could lose his life and no one would know, no one would be able to see what happened.

Schneider could feel the fear and he liked it, it made him feel strong and excited just to think that such anguish was all his doing. He bent down to Richard's left ear and whispered.

"Now, if you cooperate, I will personally make sure you end up in a prisoner of war camp with all the protections of the Geneva Convention. On the other hand, if you don't, I will torture you to death. Now, what's your name, how did you get here and what exactly are you doing. Also, I need to know where your friends are and what is their mission here? Now please don't think that I am stupid, I am far from that and don't assume I know nothing because I do. So, tread very carefully RAF, your life depends on what you say next"

"My name is Richard James, my rank is Wing Commander, I was shot down a few days ago. I am simply trying to escape back to Britain, same thing that you would do in my position I am sure"

"Yes Richard but I am not in your position am I, in fact your position, as you put it, is extremely precarious don't you think? I could pull my pistol out now, shoot you and no one would ever know what happened to you. So, I need to think you are trying to help me Richard, you are on my side, otherwise why should I keep you alive?"

"You are going to do whatever you want with me I am sure, you know who I am and why I am here, there is nothing more I can say"

"Actually Richard, I agree, and I also believe that you won't tell me anything of any use, so I will put you back in your cell and see if Sister Beverley Jane has more to add. Of course, she is a member of the French Resistance and therefore I have full discretion in what I do with her, she has no protections from any silly Convention.

Now, you can stop that by being my friend and telling me what I need to know. I won't tell anyone what you have told me, it will be our little secret. Also, it will mean that Sister Beverley will be spared from my interrogation and simply held in Police custody until the end of the war. So Richard, what do you want me to do, have a friendly chat with you or torture Sister Beverley Jane to death?"

Richard could feel the pressure in his head rising, the rapid beating of his heart was thundering in his ears, he wondered how much longer he would be able to hear that beat before Schneider put a bullet in his brain? He tried to swallow but he couldn't, he took a deep breath and replied.

"Listen old chap, please forgive me if I sound a little suspicious about your intentions but I really don't have anything more to add. Even if I did, I am not sure that it would help me or Beverley in anyway whatsoever. I am fairly certain what your plan is, and that it involves Beverley and myself being put up against a wall and shot"

"Look Wing Commander, I am a fair and generous man so here is what I am going to do. I will have you returned to your cell and at dusk tomorrow evening I will ask the questions again, how did you get here and what exactly are you doing. Also, your other friends, you see I know there are another two people missing from our little get together. It is my suspicion that they are a couple of British Agents, trying to disrupt the war in some way and I need to know about them, where they are, what they are up to. Don't get me wrong Richard, they are spies and should be shot, but you on the other hand are a prisoner of war and will be treated with the upmost respect. If you tell me exactly what I need to know, then you have my word that you and Sister Beverley will be treated correctly and you will not be tortured or killed, I think that's a very reasonable offer, don't you?"

Richard didn't answer, he just sat still waiting for the beating, but it never came. He was simply strong-armed back to his cell, his blindfold and cuffs were removed, and the door was slammed shut.

He sat there for some time, trying to come to terms with what had just happened. There was no doubt in his mind that his life would soon end, as would that of Sister Beverley Jane whether he cooperated or not. Once Schneider had everything he wanted, he would simply kill them both and there was nothing he could do about it.

June 10th. Nighttime. The Poachers cottage, downstream of the Water Pumping Station.

It was an odd little place, damp and not very square, a single room cottage or as Madeleine called it, "a crumbling dank little hovel"

It sat only feet from the riverbank and judging by the lines that radiated throughout the place, it had been flooded on many occasions. It was leaning precariously to one side, not far from losing the battle with gravity, once and for all.

It did have a couple of advantages though, firstly, the Germans had absolutely no idea it was here. Secondly, it had a table and five chairs, two of which were completely rotten but at least they had somewhere to sit. Peter, Madeleine and Claude Durand sat on the half rotten chairs around a cobweb ridden oblong table.

"Why the hell are we sitting in this hole Peter, it makes my flesh crawl, goodness only knows what's in here with us. Please tell me there are better places for us to go"

"Not at the present Madeleine, it's as good a place as anywhere, we certainly can't go back to the Doctors house, unless you have a better plan, it's here or nowhere"

"Peter is right Madeleine, we have to assume that the two people Leo Monet saw being taken away were your friends Richard and Beverley. If that's the case, we must also assume that the SS have interrogated them, and goodness knows what they have told them. I know these people and they will stop at nothing to extract what they need, no one is able to resist them, not and live to see the following dawn.

I have no reason to believe that they know anything about me otherwise they would have arrested me on the bridge. But they will be searching everywhere and that includes out of the way places like my cottage. So, we have to stay hidden until we decide exactly what we are doing next"

"I agree with everything you say Doctor, but do we have to do it here, it stinks?"

Peter reached out and took her hand, "we have been in worse places than this, it won't last long"

"Sorry Peter but I don't actually remember any places that were worse than this and the way I see it, it will last a long while yet"

Doctor Claude Durand laughed, "listen we do have a few advantages, I am pretty sure that the Chief of Police, Leo Monet will be on our side if we ask him. We are safe here for as long as we need to be, we have a car, some money and the SS don't suspect me, well at least for now. From what Peter has said, your friends know nothing about me either, so they can't give me away to the SS"

"We have to get Richard and Beverley out of there Claude"

"Yes we do but they may already be dead, we have to expect that Peter but I think, Leo Monet will help us. I will call into town again tomorrow and ask him what has happened to them"

"Let's hope that they are still alive tomorrow morning Claude"

"I am sure they will, the SS don't rush with their interrogations, they like to take their time, they seem to enjoy it. The other thing I need to find out is from Leo Monet tomorrow is how did the

SS know about Beverley and Richard, was it luck or did someone betray them?"

"There is only one person who knew what we were doing, and that is the owner of the Hotel Paris, Didier Allard"

"I was thinking the very same Madeleine, we will have to be very careful from now on, you two going back into town is absolutely out of the question from this point on. If it was Allard who betrayed them, he won't hesitate to do the same to you!"

June 11th. First light, the Poachers Cottage.

It had been a miserable damp night, the whole place was clammy, rotten and full of ill. Madeleine hadn't slept very well, she had eventually curled up in the back of Claude's car, "not perfect", she thought, "but at least nothing will crawl across me in the night"

The sun had just about pushed up over the eastern horizon, it was a glorious morning, bright, clear and full of life. The birds were revelling in the summer sun, chasing the insects, feeding themselves frantically, ready for the winter that would eventually arrive.

Madeleine pushed the car door open, Claude A Durand was standing in front of the cottage, he looked calm and ready for the day ahead. Despite the secrets he held and the potential of the things he had created, Madeleine had been impressed by his kindness and intelligence. As soon as he saw her, he started to walk towards the car, he had a wry smile on his face.

"Good morning Madeleine, did you sleep well or is that a silly question?"

"That's a silly question Doctor, let's hope we find somewhere better, very soon indeed. So, what's the plan for today?"

"I am going to try and find Leo, the Police Chief. Try and find out who betrayed your friends. I think we know who that was, but let's be sure before we do anything about it. Also, I will suggest that we need some help in getting those two friends of yours out of the clutches of the SS"

"What happened if he goes over to the SS and betrays you?"

"I have known Leo for a long time, there is no way he would do that. Also, judging by what he said about the SS last night, I think he would be more likely to shoot the lot of them, rather than help them"

"Let's hope you are right Claude, the very best of luck, it's about time we cut a lucky break"

She watched the silver Citroen slowly disappear down the track and into the woods. She shook her head at the thought of what might come back down that track later that day. This was the most dangerous part of this and perhaps any mission she had been on. The thought of freeing Richard and Beverley seemed impossible, there was a traitor in the town and the SS had taken control of the local Police, there didn't seem any chance of success.

"Good morning Madeleine......"

"Let me stop you there Peter, no I didn't sleep well, so find me somewhere better please, and do it now"

He laughed as he walked up behind her, his strong arms embracing, wrapping themselves about her waist. She could feel his head right behind hers, she wondered if she could detect something more than comfort from him. Her hands naturally moved down to hold his, this moment of pleasure and escapism was wonderful, a brief rest bite from the horrors of the events unfolding around them.

"I am sorry Madeleine"

"Sorry for what Peter?"

"Sorry for getting you into this bloody mess, I should have left you in Belgium with your Aunt and Uncle"

"Yes, but if you remember, I chose to come with you, you didn't chain me to the back of that car"

"I know and I am so very grateful that you did, but I shouldn't have even considered asking you in the first place. What was I thinking, I was going to ask you to do all of this by yourself, I must be mad, completely stark raving mad"

"I know, but I insisted that you came with me, so that kind of evens it out. Besides which, you couldn't possibly have known that it would all turn out like this. Richard, Sister Beverley, getting shot up at the border, the bloody Hotel manager and goodness knows what else"

He laughed, "I know but it doesn't make me feel any better, thanks anyway though, I couldn't have done any or this without you"

She turned around in his arms, looked straight up into his eyes, hesitated for a moment and then kissed him full on his lips. She immediately felt very awkward, should she have done that, what would his reaction be, would he pull away?

He didn't react other than to continue the kiss for what seemed like an age. She felt a wonderful rush of emotion and pleasure, it had been so long since he had shown such passion towards her, she had missed that so much. Eventually their lips parted, she buried her head in his chest and held onto him, as if her very life depended on them staying together. He ran his hands up and down her back and then squeezed her tightly before letting go.

Staring down into her eyes, he never blinked, just gazed deep into her soul, "what was he thinking" she thought, did he still feel the way she did, would she ever find out?

He took a deep breath before speaking, he looked up, somewhere off into the distance and then back down at Madeleine. His mind seemed to have moved on, away from what had just happened, she wondered if that was deliberate or a consequence of their present predicament.

"Let's hope the Doctor finds something positive this morning, I have a bad feeling about all of this. I am sure the Chief of Police is a good friend, but I am not convinced he is going to help us"

"He is all we have Peter, if he doesn't help, I am not sure what we be able to do to get them out of the cells, I fear that we have seen the last of them?"

Doctor Claude A Durand pulled up at the front of the Police Station on the square in new Chênes. There were a couple of soldiers standing at the entrance, they looked menacing, his story had to be good, or he would also find himself a guest of the SS.

He slid out of the driver's seat trying to look relaxed, as if it was another normal day. Ensuring that his clothing was in order, he tilted his head into the air and walked towards the main entrance. Before he got anywhere near, one of the soldiers advanced, he had an angry look and was not about to take any nonsense from anyone.

"Yes, what do you want?"

"Good morning sir, I am the Manager of the local prison, here are my papers. I am here to see the Chief of Police, Leo Monet, it's about an escaped prisoner, he has some information for me"

"Some prison you run old man, how many more have wandered off, you call it a prison? I am staggered how this country managed to function before we took control, wait here"

He and his colleague laughed as they exchanged glances, before the young soldier disappeared into the station. Claude turned to look across the square, nothing seemed to be out of place, all these people had absolutely no idea of the drama that was now playing out in their town. He wondered how much would change over the next few years, would this war ever end, perhaps this was the new way of life.

"Old man, come with me"

Before he had time to turn, the soldier had disappeared into the station, the main door slamming behind him. Claude hurried up the steps and without making eye contact with the other man guarding the main door, he entered.

Almost immediately he was greeted by Leo Monet, he had a smile on his face, he held his hand out to Claude. He spoke at a slightly elevated level, ensuring that the young soldier, who was standing behind him, could clearly hear.

"Good morning is it about that prisoner, bad effort on your part, we need to find him as soon as possible. Listen, do you fancy a coffee across the square, we can discuss what our next move is going to be"

"Sorry to be a nuisance Leo, but we need to clear this up as soon as possible, and yes, a coffee would be nice"

The two men sauntered out of the Police Station, down the steps and across the busy square and sat down at a table outside the Hotel Paris. Within a few seconds a waiter appeared, Leo Monet ordered two coffees and croissants. Neither of them spoke until the waiter had delivered their order and disappeared.

Leo Monet pulled a pack of cigarettes from his top pocket, and a small silver lighter. He made a big effort to look around as he was lighting up, murmuring to Claude a warning.

"They never stop watching people Claude, just keep your eyes open and your voice down to a minimum"

He blew a large stream of smoke up into the air, again taking the opportunity to glance around.

"I overheard a conversation this morning, that idiot Lieutenant Schneider is a complete fool, shouts all the time. The benefit I have, is I can hear everything he says, as can most of the town, I am sure. Anyway, he was talking about the owner of this place and how he had been so helpful. I can only assume that it was him who betrayed the two people who were arrested. He has always been a dam rogue, I never did trust him, almost arrested him on several occasions"

"Yes, Didier Allard, I know what you mean, a greasy little man, he would sell his grandma if he thought he could make a profit"

"Claude, do you happen to know who the two people are who Schneider arrested, and why he had any interest in them?"

"To be honest Leo, I do, and I might need to take you up on your offer of last night"

"All you need to do is ask, Schneider is such a dam fool, I am certain I could tie him up in knots any time I like"

The two men laughed, but in truth, neither of them really thought that Schneider was any sort of fool and tangling with him would always prove a very dangerous task indeed.

"Right Leo, I might have some information about the two of them, I know I can trust you but please don't go putting yourself at risk, you are my friend, I don't want to go to your funeral"

He laughed, "I am in no hurry to die Claude, you know you can trust me, what is it you know?"

"I think you know one of them anyway, it was Sister Beverley Jane. The other is an RAF pilot, he was shot down not far from here. From what I understand, they were staying at the hotel, as a guest of that grease ball Didier Allard. He obviously saw some sort of profit or advantage in betraying them, so went to see Schneider.

Now, we need to get them out, they have another couple of friends who need them freed before they can leave the area. Trouble is, even with my help, that makes three, it's not going to be a match for the local German army, we need help Leo and lots of it"

Leo Monet sat bolt upright in his seat, rubbed his chin and took another cigarette out of his pack, lit it and blew several lungful's of smoke straight up into the warm morning air.

"It won't be easy Claude, in fact it might not be possible at all, even with my help, we can't just take this lot on, we need to be a little more subtle than that. Let me be clear Claude, you need those two out of the cells, free to leave and you have two others to help you?"

"I am afraid that's about it Leo, not much of a threat to the German army, are we?"

"Not at all Doctor, but you know me, I love a challenge even if it means taking on and defeating the whole German third Reich, then so be it. Can't promise we will succeed though"

The two men laughed and drank their coffee, it was an impossible task, but they were patriots, and they would do their duty.

Chapter 20.
The office of Hauptman Karl Wagnor.
The manor house near Saint Aderald.
June 10th, 1943.

He stood up and dropped the telegram from the Intelligence Office Berlin, it fell onto his desk, he turned and took a couple of steps into the bay window of his office. He stood looking outside with his hands clasped behind his back. He sighed, this war asked so much, takes life without mercy, without counting the dead, he wondered if it would ever actually end?

It was an odd picture of normality outside, a local man was mowing the lawn, two others were clearing some of the flower borders, ready for the summer bedding plants. He looked left and right but there was no sign of any military at all, it brought a smile to his face, "maybe it will end one day, perhaps I will come back and live here"

He took a cigarette out of his case and lit it, he watched the smoke hit the glass and whirl upwards.

"So, you have killed Private Lena Webber English, hung for being a spy, she was a brave woman and a credit to the fatherland. One thing is for certain, I will avenge her death, she will not have died in vain. If I catch that Louis Dubois, my vengeance will be long and very painful indeed"

The phone rang, he slowly turned and walked back to his desk.

"Wagnor"

"Sir it's Lieutenant Schneider, those two won't say anything, we either torture them or save ourselves the trouble and shoot them. What would you like me to do sir?"

"To be honest Schneider, I am in no mood for killing women, especially Catholic Sisters, or at least not publicly. So far as the RAF pilot is concerned, do as you please, I am beyond tolerance of anything to do with the Allies at this moment.

On second thoughts, send them both back here, I will send the Sister to a concentration camp, let's see how her religion helps her in one of those places. I will decide what to do with the pilot, I don't think he has anything of interest to us, let me sleep on it.

Have you made any more progress on that British spy, Louis Dubois? If you manage to get him Schneider, I promise you a promotion and a posting to anywhere you choose, just deliver him to me and I will do the rest"

"Well sir, I was hoping that the two we have might have known something, but I think it unlikely, they are just a couple of fools on the run.

Also, I don't think they had anything to do with the murder of our soldiers near to the old watermill, it is too far away, how the hell did they manage to get here without transport? No, I am certain it was the local resistance from Saint Aderald"

"I agree, have you found out anything to do with this scientist?"

"I think we need to capture the British spy to find out anything about the scientist sir. He is the man who will know his whereabouts, these two I have in the cells will know nothing, I am confident about that. I will keep trying, I have a feeling he is in this area sir, if he is, I will get him don't worry about that"

"Good, you keep on it Schneider, it will be worth your while if you succeed. I have arrested three members of the local Resistance, I had them all shot this morning, so that was a pleasant start to the day"

"That's good news sir, I will report back soon, and I will send the prisoners over tomorrow morning"

"Better check with the front desk first Schneider, we are a little busy in the cells at the moment, we wouldn't want those two prisoners of yours feeling all cramped up, would we?"

They both laughed, "in that case sir, it might be a couple of days before I get them over to you. I haven't subjected either of them to any, what can I say, more persuasive techniques yet. I do enjoy that side of interrogation, I think it brings the best out in me, so with your permission sir, I would like to try?"

"Oh, help yourself Schneider, you go and do whatever you think is right, I only wish I could be over there to help. Don't get too carried away though, I know you, you will have two dead prisoners on your hands if you get overly excited"

"I can't help myself sir, I get so enthusiastic, it makes me feel so alive to see people suffer, and there is nothing they can do about it, I do love my job sir"

"That's my worry Schneider, if we left you to get on with it, most of the French population would be long dead. Just keep yourself in check, at least a little, I don't care what you do with those two, but I would like to see them alive, well at least the Catholic Nun"

"Sister sir, she is a Sister, not a Nun"

"Well, whatever she is, try and keep her alive, don't care what happens to the RAF man though, go and enjoy yourself with him"

"Thank you sir, I will be in contact soon"

Wagnor replaced the handset and sat back down at his desk, looked once more at the telegram from the Intelligence Office, screwed it into a ball and threw it into the bin. He picked up his telephone and dialled the number for the kitchen.

"Kitchen here"

"It's Wagnor, what's for lunch, I am feeling particularly hungry today?"

"We have fish as the main course sir"

"I like fish, put me down for an early lunch"

"Already done sir"

Wagnor spung his leather chair around to face the window, the sun streamed in, it was warm and very bright, it made him squint just a little. He reached for his cigarettes, lit another one up and contemplated his situation, he chewed on his bottom lip for a few seconds.

"I will get you Dubois, if it's the last thing I do, and when I get my hands on you, I will do things to you that not even Lieutenant Schneider could dream of"

Chapter 21.
The Poachers Cottage. Early morning, June 11th, 1943.

"This plan is never going to work Claude, we are all going to end up dead. I am sorry you went to see Leo Monet last night, what were you two drinking?"

"Well Peter, if you can come up with something a little better, let's hear it now"

"Look Claude, its one thing coming up with a plan, it's another thing trying to stay alive whilst you're carrying it out. This is not going to work, they will see straight through it, we will be dead within seconds, we are wasting our time"

"It's a good plan Peter, it's going to work, there isn't anything in there that could go wrong, if we are sussed out, we simply walk away. It's safe, we will get away with it I can assure you"

"So, let me get this clear, we send a bomb to the Chief of Police, he opens it, panic ensues, the place is evacuated, we rush around the back and release the prisoners, it's not going to work Claude! We will never get away with it, it's too simple, we are all going to end up in a Gestapo jail or lying dead in a pool of blood"

"We will Peter, trust me, simple is good, Leo Monet has got a couple of his trusted men prepared, once the 'bomb' has been detected, they will evacuate the place. They will kick up such a dam fuss and panic, the whole building will empty of its own accord"

"We are dealing with the German SS here Claude, they are used to bombs, bullets and explosions, people try to kill them seven days a week. They won't be fazed by it, it will be just another day in the war, trust me"

"Well, that's the beauty of the plan, even if the SS soldiers are not panicked by the event, we haven't lost a thing have we. They will need to identify the bomb, when they find out it's a hoax it will be too late. In all the melee, shouting, noise and alarm, they will be distracted, and we will be able to grab the prisoners and run. Whatever happens, we will only succeed"

"Claude, I have to agree with Peter, this is never going to work as long as night follows day. It's just way too simple, they are not going to fall for it, trust me"

"Madeleine, I have always followed a mantra when carrying out my work, and to date its always worked for me. That mantra is KISS, 'keep it simple stupid', and trust me, whatever you two think, these SS men are stupid. They will blindly follow procedures, never daring to vary, always doing what they are taught. I am relying on them 'not thinking' and so long as they don't, the plan can't fail"

Peter looked across at Madeleine and shook his head, he drew a long and deep breath, and held the sides of his head in his hands.

"Ok, it's all we have, at least the Police are in on it, that's going to help I am sure. So how will this foolhardy escapade work then?"

"Right, we send a bomb to the Chief of Police, Leo Monet, it will arrive in the morning post. He opens it, shouts that there is a bomb on the premises. His two most trusted men will then start to run around like headless chickens, screaming and shouting and generally causing a panic. They will evacuate the whole building, making everyone muster outside on the main square.

No doubt Schneider and his sidekick Schmitt will want to take control of the situation, it's in their nature, they are megalomaniacs, they can't help themselves. So, amongst all the shouting and alarm, they will make their way to Leo Monet's office to inspect the device and see if it's real or not.

Now, this is where we come in, during all this confusion we will approach the rear of the Police Station, open the back door and enter. That passage leads to a small office, and the cells, there are three, two on the left and one on the right. We grab the set of keys from the small office, let the prisoners out and jump into my waiting car and away, simple"

"Hang on a minute Claude, how do we unlock the back door?"

"We don't Peter, Leo will do that just before the post arrives, and he will also leave a small explosive charge by that door. We will detonate that as we leave, it will make it look like the door was blown open not left open, that leaves Leo and his officers in the clear! By the time the SS react to the real bomb, we will be gone"

"And when will all this fantasy plan actually happen?"

"Tomorrow morning at around ten, the fake bomb is already in the post, Leo and one of his men designed it, they are very creative, it will look very real indeed"

Peter and Madeleine jumped back in horror, "Claude, that's insane, we aren't ready, what the hell do we do after the snatch?"

"We are as ready as we will ever be Peter, delaying will only make things worse and give the SS more time to torture your friends and possibly kill them. As for where we go, well we have a few choices. We can come back here and wait until the fuss dies down a little. We can head north, get on the coast road and head for the channel. We could go east, back through

Saint Aderald and on towards the Belgium border"

Madeleine reacted to his suggestions first, "forgive me Claude but none of those options particularly appeal. If I was Schneider, I would guess we had gone on the coast road, it's a fast rout away from here. Staying in this mosquito infested shit hole is not going to happen, I am not going to spend one more day here, no matter what the consequences are. So that leaves the Saint Aderald rout, right into the jaws of death, the local SS HQ, and then on towards the augmented Belgium border, now on high alert after the escape tomorrow. That would be sheer suicide, they would have us for certain"

"Wait a minute Madeleine, I wonder if we do go towards Saint Aderald, they will expect us to run as far and as quickly as possible. Perhaps onto the coast road towards the channel, or even west past the jail, they are the quickest routs out of the area. If we move quickly, we could find a safe place near Saint Aderald and hang out until it calms down a little. I am sure they won't expect us to be close to them, not that close, we will be hiding in plain sight, that might work? Not sure what we do about getting to the radio in Belgium though, but perhaps we cross that bridge as we come to it"

"Peter, we have been in some terrible scrapes together, but going towards Saint Aderald is suicide, just stupidity"

"That is exactly what I am hoping Madeleine, absolute recklessness, suicide, total stupidity. If we are thinking that I am sure Wagnor, and the rest of his bully boys would think exactly the same thing! They will be expecting us to run, as far and as fast as possible"

Doctor Claude A Durand started to laugh, "that's the spirit, a little reckless adventure, that's what makes life exciting, or very short, or more likely both, aren't you up for a little fun you two?"

Peter and Madeleine exchange a glance but didn't speak.

Chapter 22.
06:00 hrs. The rough ground at the back of the Police Station.
June 12th, 1943.

Madeleine, Peter and Durand sat quietly in the silver Citroen. He had managed to persuade a couple of friends to part with a can of petrol, so the car was at least half full of fuel.

"So, if the post doesn't arrive until ten, why are we sitting here at six in the morning?"

"Well Madeleine, whilst it's normally arrives at ten, it could actually turn up at any time, it may not turn up at all of course, but that's France for you"

"Oh, this just gets better by the minute, can we call this off Peter, this isn't going to work?"

"I am tempted Madeleine, but I can't honestly think of another option, so let's give it a go, what's the worst that could happen. Well apart from being killed in a hail of bullets, or getting captured and tortured to death by the SS?"

The atmosphere in the car was incredibly tense, whilst there had been some humour about the job in hand, all three of them knew that this could actually go very wrong, very quickly. Even if they managed to pull it off and get away, where would they hide, was driving toward Saint Aderald really a good idea?

Peter was in a majority of one when it came to that decision, but he was banking that they would be safely tucked away, before the troops from the manor house set out to support their colleagues in Chênes. It was a huge gamble, but he was used to big risks, he had been undertaking the highest levels of jeopardy ever since he joined the S.O.E.

The one thing that kept him going through all of this chaos was the thought of going home. He had never been a willing volunteer in the first place, just a downed RAF pilot in a burning Spitfire. The rest was a series of persuasions by his boss, Lieutenant Colonel BR Smith, and possibly even lies by him in order to continue Peter's involvement.

Of course, he had found some great friends, enjoyed the exhilaration and adrenaline rush of being an Agent in occupied France. It had become more of a drug than he was willing to admit and then there was Madeleine.

Had she also become a drug, perhaps a fixation, even an obsession? No, she was just someone he had met, a great friend, a person who he would never forget, no more than that, wasn't she?

He looked out of the driver's side window, his mind drifted away to some far-off place, where there was no war. He wished this could all go away, he was about to jump once again into the unknown, perhaps this was the last day of his life, and nobody would ever know what happened.

He wished for a reality where this dreadfulness, this hate and misery no longer existed, and life could return to normality. Strangely though, this other state, this life where war did not occupy every moment, was something he no longer had a clear memory of.

Perhaps the war had always existed, was it part of life, normality? Was ordinariness and peace just a dream, something unobtainable, something far, far away. Somehow, he just couldn't think past the beyondness of war, couldn't recall a time when it didn't exist.

He had no idea how long he had drifted way for, or even if anyone had spoken, his mind seemed to come back in a rush, like racing through the end of a tunnel and back into the light.

"What time is it, where is that postman?"

"Well, if I am not mistaken Peter, his van has just arrived in the central square. I don't know where he will call first, but we need to be ready"

The tension in the car seemed to increase a hundred-fold, this was it, they were just about to find out if Claude A Durand's plan was going to work after all. There was a pause, a brief moment of serenity and calm, that quiet moment before the storm breaks.

There was no warning at all, the uproar just started, firstly a loud bell began to ring, like a piercing bolt of lightning assaulting the senses. Next there were shouts, people running in all directions, even hidden at the back of the building they could see people spilling out and running into the square. More and more noise emanated from the Police Station, screams, yells, men's voices giving commands, the whole place seemed to be engulfed in a whirlwind of commotion.

"Right, Leo said to give it a couple of minutes before we make our move, that way the SS goons will have time to get down from the first floor and make their way into the large office where the bomb is now sitting.

"Ok Claude, then let's get organised, make sure your guns are cocked and ready to fire. We don't know what's on the other side if that door, for all we know there could be ten heavily armed soldiers just waiting for us. Let's be absolutely clear though, if it's wearing a German uniform, shoot. One thing is for sure, if you don't, they will and in my experience, the regular German army soldier is a dam good shot"

They all looked down at their weapons, Peter with his Browning 9mm, Madeleine had a

7.65mm CZ vz. 27, stolen from some dead soldier no doubt and Claude with a French MAS Model 1935. They looked at each other, waiting for someone to make a decision, finally Peter did.

"Right go, and remember my instruction, shoot at the German before he shoots you, keep going, don't stop or hesitate, keep the pressure on, any questions?"

They didn't stop to ask, Claude flung the passenger door open, Madeleine followed him out. Peter opened the driver's door and sprinted towards the back of the Police station, gun at the ready.

He finally reached the rear door, he grabbed at the handle, hoping beyond hope that the door was unlocked. If the Chief of Police had been unable to unlock it, or if a guard had been diligent enough to check if it was unlocked, then re lock it, this escapade would be over before it even started.

In that moment before he reached the handle to the door, all the possibilities of what could go wrong flashed through Peters mind. It seemed like the whole action had gone into slow motion, now was the point in time to see if this insane plan was actually going to work.

Schneider sat behind his desk reading some reports, Schmitt was flicking through some files in one of the myriad of cabinets in the office. All of a sudden, the peace and quiet was shattered in no uncertain terms. The noise of the bell was overwhelming, just a few short seconds previously, everything had been quiet and calm.

It was an assault on the senses, neither of the men could react in any meaningful way, they simply shot glances around the room and finally at each other.

"Schmitt, with on earth is that noise, go and find out what is happening, if there is some kind of problem, sort it out. And stop that dam noise, it's giving me a headache"

Schmitt didn't stop to ask questions, he opened the door and started off down the stairs.

Schneider angered by the chaos and disturbance to his morning, stood up with a look of black anger on his face.

"Dam this place to hell, these stupid idiots just can't run anything properly, right someone is going to pay for this"

As he made his way down the stairs Schmitt was running back up towards the office. He had a look of fear on his face and a degree of panic. In a few steps they met halfway down the narrow stair well.

"Speak Schmitt, what's this all about?"

"It's a bomb sir, it's in the main office and by the looks of things, it's a big one, we need to get out"

"We need to stay calm Schmitt, that's what we need to do. Now go and turn that dam noise off before I shoot everyone in the building, including you"

Without answering, he turned and ran down the stairs in an attempt to find where the noise was coming from and how to stop it. Schneider followed him down the stairs, calmly looking around at the absolute chaos raging on the ground floor. People were running around from office to office, shouting orders that were barely audible above the noise of the bell.

He shouted at the top of his voice, "stop and stand still" but no one reacted to his command. Now raging with anger, he proceeded towards the main office where the bomb had been detected. He had to force his way past several people congregating in the main lobby, including two Police Officers' who seemed intent in creating as much pandemonium as possible.

Standing in the doorway was the Chief of Police, Leo Monet. He looked red faced and somewhat scared, he was stopping anyone going into the office.

"Monet, what the hell is going on, can you stop this dam noise?"

"I will send someone to turn it off sir. There is a bomb in the office, it's a big one so you should evacuate outside, it will be much safer there, I will stay here and guard the scene. I have sent for the local French explosive specialists, they should be here in an hour or so"

"Don't talk crap Monet, let me in, it's probably just a hoax anyway and stop that dam bell!"

Peter held onto the door handle as if his life actually depended upon it. Quickly he turned it to the right, to his delight it rotated, and he felt a reassuring click as the lock disengaged.

Pushing the door open he raised his pistol and stormed inside. One thing he had learned in situations like this, is if you hesitate, you die. Shock and surprise were their best weapons now, if there was anyone left guarding the prisoner they would need to be overcome. With luck they would be French Police, Peter was sure they would simply put their hands up and walk away. On the other hand, if they were Soldiers, they would fight back, there was no doubt about that.

It took a few pressures moments for his eyes to adjust to the darkness in the corridor, but thankfully it was exactly as Claude had described it. Long, narrow with and office at one end and three cells, two on one side and one on the other.

To his absolute horror, a man stood up in the office, he couldn't see what, if any uniform he was wearing but he could clearly see the look of absolute shock on his face.

"Madeleine, get down to that office now and stop that guy contacting anyone of importance. Get him onto the floor and stay with him, don't let him do anything, if he resists, shoot him"

Madeleine sprinted past Peter and Claude, gun at the ready and entered the office. The man immediately put his hands up, he stumbled back and hit his head on a shelf behind where he had been sitting.

"Claude, go and get the keys, we need to be out of here quickly, they might already be on their way down here to check on their prize prisoners, especially if they suspect that this is an escape"

Peter stopped as he came to the first cell, he checked but there was no one inside.

He switched to the other side of the corridor, he came to the first cell, fully expecting to see either Sister Beverley or Richard James but again, the cell was empty. His head started to pound with horror, his mouth dried, and he could feel his heart racing, were they already dead or on a transport to the local SS jail? He almost dared not investigate the third and final cell, but he forced himself to confront what seemed like the worse case scenario.

He reached the third and final heavy wooden door, looked through the slit but for the third time, there was nothing. He ran into the office, the man, balding, somewhat overweight and probably in his sixties had an absolute look of shock and fear on his rounded face.

Peter walked straight up to him, raised his Browning and pushed it into the man's face. He was shaking uncontrollably, beads of sweat were rolling down both sides of his temples, he was clearly terrified.

"I will ask you once and once only, don't doubt me, I will kill you if you don't tell me where the prisoners are!"

The man opened his mouth and tried to speak but nothing came out, he just stood there shaking.

"I am running out of patience, for the last time, where are the prisoners?"

The man forced the words out of his mouth, like spitting something that had almost choked him, "Schmitt, he took them"

"Schmitt took them where?"

"He took them upstairs, I think to the interview room"

Peter, Madeleine and Claude looked at each other, they had a look of incredulity on their faces. It may have already failed there and then, their mission to rescue their friends could have become a futile and pointless exercise.

"Peter what are we going to do?"

"Madeleine, we are going to act and sort this out, right now"

"Inspector Monet, for the last time, go and turn that fucking alarm off before I lose my temper and start shooting people"

"On it Lieutenant"

Monet moved out of the room, with no particular urgency. As he exited through the doorway, Schmitt barged past him and moved over to where Schneider was standing, right by the bomb.

"It looks real sir, shouldn't we evacuate with everyone else?"

"I have had a lot of experience with these kind of things Schmitt, it looks real, but it isn't. Trust me, this is a fake, it's no more dangerous than a cup of coffee, just calm down and start to get people back into the building, once Monet has stopped the alarm"

"Will do sir, who the hell has sent it though?"

"Goodness only knows, someone who wanted to piss off the Police, someone who has been arrested recently, they need to check their records. Now pick this thing up and put it somewhere where people aren't going to freak out when they see it"

"I will take it downstairs, there is a storeroom in the cells area, it will be safe enough there until the Police do something about finding who sent it"

"Then do it now Schmitt and be quick about it"

He picked up the now discredited bomb and started to walk, rather carefully, out of the office and through the lobby towards the door leading down to the basement and cells.

Peter turned again to the man in the office, "right, you are going to take me upstairs to the interview room and get those two prisoners, do you understand me?"

"Yes sir, whatever you say, you won't get any argument from me, I am a true patriot, I hate the Germans just as much as the next man"

Madeleine grabbed him by the arm, "Peter this is lunacy, that's never going to work"

"It's the only thing that will Madeleine, there is nothing else we can do, we can't just leave them here. In any case, there will be a lot of chaos up there, and no one here knows me, I will be back with Beverley and Richard in a few minutes. Get to the car and Claude, you plant that charge, as soon as I get back, we need to leave"

Peter grabbed the man by the arm and marched him up the stairs to the ground floor.

"Right, what's your name?"

"Luis sir, it's Luis, just tell me what you want an I will oblige"

"Right, well you can start by opening up that door. Just walk out and look like you are on a job for someone important. I will be right behind you, as will my Browning, understand?"

"Yes sir, clearly"

Luis carefully opened the door, they both ventured out into what looked like a lobby. The noise of the bell was almost unbearable, but it would provide useful cover for what they had to do. Madeleine was right of course, this was a step too far, in simple terms it was suicide. If just one person recognised him or questioned what he was doing, then he was as good as dead.

There were several people milling around in the lobby, mostly Policemen in their smart uniforms but there were also men and women in civilian clothes. One officer in particular glanced over to Peter and Luis, he paused for a second, frowned, look around and then back at Peter. He then broke out in a large smile before going outside via the large double doors.

Peter wondered if he was one of the Police Officers helping Leo Monet, perhaps it was just a co incident but at least his cover was holding, at least for now.

"Right Luis, where is this interview room?"

"Right in front of us sir, that door there"

Guiding Luis from behind, through the melee of people, they entered the room marked 'salle d'entrevue'. To Peters absolute delight, sat on two chairs next to each other were Sister Beverley Jane and Squadron Leader Richard James. They had their hands tied behind their back and feet tied together but otherwise they looked unhurt.

They both gazed up and had a look of absolute shock on their faces, Richard shook his head and began to laugh.

"Well old chap, it's nice to see you, have you come to join the party, who's your friend?"

"Richard, it's nice to see you also, my friend, well his name is Luis. We haven't got any time for pleasantries though, we need to get out of here"

"Can't argue with that old boy, I am bored with this place anyway and that bloody bell is infuriating"

Peter and Luis stood Beverley and Peter up, untied their hands and feet, turned and moved back towards the door.

"Right, Luis is leading the way, we exit this room, walk straight across the lobby and through the door to the cells. Don't look back, don't slow down no matter what happens, do you understand me? There is more than a good chance that we will be discovered, if that's the case just run. I can't hold them off for long, so make you way down to the cells and out of the back door, do I make myself clear?"

They both nodded and got into line behind Luis.

"Right Luis, go, and straight to the door for the cells, open it and lead the way down"

Just as Luis opened the door, the alarm bell stopped ringing. It took Peter by surprise, the silence was almost as shocking as the noise preceding it. Luis turned around to face Peter, he had a look of doubt on his face, but Peter waved him forward.

It seemed to take an age to reach the door to the cells but eventually they got there, just as people were beginning to re enter the building. Luis's hand was visibly shaking as he reached for the door handle, he slowly turned it and open the door wide. He lead the way down the stairs, followed by Sister Beverley, Richard and finally Peter.

The narrow staircase groaned as they descended but eventually, they reached the lower corridor. Luis was the first to reach the office door, he stopped and with a start, backed up slightly and turned towards Peter.

There was a voice from inside the office, it was in French but with a strong German accent.

"Ah, Luis, glad to see you, do you know anything about these two people down here in your office, I do hope not because if you did, I would have to kill you too. Good job I brought that fake bomb down to the storeroom, otherwise you would have to deal with them yourself, wouldn't you, now Luis, come in here, we need a chat"

Peter, guessing that this was one of the SS men, responded without delay. He ran alongside the three others standing in the corridor and straight into the small office. Standing in the middle of the room was a German SS Corporal, he had his side arm drawn and he was holding Madeleine and Claude at gunpoint.

Peter didn't delay for a split second, he launched himself at the SS man and struck him over the head with the butt of his pistol. The two of them went crashing into the old desk, scattering papers in all directions. The wound on the Corporals head spewed blood all over the office, covering the back wall, Madeleine and Claude. He was obviously badly wounded by Peter's strike and seemed incapable of defending himself. Peter struck him three or four more times with the butt of his gun, the man lay motionless in the wreckage of the desk and office.

There was a pause as everyone comprehended what had just happened, but Peter was right on top of the situation.

"Richard, you and Luis get this man into one of the cells and lock the door. Luis, I am sorry, but we will need to lock you in a cell as well, you can tell them that we stormed into the building, took you at gun point to fetch the prisoners. I can't see them thinking anything different, to be honest, it's the truth.

Madeleine, get Sister Beverley into the car, Claude set the charge, we will be with you in seconds"

It all seemed to happen in a flash, Schmitt was dragged, still bleeding into a cell, Luis locked the door. Without question he entered the cell next door and sat on the bench on the back wall. As Peter approached, he tossed the large bunch of keys over to him.

"Thank you Luis, I am going to lock you in, stick to the story, you will be ok"

"No, I must thank you, I always wanted to help the war effort, never got the chance, well not until today. I am proud to have served, even if for just a few minutes, my children will be proud, as am I"

Peter locked the door and took the keys with him, moved down the corridor, past Claude and once more out into the sunlight. He turned to Claude and told him to set the fuse and get to the car.

They all crowded into the silver Citroen, Claude engaged first gear and drove away, without any fuss and across the crowded square, slowly past the Hotel Paris and away toward the water pumping station near to the bridge, then hopefully off towards Saint Aderald. They were all hoping however that the Germans had not yet discovered their secret rout and exit from the area across that little bridge!

The square itself had become increasingly crowded as the news of the bomb in the Police station had rapidly spread. It was going to take a few minutes to get away, perhaps time they didn't have. Any moment now Schmitt would be discovered and the whole area would be sealed off thus preventing any escape.

Claude gently pushed through the crowd, eventually they reached the open road on the other side of the square, and the little silver car slipped unnoticed into the distance.

"Put your foot down Claude, we need to get across that bridge sooner rather than later"

Without questioning the instruction, he accelerated the Citroen to top speed and sped away from the town. It wasn't long before they passed the turn for the brewery, following the town to their left before coming to the junction towards the pumping station. Without slowing they sped down the track that would eventually lead to the bridge at the bottom of the valley. Peter could see the little bridge in the distance, there didn't seem to be any German activity in the area, so he pushed Claude on and towards their target.

It wasn't long before they reached the little bridge, to their relief, it was clear and more importantly, the Germans had not yet discovered it or its importance to the escapees.

"Right Claude, get the car to other side and let's get into that forest and under some cover"

Claude slowed the Citroen and gently drove over the bridge, it seemed to be in good order, but it certainly hadn't been used for some time and probably not maintained for longer still. Eventually they reached the other side, and the comforting sound of crunching gravel under the wheels brought some relief from the tension. A palpable sense of release from the stress of the last few minutes wafted over Peter, and a small smile developed across his face. It was at this point that Peter realised that no one had spoken during their flight, apart from giving instruction to Claude. He turned to the two liberated people in the back of the car.

"Sorry, Beverley and Richard, how are you, what did the SS do to you?"

Sister Beverley Jane just smiled, "don't worry Peter, we are ok, those SS lunatics didn't worry me one little bit and I am sure Richard feels the same"

"You speak for yourself Sister, to be honest I was frightened to death, that Lieutenant, what was his name, Schneider, was a total lunatic, I am certain he was going to have us both shot. If I get the chance, I am coming back here in a bloody aircraft and drop a big fat bomb on the lot of them"

Sister Beverly turned to Richard, "don't doubt it for a minute Richard, if these brave people hadn't got us out of there, we would have been dead by nightfall!"

The car again fell into silence, the truth was they had barely got away with the first part of the plan, now the Germans would be after them and they wouldn't give up until they had captured them all.

They were by now in the protection of the forest, working their way down the broad track which would pass the turn to the poacher's cottage and would finally emerge by the closed Military Hospital. The gravel track was dusty and dry, it made driving easy but also gave away their position, should anyone be looking in their direction.

It was Madeleine who spoke first, she had a palpable tone of fear and alarm in her voice, they all turned and listened.

"Stop, stop Claude, I saw something move in the woods, just to our right, stop the car"

"What was it, can you still see it?"

"I am sure it was a grey uniform Peter, I can't see it now, but we need to check it out"

"Ok Claude, stop the car, we need to get out and see what that is. If they have set up a roadblock, we need to know about it"

Claude Durand acquiesced to the instruction, he didn't make any fuss, just gently applied the brakes and turned off the engine.

"Right, grab a gun and out, keep the noise down. Sister Beverley and Richard, make your way to that cover over there and don't come out. Claude, you stay and guard the car, Madeleine you come with me. This could get very ugly, very quickly, so stay alert!"

Keeping low and moving cautiously, Madeleine and Peter made their way into the forest, towards the shadow that Madeleine had noticed, only moments before. The air in the dense tree covered woodland was cold and damp, never having been warmed by the sun. It was permanent twilight, the domain of creatures and spirits never seen in the bright sunlight of the day. The pine needles and leaves felt soft and springy underfoot, it made for a cushioned and silent approach.

They scanned left and right but there was nothing there, no movement or sign of humanity, just the occasional squirrel, and a Blue Jay looking for its lunch. They both crouched, turning all their senses up to full but to no avail, it seemed to have been a false alarm.

"Perhaps it was a deer or wild boar Madeleine, I don't think there is anything human out here, other than us"

"Perhaps you are right, just me being jumpy, can't say I blame myself after the events of this morning"

Peter laughed, "I would be surprised if you weren't jumpy, let's get back to the car, we need to get on"

They turned and started to make their way back to Claude, Sister Beverley and Richard. At first, they struggled to find the direction from whence they had come, but soon got their bearing and proceeded towards the car.

"We should have brought some more weapons Madeleine, it would have been so much.............."

"Peter, shush, over there by the car, that's a German soldier!"

They both fell to the ground, Peter tried to gaze through the maze of tree trunks, bramble and ivy. He moved his head from left to right trying to get a better view but to no avail.

"Wait here Madeleine, I am going to crawl forward, try to get a better sight"

"Peter, for goodness sakes be careful, let me come with you, he won't be alone"

"Stay close then and get ready, there is no way they are taking Claude, not after all we have been through"

They slowly and very cautiously moved forward, through the undergrowth, towards the car. Madeleine was right, there was in fact three soldiers standing by the car, one was frisking Claude, another was searching the car, the third was examining the pistol Claude had been carrying.

Peter turned back to Madeleine, "the game is up, there is no explaining this, we have to do something positive here before they take him away. This time there will be no springing anyone from the Police station cells, no cunning plan, I can assure you of that"

"So, what do we do, there are three of them and just us two?"

"We get as close as we can and open fire, we let surprise be our ally here. Follow me and make sure your gun is ready, this will be quick and final. Firstly, we need to make sure there aren't another twenty soldiers waiting down the track"

They got as close as they dared but there was no sign of anyone else, just an empty four wheeled personnel carrier parked several yards down the track. At least the small vehicle gave some indication that these Germans were just a small patrol, who had happened upon Claude and the car.

"Right, we stand up and start to fire, don't stop until they are all dead. You take the guy frisking Claude, I will shoot the man with his pistol and go for the soldier in the car. Once we have them all, we get in the car and go, the gunfire will be heard from a way off, we don't know who else is close by!"

They both prepared for the fight, he looked around at Madeleine, she was busy making sure the gun was ready to kill. Her beauty was evident as was her determination to rid her country of these invaders. She was truly a hero of France and the war, he wondered how many more brave people were out there, at this precise moment, preparing to die.

"Right, let's go"

Without hesitation they both stood up and ran the few yards towards the car. The soldier examining Claude's gun was the first to notice what was just about to happen. He looked up in the direction of the approaching storm, it didn't help, Peter put a bullet through his chest before he had time to react. Next to die was the man frisking Claude, Madeleine shot him twice, the first time through his right shoulder. The bullet caused him to spin like a dancer, spraying blood in all directions. He fell, writhing in agony he tried to reach for his rifle now laying some distance away. Before he made any significant gain on the gun, Madeleine put another round into the back of his head, he slumped, lifeless onto the cold ground.

The soldier in the car tried to exit the vehicle, realising what was happening, he panicked as he got out and fell backwards onto the ground. He scrambled and tried to get to his feet but to no avail. Madeleine was the first to arrive, he looked up at her and said something in German, it was the last thing he did. There was a shot from behind her, she quickly looked around to see Doctor Claude A Durand pointing his gun at the now dead soldier.

"Well, that's one soldier that won't be pissing me off anymore"

He looked directly at Madeleine, "what, didn't you think I was capable of this kind of thing, I can assure you that I am, especially since losing two brothers in the first war!"

"Sorry Doctor, I didn't know"

"It's ok, let's get on before we have more company in this black forest of death"

Gathering up a pistol and four stick grenades, they quickly got back into the car. Speed was now the imperative, they had to get away from here before it was too late. Despite the thick forest, the gunfire would have been heard for miles around, soldiers would already be on their way here. The atmosphere in the car was one of fear and dread, Sister Beverley was in tears, Richard just sat in the back examining his new Luger pistol.

"Listen guys, that was not nice, and I don't expect any of you to understand or feel good about killing. To be honest, neither do I, but it had to be done, there was no other choice"

Sister Beverley Jane was the first to reply to Peter, tears rolling down her face.

"They were someone's son, husband or perhaps brother, they didn't deserve to die, they were posted here and told to do a job. I understand the logic you applied, kill or be killed, we are all victims of that, it's not a choice it's just a need, and they no longer live because of that"

She put her head in her arms and sobbed, Madeleine put her arm around Sister Beverley, no one spoke for some considerable time.

It seemed like hours before they reached the old military hospital, each and every one of them were sore after being bounced around on the track they had taken from the little bridge. With considerable relief, they finally turned left onto the road towards Saint Aderald and away from the hornets' nest that Chênes had undoubtedly become.

"Do you think they will spread out beyond Chênes Peter?"

"I have no doubt Richard, once they have searched the Hotel Paris and any other place they can think of, they will assume we have left. I agree with Madeleine, I think they will presume we are on the coastal road heading north. With a bit of luck, they will concentrate most of their resources in that direction. After all, why the hell would we run right back into the main headquarters around here, straight back into Saint Aderald. The only fly in that particular ointment is the attack on the forest road. Once their men don't return, they will send out search parties, once they find them, they will know for certain where we are heading"

"Then we need to get through Saint Aderald and away"

"I can't disagree with that Claude but where to? There is nothing much beyond the town and on to the Belgium border, there would be nowhere to hide. We can't just drive, someone will stop us at some point even if it's just on the border itself, I am not sure what to do for the best, in fact, I am not sure what to do at all!"

Madeleine was the next to speak, "we need to find somewhere for tonight, it's been a hell of a day. I know nigh time is our friend but not this one, we need to rest, we need to sit and think, plan what we do tomorrow even if we risk the Germans working out what we have done"

"Ok, but where do we stay tonight?"

"I don't know Peter, there must be somewhere where they wouldn't think of checking, a place that would be safe at least for the next 24 hours?"

"You know madeleine, I think there might be a place, it's the old signal box by the disused rail line. I had to go there on my last mission here to check if Michelle was telling the truth when he said he had hidden a radio set there. It won't be very comfortable, but I think we should be ok there for a few hours at least. We can bypass the town, cross the bridge by the station, we could be there in a few hours, four at the most"

It was by now getting dark, they all agreed that the old signal box was their best plan. Like all signal boxes, it had clear views in all directions, and if they were disturbed, they could easily disappear into the thick undergrowth and then down to the river. Everyone was both physically and mentally worn out, it had been one hell of a day but soon they could rest, at least for a short while.

Chapter 23.
Early morning. The office of Lieutenant Schneider, the Police Station Chênes.
June 13th, 1943.

Schmitt picked up the phone on the third ring, the events of yesterday had certainly taken its toll on everyone and stress levels were very high indeed. His boss, Lieutenant Schneider was understandably incandescent with rage, he was walking around the building looking for people to blame, and probably kill and any minute now, Schmitt thought it was going to be him.

He could hear Schneider yelling at people, shouting in German as well as French, throwing things about the place, making outrageous threats. He had already sent the Chief of Police home, stating that, "I will deal with you later and best say goodbye to your family because it will be the last time you will ever see them!"

No body doubted that he meant exactly what he said, he was a violent man, prone to acts of extreme viciousness and uncontrolled savagery. Schmitt had overheard gossip from the French Detectives that Schneider had been linked to a brutal double murder just out of town. The details of which were very disturbing, but he had no doubt that Schneider was capable of such inhuman brutality.

"Hello, Lieutenant Schneider's office, Corporal Schmitt speaking"

"Where is that idiot boss of yours, I had a phone call this morning saying that you had been beaten up and two Resistance fighters had escaped. What the hell is going on over there?"

"Good morning Hauptman Wagnor, yes I was knocked about and dumped in a cell, but I am ok now, I can assure you"

"Good but what about those two escapees, what was Schneider playing at, that bloody fool, how does he think that makes me look in Berlin? Get him to the phone, I need to speak to him, get him to call me back, now, do you understand me Schmitt, now!"

He wasn't sure if Wagnor had already put the phone down, but he wasn't going to risk it.

"Yes sir, I will pass on your instructions without delay"

He rushed out of the office, he didn't fancy pissing off both Schneider and Wagnor in the same day. He eventually found Schneider holding the man in charge of the cells by the throat. Judging by the red marks he had clearly slapped him about the face several times. Now his whole head was turning dark blue as Schneider strangled the life out of him. Schmitt lacked the courage to interrupt Schneider, but he was even less happy about the prospect of making Wagnor any angrier. At least if he spoke now, the life of the cells officer would be spared.

"Excuse me sir but Hauptman Wagnor would like to speak to you"

Schneider turned around and glared at Schmitt, the look of utter animosity and hatred on his face was shocking. It was clear that he was more than just a violent man, he was a psychopath and capable of the most extreme acts of vehemence.

"What the fuck does that idiot want?"

"I think it was about yesterday sir, he wanted to ask you a few questions, I am not that sure"

"I trust you told him it wasn't my fault, it was these idiot French Police"

He turned around and dropped the cells officer to the ground, kicking him in the face. The violence of the blow forced his head back with extraordinary shock, blood and teeth flying in all directions.

He looked down at the stricken man, "If I find out that you had anything to do with this situation, I will be back to have another chat and next time, I won't be so pleasant, do you understand?"

The unfortunate man was in no position to answer, his mouth was in a terrible state. He just lay there moaning and choking on his own blood.

"Right Schmitt, I will phone that idiot now and tell him exactly what happened and what I am going to do about it"

He walked briskly into his office and picked up the phone. The exchange answered, "get me Hauptman Wagnor at the manor house, Saint Aderald"

The phone rang several times before anyone answered.

"Wagnor here"

"Sir, its Lieutenant Schneider returning your call"

"Yes Schneider, glad you got back to me, I understand you had an incident yesterday"

"Yes sir but let me explain"

"Before you go and blame everybody else for this fuck up, please answer a couple of questions for me. Firstly, how come I found out about this from my driver and not you? Secondly, where the hell are the two Resistance fighters?

I want you to think very carefully before answering those two question Schneider, especially given that I might know more about this than you think!"

There was a palpable pause before Schneider answered.

"Yes sir, sorry about the delay in reporting this, I was still undertaking....."

"Let me stop you there Lieutenant Schneider. You should have reported this yesterday, just after it happened and you didn't, why?"

"Well sir, I think I might....."

"You still haven't told me why you didn't report to me yesterday Schneider?"

Wagnor's voice rose from a quiet and in control tone, to a raging volcano that was probably audible around the whole manor house and halfway to the main gate. He was shouting so loud that it made the phone in Schneiders hand crackle and buzz.

"Listen to me you piece of useless shit, I want to know what you fucked up and why you let those two escape. I gave you a simple job, all you had to do was find the French Scientist, and you end up making me look like a total idiot. A fucking half blind geriatric monkey could have done a better job you useless fuck!

Best of all, my driver tells me about what had happened, not you, oh no, that's way beyond you. Also, I find out that three of the soldiers lent to us from the army base are missing, any clue about that, or should I ask my driver as well?

I know you Schneider, it's always someone else's fault, never yours, well I want you in my office in two hours from now, you can explain the whole debacle to me in person. Do I make myself clear or should I ask someone else if you understood, namely my driver?"

There was a pause before Schneider answered. He used a slow and calm tone, in contrast to Wagnor's explosion.

"Well sir, I do apologise about my oversight, but you must admit, I normally do a most satisfactory job. I need not remind you about that 'issue' I cleared up for you regarding your indiscretions with the wife of the prison manager. I sorted that for you, so she wouldn't be a nuisance anymore, if you get my drift sir?"

"You mean you tortured her and her husband to death, that certainly sorted her out but not in the manner I wanted. A typical Neanderthal, psychopathic reaction, you are a piece of work Schneider, trouble will always follow you about, you are a total fool"

"Well, you should have been a little more specific sir, I was only acting under your orders, sir!"

"Now listen to me Schneider, you might think you are clever, you may even think you can get the better of me, but I can assure you that you are way off target. I have been a total bastard to everyone who crossed me, and I am a fucking expert at it.....do you understand me?

If you ever even try to suggest you might have something over me, I will send someone over there right now, and have you shot. Not arrested, not disciplined, shot. I will personally strip your lifeless body naked and have it strung up from the nearest lamppost and set on fire. When I have watched it burn and fall to the ground, I will go and find your entire family and do the same to them, each and every one of them!

Now, I think you should take this opportunity to review and reflect what you have said and what I ask for. This would be an ideal moment to forget your threats and anger towards me and to be more conciliatory, do I make myself very clear Schneider?"

Lieutenant Schneiders face was purple with anger, his whole body shook violently, if anyone had the misfortune to walk into the office right now, he would have pulled his service revolver and shot them. He ground his teeth, his bloodshot eyes bulged but he slowed his breathing and tried to control his anger.

"I do apologise Hauptman Wagnor, I will be in your office in two hours, thank you sir"

"Now that's better Schneider, I do like my officers to have a controlled and dignified air. I will look forward to seeing you soon, just remember my comments about you and your family, that wasn't a threat Schneider, that was a solemn promise"

The phone line went dead, Schneider threw the handset onto the desk, if he became any angrier, he would explode.

"Wagnor, you have messed with the wrong person this time, threaten me and my family, we will see about that you piece of shit. Oh yes, I am coming over to see you, but you will regret your threats and they way you spoke to me.

I have killed for you, sorted out your dirty little affair with that French woman you got pregnant. I got rid of her and her husband, what was his name, Jacques Forelle, the pair of them cried like babies before they died.

I will see you in two hours' time......Hauptman Karl Wagnor"

Chapter 24.
Early morning. The abandoned signal box.
June 13th, 1943.

The night had been an uncomfortable affair, sleeping on coats and anything they could find to give some level of comfort to the wooden floor. At least it had been warm, so sleep was possible, if at least for short periods. Hunger and the threat of discovery though had made resting very difficult indeed.

The dawn had seen them all awake, Peter and Richard had been out to see if anything could be found to eat but with no luck at all. They huddled together in the middle of the room to discuss what they would do next, but before they could, Sister Beverley Jane called them all to order and made an announcement.

The room felt oddly sad as she finished speaking. She announced a decision that she had made and seemed very certain about it, one that had taken her several days to formulate.

"So that's what I am going to do, I remember that every day a train leaves here that connects to another service to Paris, I will be on that train today, it leaves in the late afternoon, normally about 4pm"

"But Sister Beverley, are you sure the Convent outside of Paris will accept you, what happens if they don't?

"They will Madeleine don't worry, they are a semi closed order, so someone with my skills will be very useful to them. Once this dam war is over, I will return to my house here and continue my work for the community and for God"

Madeleine looked around the room and signalled to all those present.

"We will all miss you Beverley, but I must say that I think you are making the right decision"

"I will miss you all, I hope we can meet again after the war is over. I have a secret collection of wine hidden in my cellar, it needs to be drunk, I do so hate waste"

The humour in her voice was a welcome distraction from the terrible circumstance they presently found themselves in. Nothing had really changed from last night, they were still miles away from the radio in the ditch near to Chateau Du Beck, if that radio was still there? Whilst the Germans might not be on the lookout for their silver Citroen, they would certainly be looking for them in person.

At least Sister Beverly Jane would be safe, once she reached the Convent near to Paris! What of the rest of them though, try as he might, Peter could not come up with a credible plan?

He simply couldn't see a way past the border guards, now on the lookout for them. The journey to Chateau Du Beck would certainly end in disaster, there was no doubt in that.

"Ok, has anyone got a suggestion, I am all out of plans right now?"

They all looked at Peter, then back at each other, Richard was the first to speak.

"So, we need a radio in order to summon the aircraft to pick us up. The only radio we have in miles and miles away in a ditch somewhere in Belgium. Of course, some young boy will probably have found it by now and be playing secret agents with his friend in the woods. Or a passing German patrol has found it and the local Gestapo are looking into why it was there. Either way, we are well and truly screwed, so why are we even thinking about trying to get to it?"

"Because Richard, it's the only one we have, the second radio I brought with me you shot full of bloody holes when you strafed the border post where we were parked"

Doctor Claude Durand stood up and started to walk about.

"Wait a minute, have we overlooked the obvious here?"

"I am not sure what you mean Claude, what would that be?"

"Well Peter, how do the local Resistance get the arms and ammunition they need?"

"Well, when I was here running the local Resistance and downed airmen group, I used to call up on the radio and ask for .... Of course, Claude you are right, the local Resistance fighters may have one or at least access to a radio, somewhere close by"

"So, Peter all we have to do is ask, they know Sister Beverley and Richard, I am sure they will help"

Sister Beverley spoke next, "if you take me, I can show you where the leader lives. His name is Pierre Dupuy, he is the local vet, I can ask him for you. I am certain he will help, let's go now before I miss my train"

Peter and Sister Beverley jumped into the car, and sped off down the road, over the bridge and right towards Pierre Dupuy's house.

"I hope he is in Beverley, being the local Vet, he could be anywhere"

"I am sure he will be somewhere close, if not, his wife will be more than happy to help. She actually set up the new group not long after you left last time"

"Good, we need to get that signal off and soon, the net is closing in as we speak, we have to get away!"

"Speaking of which Peter, I wonder how many people those aircraft carry, will it be big enough for the four of you, yourself, Richard Claude and Madeleine?"

"I have already thought about that Beverley and the answer is no, it will only carry three"

"So, have you decided who is staying behind?"

"I have and it wasn't an easy choice!"

Chapter 25.
Mid morning. The office of Lieutenant Schneider, the Police Station Chênes. June 13th, 1943.

"Right Schmitt, I am off the see Wagnor, he wants to shout his mouth off about how good he is and how badly I managed the situation here. I won't be long, just as long as it takes me to shut him up and drive back here, three or four hours tops.

Whilst I am away, you need to find out who sent that bomb, it's obvious that it was a distraction to allow the escape. Beat whomever you like, to death if necessary but find out who sent it. I would suggest starting with the Chief of Police, that dam stupid Leo Monet, I am certain he had something to do with it. If he won't tell you, grab the boss of the Hotel Paris, if you give him a good kicking you might be surprised what information falls out of him"

Schmitt was still shocked from the incident in the cells, and at the absolute lack of compassion or humanity Schneider showed, but he was determined not to find out just how cruel he could be. There would be no doubt he would turn that brutality on him if he even dared to deviate from his orders.

"Will do sir, is there anything else I can do whilst you are away?"

"Yes, you can phone the idiot Wagnor, tell him to meet me at Michaël's place. It's an abandoned farm, used to belong to some French collaborator. Tell him it's urgent and I need to show him something. Tell him I beat this information out of one of the locals this morning, an arms dump, with a radio, or something along those lines"

"Will he know where this farmhouse is?"

"Oh yes, it's where he used to fuck his mistress, the wife of one of the managers of the prison here. He would pick her up from Chênes in the morning, after her husband had gone to work, and take her there, nice and private you see. It was going so nicely until she got pregnant, that put a stop to his dirty little game, and I had to clear up his mess"

"What happens if he refuses?"

"He won't, tell him as well as the arms cache, I have brought a little gift by way of an apology, her name is Isabelle, seventeen and stunning"

"So where is she, this Isabelle, is she that nice?"

"No you fool, I just made her up, there is no such girl, but Wagnor won't be able to resist, trust me, he will have to see if I am telling the truth. Tell him that she is a present, and that he can do with as he chooses, no matter what that might be. No one knows that she is there, so there will be no questions asked, if you see what I mean. He will like that, the opportunity to indulge and express himself with the young girl"

"Will do sir, I will make sure he understands, you can rely on me"

Schneider looked down at Schmitt and smiled, he was very keen to please and reminded him of his younger brother and he certainly followed his orders to the letter.

"You are shaping up very nicely Schmitt, if you stay close to me you will certainly go places. When I get back, I will see about getting another stripe added to your uniform and who knows what next"

Schneider pulled up in front of the abandoned farmhouse, the former home of Michaël Bécaud, the past leader of the local resistance, turned traitor. The once proud building had been neglected for some time now and it showed. A couple of the shutters were handing precariously from their frames, the white paintwork was now faded, peeling and green with algae. A profusion of plant life had forced its way through the gravel on the drive as well as implanting itself in various parts of the building.

He got out of the car and began to walk around, past the small kitchen garden and through the old barn at the back. He glanced in through some of the ground floor windows, there was still furniture inside the house, carpets on the floors, even a kettle and two pans on the stove. It was an odd frozen picture, still full of life but now lifeless and dead.

He looked around, there was no sign of Wagnor, perhaps he had not taken the bait, maybe Schmitt had not managed to convince him? For all his weaknesses, Wagnor was certainly not a stupid man, there was no doubt he would be cautious about this meeting, but Schneider was convinced that Wagnor would turn up. Lieutenant Schneider looked around for somewhere to sit and wait, when a familiar voice rang out from behind him.

"It used to belong to a Michaël Bécaud, he was the leader of the local Resistance. He started to work for my predecessor, I think he enjoyed the excitement, I can't think it was for the money, this place was not built on poverty, there was old money in his family and plenty of it. Anyway, he did a lot of work for me before he disappeared, goodness knows what happened to him. The Resistance managed to kill my head of security, the thinking was that Bécaud was killed by the Resistance at the same time"

Schneider turned slowly to find Hauptman Karl Wagnor standing no more than twenty feet behind, his Walther pistol pointing directly at him.

"I love that story about 'Isabelle, seventeen and stunning', just for a moment I actually fell for that one, well done. The thing is Schneider, people like us, know people like us, if that makes sense. In other words, we don't trust a single thing we actually say or do, you think and act like I do and vice versa. So given that you would never fall for such a hoax, what made you think I would?"

Schneider laughed as he looked around, "I see your point Karl, but you see, I am not like you, and I never will be. I don't suffer from any form of conscience, I don't feel any compassion, I always get my own way and if anyone tries to stop me, well I just get rid of them"

"You see Schneider, that's where you fall down, you are very arrogant and that leads you to think you will always succeed. You need to be a little humbler, expect the unexpected, assume that there are more intelligent people out there, accept that you won't always win. That way you won't fall into traps like this, you won't find yourself in front of the barrel of someone's gun.

Anyway, what am I to do, you were obviously going to kill me, does that mean I should kill you? I guess if I don't, you will put a bullet in my back the first chance that you get, am I right Schneider?"

Schneider laughed again, looking down at the ground as he kicked the dry earth into a small dusty cloud.

"You are right Karl, on all those points, including killing you. The thing is though, you won't kill me, you are not that kind of man, are you? You could no more pull that trigger than get rid of your pregnant mistress. No Karl, you even had to get me to do that for you, thing is, you haven't got that killer instinct. That's what separates men like you from men like me, your kind make threats, whereas we carry them out!"

"I see your point Schneider, but you and that woman I got pregnant are not the same, I actually did care for her, but I don't give a toss about you. The other thing is, she was not going to kill me the first chance she got, unlike you. I need to ask you a question though, why did you do what you did to them, torture and butcher them, there was no need for that?"

"That's simple Karl, I did that because I enjoyed it, it was one of my best days work, I only wish I could do it all again"

This time it was Wagnor's turn to laugh, he chuckled as he walked a few steps closer to Schneider.

"Right let's get this over with, do you want one in the head or two in the chest?"

"Do what you want Karl, I am not afraid of dying, just get on with it"

With that, Hauptman Karl Wagnor raised his pistol and pointed it at Schneider's head, he looked his Lieutenant straight in the eyes as he began to pull the trigger. He gently squeezed the trigger all the way back, the hammer fell and struck the back of the round in the gun, but nothing happened. He pulled the trigger again and then again, but the gun refused to fire.

Schneider didn't need a second chance, with all the force he could muster he launched himself at Wagnor. In two or perhaps three paces the two men were engaged in a life-or-death struggle. It was clear to both of them that there would only be one survivor of this duel to the death.

They rolled about on the ground, grey, brown dust flew into the air. Punches flew in both directions, it was a violent and frantic struggle. Wagnor's pistol flew from the fight and spun across the ground just beyond reach but he was not the only man to be armed.

Schneider grappled with Wagnor but also tried to pull his own pistol from its leather holster. Eventually he managed to get it free and pushing Wagnor to the ground, pointed at his head. Wagnor was not finished though, he grabbed the Lieutenants wrist and tried to turn the gun in the other direction.

Back and forth the battle raged, neither man getting the upper hand, dust filled the air, a smell of fear and exhaustion saturated the atmosphere. Eventually though, the conflict ended, a crack and then another as a weapon was fired. Suddenly the fight stopped, and silence prevailed as a large pool of blood seeped over the dry and dusty ground.

Chapter 26.
Late morning. The abandoned signal box.
June 13th, 1943.

Peter and Sister Beverley Jane had returned from the meeting with Pierre Dupuy, the local Vet and leader of the Resistance group. He had agreed to allow Peter to send a message to the British, later that day, asking for an aircraft for a pickup. The time and place for the rendezvous would be set, but that was the easy part, now he had to tell the four people present in the railway signal box who was staying behind. He stood up in front of the group and drew a deep breath.

"Well, we called in at the station on the way back to buy a ticket for Sister Beverley Jane, she will be on the 2pm train. So, if you are going to say goodbye, I suggest you get on with it before she has to go"

The other three gathered around, giving Sister Beverley a hug, but Peter had another task to undertake and one he hadn't been looking forward to.

"Madeleine, would you like to come for a walk with me, down by the river?"

She looked at Peter with an expression of puzzlement on her face. "Sure, when do you want to go?"

"Now would be a good time, I need to tell you something"

They stepped outside into the warm June sunshine, it was a glorious afternoon, perfect for a walk down by the river. He reached out and took hold of her hand, she squeezed his gently as they set off for the river.

"So, what's this all about Peter, have you become very romantic all of a sudden or do you need to tell me something I don't want to hear?"

"There is some truth in both parts of that Madeleine, you must realise that I am coming to the end of my mission here and things are going to change shortly?"

"I had worked that out Peter and I must admit to being somewhat worried about what happens next?"

"What happens next is the evacuation, and in there lays the problem. You see, the aircraft that will be sent will only carry three people as well as the pilot. So, one of us has to stay behind. That means someone having to cope by themselves, they will be all alone, there will be no friends around them to help.

Now, Beverley will be making her own way out of here, obviously Claude and Richard have to go back, so that's leaves you and me. Now, the question is, which one of us stays, it won't be easy for whoever it is"

There was a long silence as they walked along the grassy path and eventually, they reached the river. A myriad of insects buzzed all around, some dancing above the water, some around the bank. Occasionally a fish rose and took a bug off the surface, it was a tranquil and restful scene.

"Are you asking for volunteers Peter or are you going to tell me who it will be?"

"I am going to tell you Madeleine, you see there is only one logical choice. I am a serving S.O.E. Agent and an experienced fighter pilot, as such, I need to return home. Additionally, I have a wife and baby daughter, they have not seen me for months, there is no choice really.

On the other hand, if I did get on that aircraft, I would be leaving you to a very uncertain fate, one that would almost certainly end up in your death. We have shared an awful lot together Madeleine, not just physically but together as a team fighting a common enemy. I couldn't get on that plane and simply leave you to die, that's not going to happen, that's why I have decided to stay here"

She turned with a shock and looked straight into his eyes.

"Peter, there is no way I am getting on that plane without you but also, I could not ask you to stay here without me either. You have a job to do, a very important one as well as having a family to go back to. There is only one option and only one, you have to get on the plane. I will be fine, I will drive back to my Aunts and Uncles in Belgium, I will be safe there. They are not looking for a single woman in a silver Citroen, I will be ok"

"I had thought about staying behind with you, I must admit, but I have another life away from here and a job to do, but I can't leave you here, I could never do that"

She reached out and took hold of him, holding tighter than she had ever done before. He could feel her sobbing, this was an inevitable moment, something that was always going to happen. Ever since that first meeting when they dragged him out of his burning Spitfire and those glorious afternoons spent in the old barn and the two cottages, this moment was inescapable.

"Peter, you must go, I will be fine, maybe you will parachute into my life again one day soon"

"I have to be honest with you Madeleine, I don't think I will be doing that again, not ever. I have got away with it too many times, eventually someone like Wagnor will catch up with me and kill me. I have told my boss that I will not be returning, not for any reason whatsoever.

It would be easy for me to say something different, pretend I will be back soon, but I owe you the truth Madeleine, I won't ever be coming back again"

There was a complete silence around them, even the buzzing insects and singing birds seemed to fade into the background. The hush was almost overwhelming, he pushed her gently away and looked down into her tear strewn face.

"I am so sorry Madeleine, I don't see any other way, I will never forget you. I won't make any empty promises about meeting up after the war, you are more important than that, the truth is Madeleine, this is goodbye"

She tried to speak but no words came out, she wanted to say goodbye, but it was impossible, this was the end, she knew that, but she couldn't possibly accept it. She let go and turned to walk back, without Peter Parker, without the only man she had ever loved, her heart was broken, the pain was overwhelming.

Eventually, the time to say goodbye to Sister Beverley arrived, Peter was already sat in the car with the engine running. They took it in turn, tears flowed from them all, whilst this was the beginning of the end of their time in France, it was still very difficult.

"Well old girl, been nice seeing you and all of that. Tootle pip and stay safe, if I fly over that Convent near Paris, I will land nearby and say hello"

"Thank you Richard, I will look forward to that"

They all laughed, the image of Squadron Leader Richard James with his huge handlebar moustache knocking on the door of a Convent in France, seemed a strangely humorous one. The only person not smiling was Madeleine, she just gave Beverley a hug and turned to walk away.

"Madeleine, I think I know what's making you so very upset and for what it's worth, I fully understand. I lost the only man I ever loved, he was killed in a car accident, I guess it's what made me turn to God and the church.

I thought that I would die from a broken heart, to be honest I wanted to end it all, but I struggled through"

She smiled at Madeleine, "I know it's pointless me saying anything to you now, nothing will make you feel any better, but things will improve, I promise you"

"Thank you Sister, I know you are right but I feel so cheated, if it wasn't for this dam war, we could stay together"

"Yes Madeleine but if it hadn't been for the war, you would never have met at all. Remember that old saying, 'better to have love and lost, than not to have loved at all'. Who knows what the future holds, one day the sun will come up and you will fall in love all over again"

She smiled at Beverley and unable to control her emotions, left the gathering and walked outside.

Peter turned to Sister Beverley as they stood on the station platform. "Well Sister, this is it, I must say that this is the first time I have fought a war with a sister of God, bust her out of jail, been chased across France and been introduced to the local head of the Resistance by one. I will never think of a woman of God in the same way again, it's been a blast"

"Thank you Peter, it's been fun, not to say a little exciting at times. My life from now on will never be the same, perhaps that's not a bad thing, it certainly will be a lot safer once I reach the convent in Paris and you have flown back to England"

They both laughed, looked at each other and embraced warmly. They could hear the distant noise of the approaching train as it puffed it way towards the station.

"Sister, please promise me that you will take care of yourself, stay out of trouble and don't come back here until this bloody war is over"

"Peter, my life is not important, my calling is to help those in need and to that end I will continue to do my work. If that brings me back here in times of war, then that is what I must do.

However, I will take your advice and try to stay away from S.O.E Agents, downed RAF pilots, French Scientists and ex Resistance women, especially if they are all in the same group"

They laughed again, Sister Beverley had been a steadying hand on the tiller, they simply couldn't have managed without her. There was one more embrace as the train pulled alongside, one small tank engine and three carriages. In a cloud of steam and squeaking breaks it stopped, a couple of doors opened, and two passengers got off.

"This is it Peter, please pass on my love to the others, I will miss you all, maybe we will meet once more in times to come"

She didn't speak again, turned and boarded the second carriage and slammed the door behind her. There was one more glance and a wave before she sat down. Peter wasn't completely sure, but did he catch the glint of a tear on her cheek, glistening in the afternoon sun.

There was a whistle from the station master, a huge chuff from the engine and blast of steam as the little train pulled away, off to the connection for Paris, carrying away Sister Beverley Jane.

Peter felt a huge wave of relief as it disappeared into the distance, relief that she would be safe. At the same time, there was an overwhelming sense of sadness that he would never meet such a fine woman and a brave soul ever again.

Chapter 27.
Late evening. An unknown location.
June 13th, 1943.

The leader of the local Resistance, Pierre Dupuy had driven Peter out into the countryside, somewhere west and south of Saint Aderald. It was dark and the best he could tell, they were very close to the turning for the stone quarry.

It flashed up memories of Michaël and chasing him down into the quarry with Philipe. It seemed a lifetime ago, but it was just a few months.

"I wonder how they are all getting on, Philipe, André and Laurent?"

He desperately wanted to ask Pierre, but he was scared of the answer, terrified that they may all be dead, murdered by the SS. He had become harder now, less influenced by guilt, but their loss, he would not be able to cope with that, it would break him in two.

They pulled off the road, onto a bumpy and ill maintained track. He eventually stopped and turned off the engine.

"Right Peter, this is as far away as we need to be. No doubt that the Germans will pick up this transmission, but we will be away before they get anywhere close to us. You need to keep it very short Peter, the less time we are on air the better, quick message and away"

"No problems Pierre, I am quick enough at morse code. I will tap out my message and wait for the reply, we should be done in a minute, two at the most"

The two men got out of the car and fumbling about in the dark energised the radio, extending the ariels above the car. Pierre connected the morse key and waited for the set to warm up.

"Right Peter, send your message"

He engaged the key with and amount of rapidity, tapping out his call sign. Within seconds there was a reply from Grendon asking for his response code and message.

Tapping furiously, he sent the details, when and where he wanted to be picked up and the total numbers to be taken back to England. Again, the response came and confirmation of the pickup. For a second time they asked for an answer from Peter, one carefully planned by the S.O.E, requiring a response only known by Peter and one designed to alert Grendon to a potential problem.

Your wife and child are safe after the bombing raid last week.

Thank you Grendon, I was worried about Susan, there house is on the main road.

If any other answer had been sent by Peter, the whole mission would be cancelled, Grendon would have been alerted to a compromise in security or that Peter had been captured and forced to send a message.

"Right Pierre, I am done"

He snatched the morse key away from Peter, and quickly dismantled the equipment. They both jumped back into the car and sped away from the scene and back towards Pierre Dupuy's house and relative safety.

"Thank you Pierre, I couldn't have managed this without you. The alternative would have been to make our way across Belgium, we couldn't possibly have succeeded"

"No problem Peter, it's more than I could do for Sister Beverley. You need to be away from here though, I must admit that the extra patrols and activity from the Germans is most certainly not welcome. Once you have left, I do hope that things settle down around here and we can get on with our work"

Peter detected a certain amount of resentment in Pierre's voice, but he couldn't blame him, this was his country not Peter's. Soon he would be away and back to England with Claude A Durand and Squadron Leader Richard James. It wouldn't be a moment too soon, he loved France and the people, but he had a feeling of impending doom. He had been on several missions here and he was still alive, that in itself was a miracle but he knew all to well that miracles aren't real, it just luck, and luck always runs out.

He said goodbye to Pierre and got into the silver Citroen and started to drive back to the disused signal box. He couldn't help thinking about Madeleine and what would happen to her. She would be a 'woman alone in a silver car'. That's what she had said, he was certain that would be fine, why would the Germans suspect anything other than her cover story, which happened to be the truth. She was travelling back to her relatives in Belgium!

He still needed to say goodbye to her, this was going to be one of the hardest things he would ever have to do. She meant so much to him, perhaps he was in love with her, but what was he supposed to do? It was certain he would never return to France, at least not during the war. Perhaps one day he could return but when would that be?

There was something else troubling him and in truth, he knew what it was. It was that same feeling he had when he returned to England after being chased out of France, following the attack on the cottage in the woods.

It was a sense of knowing what he could have, what was in reach, but it was beyond his ability to truly choose. He would be lost forever in a nightmare of hesitancy and torment and the need to decide between his lives.

The first in England, safe with his family, the other in France trying to stay alive, feeding off adrenalin, passion and excitement. It was probable, even likely that he would never really find an inner piece, forever being lost in the beyondness of things.

It was not altogether a situation of his own making, he had crashed landed in France. He had stayed with the Resistance, partly because of his injuries and partly because he was good at organising them. If the powers that be in England had not noticed what he was doing and ordered him to stay, none of this would have happened.

"That's just an excuse Parker" he mumbled to himself, "I could have stopped all of this some time ago". In that part of his mind where honesty rules, that place which sometimes is ignored, was a nagging doubt that he actually wanted this life.

"Why am I so sad to leave, what is it that keeps drawing me back? I know how to say no, so why do I keep saying yes when my boss asks me to return?"

There was of course an answer to all of this, and Peter Parker knew it all too well, but he would never admit it, just in case he could not finally walk away.

Chapter 28.
Departure?
June 14th, 1943.

Peter woke first, he wasn't sure if something had disturbed him, or he had naturally returned to the land of reality. The old signal box was silent other than a little snoring from Richard James, and the noise of a loose window knocking against its frame in the morning breeze.

It was still dark outside, but the first rays of the morning sun were just visible in the eastern sky. This was the last day Peter would see dawn in France, tonight, just after midnight, the Lysander aircraft would pick them up, just north of the disused slaughterhouse. He had used this location before, but he was prepared to gamble that the Germans would not be watching it. The fields around there were open and flat, perfect for the aircraft to land and take off safely.

It was going to be a long and tense day, waiting for their departure but they had things to do. Firstly, they had to clean up the signal box, Pierre Dupuy had supplied them with food and drink, all this had to be moved. It had turned out to be a perfect hideaway, they didn't want a German patrol finding what they had been up to just in case someone else needed to use it again in the future.

They had to get to the slaughterhouse ready for the evacuation, this was fraught with danger and the possibility of discovery. Pierre Dupuy would be joining them along with a few volunteers. They would be used to light the landing zone with torches, much as André and Philipe had done during his last escape.

They aet their breakfast in complete silence, it wasn't much, some half stale bread and a few bottles of water but it was enough. No one was in the mood for eating anyway, the tension around the group was palpable. There wasn't much to do but there was plenty of things that could go wrong.

Once everyone had finished what they wanted, Peter stood up and addressed the group.

"Right, we need to get cleaned up around here, nothing to be left behind, we don't want the Germans knowing we were here. Next, we need to move to the pickup sight, the sooner we get the, the sooner Madeleine can get on her way. If we move now, she can be over the border by nightfall, any questions?"

He tried to avoid looking at her, but he simply couldn't evade it. He naturally looked over to where she was sitting, on an old coat and a sack. She didn't look at him, she was staring into nothing, a blank look on her face.

"Right, let's get busy, we need to be off sooner rather than later"

The group started to move, the couple of nights sleeping on the wooden floor had made them all rather stiff, their bodies reluctant to obey. It wasn't long before everything was cleared, and any rubbish hidden away. Peter looked around the signal box, it was just how they had found it, no one would be any the wiser about their presence.

"Right, Claude, it's your car, so you drive, I am in the front, Madeleine and Peter in the back. Keep your weapons ready, you never know who we might meet. We need to get across the two bridges and onto the other side of the river, once there we will stay on the backroads and then on to our target"

This was going to be the most hazardous part of the whole operation. There were just too many opportunities to be caught by a German patrol. They had no choice though, they had to make the dash to the abandoned slaughterhouse, and they had to do it today.

It was a calculated risk on the part of Peter, they could have left it until the darkness and safety of the night but that would have meant no time to correct any issues that might have arisen. Also, he wanted to see Madeleine away and safe in the daylight. She had to make the Belgian border before the alarm was raised by their flight, so the sooner she got there the better.

Claude got into the driving seat and reached forward to start the engine. He turned to Peter with a look of concern on his face.

"Peter, just look at the four of us in this car. If any patrol sees us, we are done for, we might as well put a sign on the top of the car, 'escaped prisoners, come and get us"

"I don't see that we have a choice Claude"

"Well, we could space things out a little. There is plenty of fuel in the car, its only early morning, why don't I take you one at a time, that way, things will at least look a little more normal?"

Richard leant forward from the back of the car, "he's got a point old chap, two people in an old Citroen car, on their way to work in the morning, it's just an everyday sight. I don't think a patrol would even think about it, just part of the background scenery around here"

"You two are right, ok let's do that, as you say, no rush, let's make the best use of the time we have"

"Right Peter, I will do all the driving, it's my car and I know what she will or won't do. I will take you first, I don't know where the slaughterhouse is, so you can show me. I will bring the other two, one at a time"

Madeleine and Richard moved back into the signal box whilst Claude and Peter set off to their destination.

"I will bring Madeleine next Peter, it will give you two a chance to say goodbye"

"Thank you Claude, I appreciate that"

The door on the Citroen slammed shut, Peter heard the car pull away down the old lane that connected the slaughterhouse to the main road. He couldn't see who got out of the car, but the plan was Madeleine would be the next. It was Claude's suggestion, Peter didn't want to agree but he knew it was for the best.

He lacked the moral courage to actually say goodbye, in truth he didn't want to face the situation that he found himself in. Of course, he owed it to her, why should he just walk away without saying goodbye. As he waited for whomever had got out of the car to round the corner and enter the remains of the old building, he felt the urge to turn and run.

"Come on you dumb fool, just get on with it, there is no putting this off. Don't know why I feel like this, it's just a goodbye, it was always inevitable, wasn't it?"

As he was mulling over his situation, she came around the corner. She was a portrait in beauty and perfection, a slight air of vulnerability. She looked straight at him, then away, her hair was backlit by the sun, her shape defined in the golden light.

She stopped and half turned away, it seemed that she had the same feelings as he did, a reluctance to say goodbye, forever apart. Eventually she turned back, and head held high started to walk towards him, with a slightly sad expression on her face.

"Well Peter, I guess this is it. I knew this day would eventually arrive, to be honest I thought that day had, when we said goodbye at the cottage, before the attack. Somehow, I knew we would meet again though, I knew that you would be back, but I don't have that feeling this time. This is the last time I will ever see you Peter and it breaks my heart, but I know you have other priorities.

Saying goodbye hurts me more than you will ever know, I will move on of course, maybe love again, but I will never forget you Peter Parker, never!"

She held onto him so tightly that he struggled to breath. He could smell her hair, it always seemed to remind him of a summer's day, a perfect sweet perfume.

"There's no easy way to do this Madeleine, I can't pretend that there is. Nor can I pretend that

I want to do this, I just must do it, it's not a choice I have. I have to return to England with Claude, it's my duty. I have a wife and baby girl waiting for me, they need me, and I love them both. Dam I wish things were different, but they are not, this is the hand of cards fate has dealt me and I have to play the game accordingly.

I wish I had never involved you in this bloody awful mess, I should have left you alone in Belgium. You have done your bit for your country, what the hell was I thinking? I have a terrible habit of fucking up people's lives Madeleine and you are no exception, I am sorry for that.

I lay awake at night trying to count up all the people who have died because of me, every night I come up with a different number. When I close my eyes, I see more faces I hadn't counted the night before, like ghosts wandering around in my consciousness. If I tried to add on the people whose lives have been ruined because of me, that number would be incomprehensible"

She pushed him back slightly and looked directly into his eyes.

"Yes Peter, you have done that, many people have died because of you but only because you had to do it, not because you wanted to. How many people died today in this war because they had a job to do, they didn't ask why, they just acted for the greater good.

Try not to beat yourself up for doing your duty, many brave people have died just doing that. No Peter, you are not a monster or a bad man, you are just a man trying to do your best in an impossible situation. Best of all though, that has included me and for that I will always be grateful.

Sister Beverley said something to me before she left, she said, 'it's better to have love and lost than never to have loved at all'. She is right, I have lost you, but I count myself lucky that I had the chance to love you in the first place"

They held each other tightly, neither of them spoke for some considerable time, they wished that this moment could last forever, but they both knew that it couldn't.

Chapter 29.
Crack, crack.
June 14th, 1943

The gun had gone off twice with a crack, crack, the bullets tearing into flesh, ripping skin open, splintering bone. At such a close range there was only one possible outcome and that was death.

Both men fell backwards, the sheer concussion of the guns discharge blew them apart, flung them in opposite directions. There was a spray of blood, fizzing through the air like a deep red firework, coating both men and the ground around and about.

The whole scene seemed to slow down into a morbid blood-soaked cascade, a gruesome, macabre death act played out in the open. Neither man made a sound, there was no pain, a terrible numbness had enveloped both of them, a combination of shock and adrenaline protected them both. They both looked down at their abdomen, feeling for that sticky warm discharge that forecast their end.

Wagnor was the first to speak, he looked up at Schneider who was staring directly back at him.

"Well Schneider, it seems you have lost this particular argument, trouble with you young fools are that you don't know who your betters are.

You all seem to think you have a right to throw your weight around and be the boss, well it takes more than bullshit and aggression.

Thing is, I don't really give a fuck about you, but at the same time I do respect what you are capable of doing to me. That is the difference between you and I, you don't give a dam about me, but you seem to forget what I am capable of, especially when it comes to dealing with little trumped up shits like you.

Now just lay down on the ground and die in piece, there is no way you are living through that mess, so just relax and enjoy your trip to hell"

"I am going to hell Wagnor, there is no doubt about that, but I will be waiting for you because you won't be far behind me. The things I did for you, the trouble I cleared up and you never said thank you, you never acknowledged what I achieved, you are a wanker of the highest order"

"You see Schneider, that's another difference between me and you, you did as I told you and you expected a reward. I do things for my superiors, and I don't expect anything, so I never feel angry. In fact, I don't give a toss, I just get on with it and hope that tomorrow is a better day. When this shit storm is over, I just want to return to my family and pretend none of this ever happened, simple really!

Do you know how many men and women I have personally killed, some might say murdered, to be honest I can't remember. I think there was 4, or 5 downed airmen, 10 Resistance fighters, half a dozen SOE Agents, there was even a local girl who thought that I loved her. I put a bullet in her head, and she died, just the same as the airmen and the local Resistance fighters. There have been others, but I lose count, I must be getting old. The odd thing is, I didn't feel anything much above a little bit of excitement. I know that one day I will be called to account for that, but I don't give a toss. Maybe I should but any day now someone might put a bullet in my head, so why worry, just enjoy the journey. In the meantime Schneider, I have to manage people like you, pointless little men who think they are important, when in fact they are not.

That might have been a lesson you should have learnt Schneider, it would certainly have saved your life. You shouldn't have got angry at me, you should have just got on with it, but you didn't and now look at you"

He opened his mouth to say something but the damage to his body and the enormous loss of blood had now taken its toll. He fell rather stiffly into a sitting position, looking down and the blood-soaked ground and then back up at Wagnor.

"What will you tell my family, what will they find out about my death?"

Wagnor started to laugh, "that's a dam odd question to ask, I don't know, I will tell them you ran away crying like a baby and the Resistance shot you, how about that?"

The colour had completely drained from Schneider's face, he slumped a little more. His end was very close now, the blood and stopped oozing from his wounds, he fell to his right, now laying on the ground, he coughed several times.

"Oh well Schneider I guess this is goodbye, don't worry, I will send a truck to pick up your body, but I will leave it for a week or so, it will be nice and rotten by then"

He stepped up to where Schneider was now laying, he could see the slightest movement in his chest, his breathing was very shallow and rapid.

"I don't think I will order a formal burial for you, I will just get the men to throw you into a ditch, no wait into that lake at the old quarry. Yes, weighed down with a few stones, forever undiscovered, cold and alone, I like that Schneider, that idea appeals to me immensely.

Anyway, are you dead yet, it would be remiss of me to leave you here alive and breathing? I wouldn't be doing my duty as an officer in the SS if I didn't take care of my men"

With that, Wagnor took another step towards Schneider and levelled a huge kick into his midriff, causing his whole body to writhe around like an old rag doll.

"I guess you are dead then, well best of luck and enjoy your trip into hell, I will see you there one day, of that I am sure"

With that, Wagnor stepped over the lifeless body of Lieutenant Schneider and walked off, behind the barn and got into his car. He had a large smile on his face as he drove past the now dead Lieutenant, "So, I wonder what's for dinner in the mess tonight, I hope it's fish, I am starving?"

Chapter 30.
Return Home.
Early evening, June 14th, 1943

Peter, Madeleine, Doctor Claude A Durand and Squadron Leader Richard Burton were sitting in an outbuilding at the disused Slaughterhouse. It was a little distant from the main building, perhaps an old boiler house or the like, made of concrete with a grey slab roof. It had one door with a couple of windows either side, a rough concrete floor and several broken lights hanging from the ceiling.

The evening was calm and peaceful, warm with the slightest suggestion of a breeze wafting about the doorway. They sat on the hard floor, no one had spoken for a considerable amount of time, the tension and perhaps fear in the building was palpable. Peter and Richard stared at the floor in front of them, whilst Madeleine and Claude watched the view though the open door.

"Right", Richard announced, "I have one cigarette left, so I am going outside to enjoy it. If anyone feels the need to join me, please don't engage me in any conversation until I have finished smoking this last one, it's the last bit of stress relief I have"

Claude Durand chuckled, "I will join you Richard and if it helps, I might just have a half-smoked pack in my car. I don't normally indulge except when I go fishing, I can't help reaching for my pack of Gitanes, I don't know why? Anyway, we can enjoy the last few together before the flight"

"That's a deal Claude, let's go and enjoy the evening"

They rather stiffly got to their feet and made their way outside. It wasn't long before they were both enjoying a couple of Claude Durand's Gitanes and strolling aimlessly around the old buildings.

"So, what are you going to do once we get to England Richard, will you return to flying?"

"It's what I do Claude, I used to help my father with his aircraft charter business from when I was a young boy. It's where I learnt to fly, to be honest it's all I really know. When this bloody show started in 39, I joined up straight away, became a pilot. I managed to stay alive long enough to get promoted a couple of times and here I am, a jolly Squadron Leader. My father says he is very proud of me, but I can see in his eyes that he is terribly worried, goodness knows what state he is in right now.

I was offered a training post just before this last jaunt, I think I might take them up on that offer, for my father's sake you know"

"What about your mother, what does she think of what you do?"

"She won't even talk about it, she just pretends I am working in an office somewhere, I am sure. I don't even go home in my uniform anymore, you should see her face Claude. What the hell she is going through right now, I dread to think, I must be killing her, I need to sort things out Claude, save them both the torment. I am sure it will kill her one day, just the stress of knowing that I am a pilot, but it's war, what am I supposed to do?"

"I guess there are many, many mothers out there feeling the same way Richard, you just get on with your job, the sooner this lunacy is over the better"

"What about you Claude, this weapon thing, will it end the war?"

"I don't think so Richard, it's more likely to end the whole of humanity, kill every living thing. So, faced with that outcome I don't think anyone will actually be stupid enough to use it, or am I being a little too optimistic? Seems at odds really, if it's that terrible, why do they want me to complete my work? I guess it's better them having it rather than the enemy.

Anyway, I will do my duty, much as you do and complete my work and hope that the war is over before the weapon is complete. At least that way it will sit in a dusty warehouse somewhere, never to be used"

"In my experience Claude, things never sit unused, they just wait until the right time!"

"Can't argue with that Richard but that's their decision, they will need to explain it one day and look into their families' eyes before they kill them all, kill everyone. Now, can I tempt you with another Gitane, or do I need to smoke them all myself?"

The two men laughed, just for a moment the tension and anxiety disappeared into the perfect summers evening. They strolled, smoked their cigarettes and pretended nothing was wrong, and the war didn't exist, the world was a perfect place, and just for those few brief moments, it was.

Back in the building, Peter turned to Madeleine and looked straight into her eyes, it seemed like a dream, this was the end and he knew it.

"Are you going straight back to your Uncles and Aunts bakery, you will be safe there, no one will know who you really are?"

"Yes, they are a lovely couple, I might even get my old job back in the bar, I will sit out the war, watch the world go by and see what happens then"

"You will have to drink a toast to me every evening, I will do the same when I get home"

Madeleine leant over onto his shoulder, "tell me you will come and find me when the war is over, even if you don't mean it, just say that you will"

"I will always think of you Madeleine and I do mean that, who knows what the future holds?"

Madeleine was just about to reply when a familiar noise drew her attention.

"Did you hear that, Peter?"

"No, what was it?"

"Sounded like a gun being cocked, it's a noise I have dreams about, horrible black nightmares, I am sure that's what it was"

"Probably those two outside, they have nothing better to do, probably found an old hunting rifle"

"Why would they do that Peter, there is nothing out there, no guns or anything, we have looked?"

She was right of course, in any case, they had their guns already cocked with a round in the chambers. There would be no reason to do that again and their talking had faded away into the distance, it was strangely quiet, but only now had he actually noticed. He looked at Madeleine, her eyes were wide open. She sat up and then got to her feet, putting her index finger over her lips, she made her way to the door.

She very cautiously looked outside, firstly to the left and then to the right before turning back to face Peter. She looked fairly relaxed, the immediate tension had faded from her expression.

"Can't see anything, perhaps it was something else, a fox standing on a stick or chasing a mouse"

He looked at her, she was a very practised freedom fighter, experienced in simply staying alive. If her senses had been alerted, then it was very likely to be genuine.

"Hang on a minute Madeleine, I have never noticed you hearing things before, not that weren't actually there, if you heard a gun being cocked, that's what it was!"

She looked outside again but there was nothing, she cautiously stepped outside and then quickly back in again.

"I can't see anything Peter, it's pretty open out there, if someone was around, I would have seen them"

"Can you see Richard and Claude, are they about anywhere?"

"No Peter I can't, and I can't hear anything either or smell their Gitanes anymore. I think they are a way off towards the main building"

He crept up to the other side of the door, whispering just loud enough so she could hear him whilst standing on the other side of the opening.

"Perhaps they are behind the building Madeleine, we need to get out there and check. If there is anyone out there, I don't fancy them throwing a grenade in here and us surviving do you? I am going left, I will stick to the wall, you stay here and protect my back, I don't want one of them creeping up behind me"

She nodded and mouthed the words 'be careful'.

He smiled and lowering himself onto his haunches, he slowly made his way outside. At the same time, Madeleine looked right, she tried to open her senses up, could she see or hear anything but there was nothing.

Peter slowly crept around to the back of the building, his Browning 9mm leading the way. He could hear his heart pounding, it was so loud that he feared anyone around would also hear it beat. Eventually, he made it around to the back wall but there was nothing or no one there.

He pushed his back up against the building, the sensation of warm hard concrete gave him a feeling of safety even though he knew it gave him nothing close to that. Directly in front of him was a thick entanglement of brambles and impenetrable bushes. It was clear that no one was hiding in there, perhaps Madeleine had mistaken the noise of some local wildlife for something more sinister. He shook his head, he had learned to trust her and others like her, they had the instincts and senses of a local fox, they had to have in order to stay alive.

One more side of the building to check, perhaps this would be the hiding place of the stranger? He slowly and very quietly moved his head out, just far enough to see if anything was there but again, nothing. Scanning the area, he slowly stood up and moved back to the front of the building.

"There is nothing there Madeleine, maybe it was a stray cat or a bird?"

"It must have been Peter, I guess we are all stressed out, it's just that noise, a gun being loaded, it's seemed so real and very close by?"

"Well, I can't see anything and there is nowhere to hide behind us. Why don't we go for a walk, see if we can find the other two, if they haven't smoked themselves to death by now"

She smiled and reached out with her hand, he instinctively took hold, it felt warm and soft in his. He lead them outside and into the bright sunshine. The brilliant light made her squint, she took a second to readjust, as they waited, he could hear someone talking somewhere ahead of them.

"I don't think they have died yet Peter"

"I think it will take a little more than half a pack of Gitanes to kill those two, thank goodness"

He could feel the hot sun on his back as he walked towards the laughing. Despite the lateness of the afternoon, there was still a considerable amount of power in its golden glow. He looked up into the faultless blue azure sky, a couple of birds fluttered past, it was a scene of perfect piece.

In a few short hours the aircraft would arrive, and he would be gone and back to his former life. Back to Susan and the baby, back to a relative level of safety, no more SS chasing him, no more sleepless nights, no more Madeleine. He smiled at the enormous difference between now and then, this life and that. Peter wondered if he had been lucky to experience such a contrast or if it had been a curse, but not of his own making.

"I didn't get a chance to meet Philipe, André and Laurent this time, if you ever see them again, please pass on my thanks. If it wasn't for their help, I couldn't possibly have succeeded or even stayed alive"

"You should thank them yourself Peter, next time you visit"

He didn't reply, he just squeezed her hand a little tighter and continued on towards Richard and Claude. They rounded the corner of another concrete building, this one was two stories high and at least three times the size of the one they had come from.

Their steps kicked up little puffs of dust as they walked, Peter looked down at the sprites of light brown clouds whirling around their feet. It was at that moment that he felt a shock of unease flow through him, he stopped and looked up.

"What's wrong Peter, have you forgotten something?"

"Something's not right Madeleine?"

She looked around, quickly turning from left to right but she couldn't see anything out of place.

"There is nothing here Peter, what's set you off, what have you noticed?"

"I am not sure?"

He looked back down at the ground again and it was then that he realised what it was.

"Look Madeleine, look at the ground and tell me what you see?"

"Footprints, that's all, just footprints"

"No, not just footprints, these here, they are military boots, look at the hob nails hammered into them. These aren't our prints, these are army boots, and more importantly, they are fresh"

She looked down and there, right in front of her were several sets of heavy footprints. A hot flush flashed through her, he was right, they were army boots, and the prints were sharp and very recent.

She let go of his hand and reached for her pistol from the back of her waistband, she snicked off the safety and prepared to fire.

"Over there Madeleine, there is a wooden shack, it's only 10 perhaps 15 yards away, go"

They both turned and ran, staying as low as possible, expecting to be cut down in a hail of bullets at any moment. The absolute surge of terror running through them made it difficult to breath. They had to force one foot in front of the other, staying focused on their destination.

It felt like they were running in thick sand, pushing against an incredible force, preventing them from reaching safety. Every stride brought them closer and after what seemed like an age, they finally reached the broken wooden door of the shack.

The darkness of the interior confused their eyes, transiting from the bright evening sun into relative darkness left them almost blind. The surge of panic in Peter only increased, they had run headlong into a dark building, now unable to see and unaware of anyone else who might be present.

He tripped headlong over something small but with a narrow edge, as he crashed to the ground, whatever he had hit fell on top of him.

He rolled over a couple of times before hitting the wall on the other side of the building.

He could hear that a similar fate had befallen Madeleine, she crashed at least twice into objects before falling somewhere close by. The silence washed over them, the dust sticking in his throat. At least he was now certain that no one else was in here with them.

He tried to sit up and then get to his knees, but a searing pain shot through his ankle, the likes of which he had not felt before. He didn't remember letting out a cry of pain, but Madeleine's voice came out of the dusty darkness.

"What's wrong Peter, are you ok?"

"Not sure, I think I have done my ankle, must have hit something as I ran in"

"I am not surprised, you crashed into an old table, wait I will get over to you"

The dust was beginning to settle, and their eyes were becoming adjusted to the dim and deeply shadowed light. He started to see shapes emerge out of the dust, a broken table and two chairs, and in the corner Madeleine. She was untangling herself from what looked like a smashed bookshelf, she kicked away several shelves and a couple of small boxes.

Eventually she got up and slowly made her way towards him but as she squatted down to examine his damaged ankle the light dimed once more. Instinctively he looked towards the door and to their complete and utter horror, there standing in the opening was someone dressed in a German army uniform with Sargent's striped on one arm.

"Well, if it's not......not sure what your real name is, I would take a guess at Peter Parker?"

The voice and the uniform was very familiar to Peter, it was Lina's Sargent, the very same woman who had threatened his testicles the last time he was here and had been held prisoner in the basement of the water mill. She stood with a pistol in her left hand, pointing directly at his head.

"It seems that our lives are linked Parker, it started with Lena and you taking advantage of her, ups sorry, she is taking advantage of you. Then you held me prisoner in the mill, until that stupid RAF fly boy let me escape. How on earth are your RAF putting up any kind of fight with officers like that, they are a joke!

Looks like I have the upper hand this time. You should have killed me when you had the chance, I would have killed you if the circumstances had been the other way around.

Anyway, I will be taking you back to have a chat with Hauptman Wagnor, he does enjoy his little tête-à-têtes. Trouble is, I am not sure you will enjoy it in the same way, especially when he starts to get rough with you"

She laughed and half turned, "they are in here, bring the cuffs, we need to get them into the lorry and back to the manor house"

Madeleine turned to look at Peter, the expression of utter surprise mixed with terror was clear to see. Just for a split-second Peter thought she was going to start shooting, he was about to stop her when there was a fizzing and a thump as something hit the side of the building.

The Sargent ducked and then fell backwards out of the doorway as another thump hit the side of the shack, sending clouds of dust raining down from all parts of the roof. It took Peter a second or two to comprehend what was actually happening, someone was shooting and judging by the actions of the Sargent, they were shooting at them.

"Quick Madeleine, get to the door, if you can see where she went, shoot, and don't think twice about it"

She sprang to her feet and cautiously made her way towards the door, there was another volley of fire from outside and then another. The whole area seemed to have changed from a peaceful summers evening into a war zone without any warning at all.

Madeleine cautiously looked outside in the direction of where the German Soldier had stumbled but she didn't fire. Peter assumed that she had made an escape with assistance of the confusion generated by the situation.

"I can't see her or anyone else Peter, I don't know what the hell is going on?"

The statement was met by another volley of fire at least one of which hit the doorframe just above Madeleine's head. It sent a shower of splinters and dirt flying into the shack, causing Madeleine to fall backward into the room. She quickly got to her feet, and took up a position just inside the opening, trying to understand what was happening outside. There was another burst of fire but this time there were impacts on the shack.

"There is fire going away from us and towards us Peter, I can only assume that there are several groups out there, goodness knows who they are though?"

"Well, I can only assume Richard and Claude are two of them, let's hope they get through this, ok?"

Again, Peter tried to get to his feet but the intense pain raging in his ankle made any such attempt utterly futile. He collapsed once more onto the dirty floor.

"Listen Madeleine, you are going to have to help me get to the door, I can't move, I think we are stuck in here, we need to hold out until Richard and Claude can get to us"

She quickly started to remove the tangle of wood and debris surrounding Peter. He was right of course, the Germans might be back at any moment and this time there would be no second chance.

Richard and Claude had heard the lorry pull up outside the main building of the slaughterhouse. Four soldiers had got out of the back, jumping down holding their rifles, ready for the fight. From the cab of the truck exited another soldier and a female Sergeant, she gathered the group together and moved off into the complex of buildings.

"They don't know we are here Claude, let's keep it that way. They may just be searching the area, if we can stay out of the way they will eventually leave"

"Trouble is, Peter and Madeleine don't know what's coming their way, we need to find and warn them"

"Right, well let's keep our distance, see where they go. If it's anywhere near the other two we will open up, kill the lot of them before they can work out what's happening. They clearly don't know that we are here, let's keep it that way, maintain the element of surprise"

They cautiously followed the group of soldiers as they methodically moved through the collection of disused buildings. It didn't take very long to search any particular area, most of the buildings were empty concrete shells, abandoned long ago, rotting and falling back into the grip of nature. The grey uniformed soldiers moved about like a veil of danger and death, one false move and they would be dead.

Richard and Claude trailed them through the complex, hoping beyond hope that they would find nothing of interest and leave empty handed. Eventually they came to an open area, bounded on two sides by metal frames, rusting with peeling paintwork and on the third by a wooden shack.

In the door of the shack stood a female soldier, perhaps a Sergeant, she seemed to be talking to someone inside. Richard and Claude observed from the safety of a ledge on a nearby building.

"She was the woman we held prisoner in the water mill, the slippery eel managed to escape"

"You should have put a bullet in her head, she would do the same to you in a heartbeat. Who is she talking to, it can't be Madeleine or Peter, they are on the other side of that building in that shed?"

"Let's get closer Claude, we can crawl along this ledge, see who it is in that building?"

The two men slowly crawled along a narrow ledge on the outside of the concrete building. It was two stories high and the drop to the ground below would be fatal. It wasn't long before they reached a window opening, the wooden frame had long since rotted away, leaving an empty void into the building beyond. With a huge amount of relief, they edged through the window opening and into the building, turning to try and listen to the conversation somewhere below.

They strained to hear what was being said, it didn't take long for them to realise who the conversation was being directed at.

"Dam, it's Peter in there, she is talking to Peter"

"You're right Richard, we can also assume that Madeleine is in there with him"

"What do we do Claude?"

"We need to get them out, we need to start shooting, give them a chance to run for it. First, we need to find all the other soldiers, they need to be shot or at least tied town whilst we get them out"

"Right, well I can see three of them and the Sergeant from here, it's the other two who have gone missing"

"I am not sure we have time to find where they are, if she starts shooting it will be too late, we need to act now"

"Right Claude, you shoot at her and I will pour some fire on the others, it should be enough to scatter them, maybe I can wing one or two. If we can keep it up for just a few seconds, that should be enough for Peter and Madeleine to make a run for it"

Claude looked at Richard, it was quite normal for this RAF Squadron Leader to start shooting, blazing red hot missiles at people, he was a fighting man. He on the other hand was a scientist, the quintessential quiet person working alone in a lab. What the hell did he know about killing people, it was one thing talking about it, it might prove a whole lot more difficult actually doing it.

Richard looked back, "before you say anything Claude, I know you haven't shot at anyone before, let alone killed anyone. I have seen that look on a hundred young pilots faces, just before they go into battle, you all have that visage of terror mixed with doubt. Just point the bloody gun and shoot, they will move out of the way, trust me. If you hit anything, it will be sheer bad luck on their part"

Claude smiled, "thanks Richard, I am sure they will but it's what happens when they shoot back, that I am worried about"

"Then we will move out of the way, you will I promise you, just do what I say and don't think about it too much. Thinking can get you into a lot of trouble, just go with your instincts, they will take care of you"

Without any further conversation, Richard took aim at the three soldiers in the courtyard below as Claude nervously pointed his gun at the Sergeant. The sound of Richard's gun going off caused Claude to jump slightly but he quickly regained his composure, pointed the barrel at the female German and pulled the trigger.

The smoke and the noise was overwhelming, Claude tried to do as Richard asked, "just act, don't think". It wasn't long before the bullets started to come towards them, ricocheting of the wall behind them, sending sharp grey splinters in all directions.

"Keep firing Claude, keep their heads down, she has run for cover, Peter and Madeleine will be out of there any second"

Another volley of fire hammered into the wall behind them, this time a little closer, the next shots would be on target, they had to take cover.

"Richard, they aren't coming out, there isn't any movement from them at all"

"Ok, we need to take cover and move, let's work our way around to the other side of the building, we might get a better shot from there"

They moved back, just in time to miss the next volley. Traversing to another window they both continued to fire at the German soldiers below. One went down holding his right leg, but it was clear that their action was having little if any effect.

"Listen Claude, you need to get out of here, make your way towards the main road, I will hold them for a while. Out of all of us, you are the only one that has to get back to England, the rest of us are expendable"

"No chance Richard, we do this together"

"You have to listen to me Claude, get to the road, make contact with that Vet and set up another pickup for yourself, now go before it's too late"

"I am not leaving you, now let's get on with this"

"Claude, I have a few rounds left in my pocket and a couple in my gun, I have nothing else, perhaps five or six more shots and that's it. Now go before it's too late"

Claude stared at Richard, his mind was screaming 'leave, get out' but his conscious wouldn't let him go. Richard was his friend, he would never leave him, come what may until this situation had resolved itself, even if it meant death.

The firing stopped, a strange an uneasy peace rolled over the wooden shack. The tiny dust particles, stirred up by the action were spinning and flowing like a million-star studied river, whirling about the space above their heads. Madeleine looked around at Peter, she didn't say anything, but he knew full well what's she was thinking, 'have they gone?'

He looked again at the open door, there was no action evident, but his instincts told him that this was just a lull and not the final chapter.

"They haven't gone anywhere Madeleine, they are just re organising themselves. Richard and Claude have only got a phew rounds of ammunition, they can't hold this force off for more than seconds. They were giving us a chance to get out of here and because of my ankle, we couldn't move. She will be back at any minute and at the same time, her troops will be hunting down the other two. How many rounds have you got left?"

Madeleine counted the remaining bullets, "three, what about you?"

"None"

There was a noise from outside of the shack, the approach of footsteps and then a woman's voice.

"I think we can assume that your colleagues aren't able to help you anymore. My men are, as we speak, taking them into custody. The best thing you can do is to throw your guns out here and give yourselves up.

Despite your status as infiltrators and criminals, I can assure you of fair treatment under the Geneva Convention. So, what do you say, give up and live or have my men blast you and this shack to oblivion?"

Madeleine looked at Peter, "so what do we do now?"

"There is only one thing we can do and that's exactly what's she says"

"Then what?"

"Sorry Madeleine but this time I don't have a plan. One thing is for sure though, if we don't give up, she will kill us both, right here right now. At least out there an opportunity might present itself, perhaps I can even convince them that you were not part of our group, perhaps just a local girl I met"

"You can't do that Peter, I want to be with you, even if that's the last place I go"

Without replying, he threw his gun outside, it bounced off the doorframe as it exited the building and into the dusty yard beyond.

"Go on Madeleine, we can't fight his lot off with three bullets, throw it out"

Madeleine looked down at her gun, then across at Peter, with a tear in her eye she tossed the weapon outside with a disdainful scorn.

Again, the voice of the female Sargent came from outside.

"That's very good, an excellent decision, now come out with your hands up, one false move and I will shoot both of you"

Madeleine moved over to Peter and with a great effort helped him to his feet. If his ankle was not broken it was certainly very badly injured. Together and with their heads held high they slowly shuffled out into the dusk of the early evening.

It had become noticeably darker since their dash to get inside, the whole atmosphere had changed, it was distinctively cooler, bird sound had ceased, the world was preparing for the night.

Outside they were greeted by the woman with three stripes on her arm and one other soldier, his rifle pointing directly at them. She had a sickening smirk on her face, a visage of self-importance and gratification.

"Well Mr Parker, so nice to see you again. You and your friends have certainly led me and my colleagues a merry dance over the past few days but never mind, we are all together again now.

I am sure that Hauptman Wagnor will be very pleased to see you and more than happy to have a chat, especially with your lady friend. He does enjoy a chat with the ladies in his interrogation room, I am not sure that they ever enjoy chatting with him though"

She laughed, as did the soldier standing in front of them. She walked slowly over to where Peter and Madeleine were standing, she looked down at his injured ankle.

"That must be painful Mr Parker, I assume that's why you didn't run when you had the chance?"

She took another step forward and without any warning, kicked out at his injured ankle. The explosion of pain was beyond tolerance, with a yell he collapsed to the ground.

"Oh, sorry Mr Parker, is that ankle painful, I must remember to tell Hauptman Wagnor, he will be most interested in that"

Madeleine turned towards her, but the Sergeant took one look at the approaching Madeleine and elbowed her right on the nose. It caused Madeleine to stumble backwards, blood streaming down her face and onto her shirt.

"You two must learn to control yourselves, you are in my care now and any attempt to harm me or my men, or any attempt to escape will be met with force"

She looked over to the waiting soldier and nodded at him before gesturing over to Peter. The soldier swung his rifle around, walked over to Peter had hit him on the head with its butt. The sickening sound rang out all over the yard, Peter was forced flat by the impact, his damaged head bouncing of the ground. He didn't make a sound, he lay prostrate on the dusty earth, at best unconscious, at worse dead, blood pouring from a gash to his forehead.

Instantaneously the Sergeant turned on Madeleine, grabbing her by the throat, she forced her backwards to the side of the shack. Pinning her to the rotten wooden wall with one hand she punched her in the stomach with the other. Madeleine bent over both in agony and shock, two or three more blows sent her to her knees. She knelt coughing on the ground before a kick to her head sent the world spinning out of control.

There were voices somewhere in the background, they seemed to fade in and out. She was laying on a hard floor, her fingers stretched out, it was cold, it felt like wood. There were more voices, angry, frustrated, a woman was giving orders, a man was arguing back.

She had a taste in her mouth, what was it, she had experienced that before, it was blood. Where had that come from, why was she here, what had happened to her? Someone walked past, she could hear the boots as they clanked nearby, more voices, someone sounded familiar, but who?

The room slowly stopped spinning, she tried to force her eyes open, they were dry, sore, one wouldn't open at all, why? She was laying on her back, a canvas cover was above her head, she slowly turned her head, a lorry, she was laying in the back of a lorry. To her left were two recognisable faces, they were sat on one side of the truck, it was Richard and Claude. They had their hands tied behind the back, they were looking to their left, out of the open back, into the dark night beyond.

"I thought they were good at engineering Claude, this is the second time I have been stranded in a broken German lorry. Their bloody fighters scream around the skies with consummate ease. One of them shot me down, that didn't have any mechanical issue I can assure you of that"

"Maybe their trucks aren't as reliable Richard, perhaps we will be broken down here until the end of the war, then we can all go home and have a Cognac?"

Richard laughed and turned to his right, "well hello Madeleine, that's a nasty gash on your forehead, but nice to see you back in the land of the living. Not sure you will be seeing much out of that right eye for a while, maybe that's not a bad thing hey? I bet you have a thundering headache, Peter is outside, I am afraid he looks rather bad. I wish Sister Beverley Jane was here, I am sure she would be able to help"

She tried to sit up, but the truck started to spin and the thundering pain she had in her head made her lay down again. Despite the hardness of the wooden floor, it at least was stable and felt safer than trying to sit up.

"I should stay down there for a while Madeleine, we aren't going anywhere, and neither are you. This dam truck won't start so we are stuck here, thank goodness, I don't fancy going back to the manor house and that Hauptman Wagnor they keep talking about"

Richards words were like a jack hammer pounding through her head, she wanted to say 'shut up' but her mouth didn't want to respond. She managed to turn her head slightly to look at the two men sitting, waiting for their fate.

"We have to get out of this, if they get us back to the manor house we will be killed for certain"

"We kind of figured that already Madeleine, if you can come up with a cunning plan, please be my guest. There are at least five armed soldiers out there, whatever we do would simply end up in us getting slaughtered. Perhaps that is a better way to go, what do you say Claude?"

"You might have a point Peter, like Madeleine said, if they get us back to the manor house then we are dead, no doubt about that. Running into the night would most likely end up in all of us getting shot, that's no different than going back to see Wagnor I guess. At least running might just enable one of us to get away, that's better than just waiting to get tortured and then shot by a firing squad"

"I like you're thinking Claude, but I don't see Madeleine or Peter doing much running do you? Still, what do we have to lose, let's try and loosen these ropes, give ourselves a chance. Maybe we can grab a rifle, at least kill one or two of them before they get us?"

"That sounds like a plan Richard, not much of one I have to admit but at least it's a plan. There is no talking our way out of this, they will torture the lot of us for being spies, then kill us in some slow and miserable way. I think I prefer a bullet from one of those rifles, nice and quick, and as you say, maybe we can take one or two of them with us"

The two men turned one way and then another in an attempt to loosen the ropes that held them.

Eventually, Richard managed to loosen his just enough to slip one hand out and then the other. He quickly untied Claude, they were both free but with no real plan other than to see what happened next.

Claude looked down at the still half unconscious Madeleine, she was perhaps a little more lucid than before but nowhere near her normal self. He knelt down by her side, her face was white and glistening with sweat, the lamp on the rear bulkhead of the truck illuminated her in a ghostly and lurid yellow light.

The severe bruising on her face was angry, purple and completely closed her eye. Blood streaked her face, stuck her hair together in clumps of dark red matt. She looked up at him, reached out and took his hand. He could feel her trembling, her clammy flesh had no real strength, but the contact with him made her smile.

"Listen Madeleine, I think this will be goodbye, it's been fun I have to admit. A few days ago, I was a prison Warden, fishing in the river by my house, drinking Cognac with my friends in the bar at the Hotel Paris. Now look at me, I am a bloody hero, a prisoner of the SS, a fugitive, you could write a book about me. I don't think the story would go past tonight though, so I must say adieu and take care"

"It's been a wonderful story Claude, thank you for the fun and please don't leave me here, if you do manage to grab one of those rifles, save a bullet for me"

"I will Madeleine, I promise"

Richard stood up and looked down at Madeleine, "I hate goodbyes, so I won't say one, I have said too many farewells to lots of good men. To be honest, I have lost count of those brave young souls who have left the mess, never to return. I have learnt to simply accept what fate can do and not to question it too much.

I often wish I could have been born twenty years earlier, so I would have been too old to join up. I could have been a tractor driver or a traffic warden, something honourable but with little risk to life. I am no hero you see Madeleine, far, far from it, I class myself as a victim of circumstance.

So, if I can grab a rifle, I will make sure you don't fall into the hands of Wagnor, that's my promise. Until then, thanks for the fun and trying your best to get me back to blighty. I won't be going to see Bob Swanbourne's wife after all, just another broken promise I guess in amongst a lot of useless guarantees in this war. What a fucking mess, I didn't want it to end this way, I really didn't!

Right professor Claude A Durand, fate awaits us, in the RAF, we would say, tally ho"

"Well said Squadron Leader, will you lead the charge, or should I?"

"I have never been one to shirk my responsibilities Claude, so follow me"

Chapter 31.
The office of Lieutenant Colonel BR Smith.
S.O.E. Headquarters London.
Early evening, June 14th, 1943

Lieutenant colonel Smith was finishing of a mountain of paperwork, most of which was classified as top secret, much of which would involve brave people risking their lives for the greater good.

Every time he signed another piece of paper it meant someone else being dropped into occupied Europe, another hairbrained scheme, another impossible mission. He tried not to think of all the lives he had simply signed away, he did catch himself wondering how many sometimes, but in order to maintain his sanity, he quickly moved on to something else.

If he was being honest, the stress of doing what he did was becoming almost too difficult to bear. He wished he could be one of those brave men and women jumping out of that aircraft, leave his part to someone with a tougher and more cold nature. Someone who wouldn't wake up at night sweating or shaking in the sure and undeniable knowledge that he had sent so many people to a certain death.

He looked at the clock on his desk, it was the one his grandson had bought him for Christmas. It was six pm, he couldn't remember if he had eaten lunch, or even what time he had come to work that morning. He felt himself drifting away again, into a semi dream world, one that didn't involve war, killing, sacrifice and sadness.

He was shaken back to normality by a ringing sound, he jerked back in his seat, blinking several times. It was the red phone, ringing and with a flashing red light on top.

"That's bound to be another pile of shit coming my way. I wonder what would happen if I just ignored it, got up and went for a walk? It wouldn't help I don't suppose, they would come and find me, wherever I was hiding"

Hesitating for a second, his hand hovered over the receiver, he felt like picking it up and throwing it out of the window. Eventually he snatched at the handset and put it to his ear.

"Smith here"

"Ah Smith my old man, it's Colonel Wavertree here, Porton Down chemical and biological research centre, how are you?"

"Sir, I am fine thank you, how is your beautiful wife, it's been a while since we last met?"

"Ah yes, Audrey, she ran off with some chap from her work you know, never saw that coming.

You never know what's going on behind your back you know"

"Oh, sorry to hear that sir, you are right, you never know what's coming next. Now how can I help?"

"Well, I know it's all hush hush, but I am aware that you lot are bringing back that Claude A Durand. He worked here for a few years before the war, are you familiar with his work?"

"I do know the general outline sir, much else is beyond my capabilities to understand, I am just a soldier you know"

"Right well that's expected I guess but I have some news for you. This project he was working on, Simurgh, we managed to work out where he had hidden his notes, in a bank vault in the centre of London.

Strange how things work out, but he was having a fling with one of our women here. She remembered him going to this bank vault several times, told her never to say anything. He never had any money, so she was always curious about what he was hiding there, all seemed a bit strange you know. You must be careful in times of war, you never really know who you are dealing with, even with the likes of Claude A Durand!

Anyway, the chaps over here kind of put one and one together and speculated that he had been hiding his formulars and notes, in this vault, just before he returned to France. It kind of made sense, why take them back there when he might be picked up by the SS at any time. If he had taken his notes with him, it would have been a gift for Adolf Hitler!

So, hide them in London before you leave, it's exactly what I would have done. Anyway, they thought it was worth a look, so I got the intelligence spooks to get an order to open the vault. Hey presto, there it was, notes, formulars, plans, workings out, the bloody lot.

Now, this allowed our chaps to have a go at resurrecting his work, trouble is, it's a dud I am afraid. We have tried and tried to get the thing going but no luck at all. Some of our best people have been trying to replicate it but it's a no go, it doesn't work.

No matter how they try, they just can't get the dam thing to come together. It's a good idea, maybe even a brilliant one but it's flawed, it's no good. So, you can save yourself a lot of trouble and let the Germans have him because they will be wasting their time as well. No need to send anyone over there, leave him to his fate Smith, do I make myself clear?"

Lieutenant Colonel Smith didn't bother replying, he just replaced the handset in a calm and controlled manner. He could have been much more emotional, angry perhaps, but he had to pull himself together. He wasn't sure if he was furious with himself, Colonel Wavertree for not saying something the last time they had met, or the sheer waist of life in this utterly fruitless venture.

In all honesty, it was a combination of all three and in addition, the sheer effort so many people had put in and all for what? At least one dead S.O.E Agent, the RAF crew who had risked their lives getting them there, dead Resistant fighters, waisted resources and all for nothing.

He knew the Lysander aircraft was scheduled to pick them up tonight, that mission had to go ahead, Peter Parker and the RAF Wing Commander were certainly needed back in the war.

That wasn't the point though, if he had just known about this bloody stupid Simurgh flop sooner he could have stopped so much death, so many risked lives. Now Peter Parker, Wing Commander Richard James and of course Claude A Durand were waiting in a field in France, sure in the knowledge that all the sacrifice had been worth it.

He couldn't control himself any further, he erupted in a volcanic explosion of frustration and emotion. He stood up, swiped the whole contents of his desk to all parts of the office. He yelled at the top of his voice, unable to control the upwelling of years of lost lives, sacrifice by people too young to really understand and all because he had ordered it to be done.

"How many more lives is this fucking war going to screw up, how much more can people give. The sheer bloody arrogance of people like me, who the hell am I to say who lives or dies, what qualifies me to send people to a certain death?

Then there are the people who tell me that I am doing a good job, or just get on with it Smith, follow your orders. Well screw your orders, fuck the lot of you, I am not doing this anymore. I am sick of so many brave people dying because I say so, or because some bloody jumped-up scientist thinks he can end the war when in actual fact, he hasn't got a bloody clue. What a waist, just piled up on top of so much waist and misery, that's it, I am finished"

With that, Lieutenant Colonel BR Smith picked up the red phoned and hurled it against the wall with such ferocity that it smashed into a thousand pieces. Crunching through the broken pieces of red plastic and twisted wires, he stormed out of the office, slamming the door behind him.

Chapter 32.
The old slaughterhouse.
Nighttime, June 14th, 1943

Richard James turned to Claude A Durand as they stood one the lip of the lorry, ready to jump out. The night air was sweet and calm, the warm breeze floated around, occasionally wafting into their faces. There was the intermittent sweet scent of the nearby honeysuckle, for one moment it all seemed quiet and tranquil, after all, nature was ever present, even in times of war.

"Right Claude, this isn't going to end well so I will say ta ta and thanks for the company. Grab whatever weapon you can and don't forget Madeleine and Peter, let's not let them fall into the hands of that lunatic Wagnor"

"Understood Richard, it's been nice knowing you, it could have been even better but for the war getting in the way. I tell you what, I will buy you lunch at the Grosvenor after this war has finished, I will send you an invitation. Are you going left, or right?"

"Yes, send it to the RAF base, I will look forward to that. Now, left or right, good question, I will go right, tally ho"

With that the two men jumped out of the back of the truck. For an instance the guards were taken by surprise, they spun around and froze as the two men ran towards them. The closest soldier was quickly overcome by Claude, knocking his rifle to the ground but the second was a little further away. This gave him the opportunity to take his rifle off his shoulder and level it at the advancing Richard.

The soldier cocked the bolt on his gun, click and then another click as the bolt of the Karabiner 98k Mauser loaded a bullet into the chamber. He pointed to weapon at the head of Richard, any moment now there would be a flash and then the end.

Richard kept running, memories racing through his mind, his dead friend Bob Swanbourne, his life back home, the friends he had made out in France. He closed his eyes and waited for the impact, life seemed to slow down and then there was a loud bang, and a second.

He wasn't sure how many more strides he had taken but with his eyes still closed, he tripped over something, sending him sprawling head long onto the ground. He crashed heavily, rolling over in the dust, scraping his hands and arms on the small stones and pieces of concrete that lay all about.

There was another burst of fire, this time from an automatic weapon, he felt the heat of a couple of bullets as they passed close by. He rolled over onto his back, his arms stinging with the myriad of small cuts and grazes. He tried to open his eyes, but they were full of dust, he rubbed them in an attempt to clear his vison, coughing the dust from his throat.

Someone jumped right over him, he was carrying a British issue Bren light machine gun. This confused Richard, why would a German soldier carry such a weapon? Perhaps he was already dead, and this was just a vision, the machinations of a dying brain, confusions wrought by impending death.

Another burst of gun fire, something wet and warm splashed onto his face, sticky and viscous, it ran down his temple and onto his cheek. In an attempt to understand his current predicament, he sat bolt upright. He looked to the left and the right, into the darkness, people running, shouting, muzzle flashes of guns being fired.

At his feet was the body of the soldier who had pointed his rifle at him, he was covered in bloody holes, his motionless body oozing his life onto the dirty ground. He kicked the body further away from him, shocked and confused by where he found himself.

Then, seemingly from nowhere a hand caught him by the collar of his shirt and began to drag him away, further into the shadows, further from the killing grounds. He resisted, terrified by the circumstances and his lack of understanding but it didn't help, whoever had hold of him wasn't going to let go.

"English, it's Pierre Dupuy, you will remember me, I am the leader of the local Resistance. Stop fighting me, we need to get to cover, there are still a couple of them out there somewhere. Get up and follow me, we need to get around this corner, we will be safe there"

Still dazed Richard got to his feet and scrambled behind a wall, Pierre Dupuy forced him to the ground.

"Stay here English, don't move until one of us comes to get you, do I make myself clear?"

"Perfectly"

Still confused by the events of the last few seconds, Richard did as he was told. He couldn't work out if he was actually dead and this was the dream of a dying man, or he had been rescued by the local Resistance? A minute later, Claude A Durand came around the corner, deposited onto the ground in a no less ignominious way by a young man with a Lugar pistol in his hand.

"Claude, seems like things have turned out for the best, I do like being rescued, makes me feel somewhat important"

The fighting was still ongoing but noticeably less as the seconds passed by. The shooting seemed further away, small bursts, occasional shouts.

"I guess they were coming to help with the evacuation Richard, Peter did say they would, seems like they arrived just in time"

"Just in time is good enough for me, I am going to find Madeleine and Peter, they must still be out there. The fighting has moved away, it should be safe enough"

The two men carefully moved around the wall and back towards the yard and the lorry where Madeleine had been laying. There was one body on the ground, the soldier who died right in front of Richard, otherwise the vista was calm.

"The lorry Richard, let's get to it, see if she is ok"

They quickly moved to the back of the lorry and peered inside. Madeleine was sat with her back against the bulkhead with a huge smile on her beaten and bloodstained face.

"It's nice to see you two guys, I assume you didn't kill everyone then?"

The two men laughed, Richard turned to Madeleine, "we did our share of killing Madeleine but the local Resistance kind of helped, just a little bit"

Madeleine slowly made her way to the edge of the truck and with the help of Richard and Claude jumped to the ground.

"Come on Madeleine, we can't just stay here hugging each other, we don't know what's going to happen next"

Before she had a chance to reply to Richard, a familiar voice came out of the darkness. It was the SS Sergeant, she advanced from the gloom, illuminated by the yellow flames and flickering light of the brazier.

Her features were distorted by the dancing illumination of the fire, she seemed to have an evil angular aspect to her face. She advanced forward, a pistol in her right hand, her left holding a blood-soaked field dressing over a wound to her stomach. The blood ran into her tunic and down towards her crotch. She stumbled a couple of times before coming to a halt, slowly bringing the pistol up with a trembling hand.

"It seems you have won a victory here tonight, but I am going to take my revenge. I will kill all three of you and that Parker before I die, so we can all travel to hell together.

I will however give you the choice of who dies first, I really don't mind but please be quick, I am not sure how long I have left. Anyway, where is Parker, don't tell me he has run off again. He did that last time he was here, flew back to England like a little sobbing child. He thought he had the better of Wagnor and the SS but he was wrong, we knew about him from the very start, he is pathetic"

She swung the gun from left to right, pointing it at each of them in turn. But before anyone else could speak, a dark shadow began to emerge out of the blackness. Slowly at first but becoming progressively recognisable. The outline moved quietly in behind the SS Sergeant, right up to within a pace of her.

"I do agree with you about going to hell, but we won't be going together. Don't turn around, this object pointing into your back is my Browning 9mm and I will gladly pull the trigger. Now drop your weapon to the ground, if you value your life.

As for the SS knowing everything about me, I very much doubt that, you believed exactly what I wanted you to. I must admit you had me with Lena, at least for a while but not for long, it was way too obvious what she was up to. I guessed early on about her real mission in all of this, I presumed Wagnor had something to do with it.

As for the rest, well I managed to get rid of the three original men in charge, shot the Sergeant Major in his office and blew the other two up in front of Laurent's lock up. I managed to kill Wagnor's number two and a couple of your soldiers at the bridge, oh yes and three Gestapo men on my first visit at the same place.

So, you see things haven't been that bad since I arrived and now, I get to take the famous French scientist Claude A Durand back to England. Best off all, I get to kill you, right here, right now, have you anything to say before I do?"

"You won't kill me Parker, you don't have to courage to do that, if you did you would have killed me when you last had the chance in the watermill. No, you will end up tying me up and leaving me here, so why are you even talking like that?"

She slowly turned around to face him, she had a sickly smile on her face but with a look of contempt in her eyes.

"So, I am facing you Parker, can you shoot me when I am looking into your eyes, can you stomach killing me whilst I face you. I don't think you can, you haven't got the guts for this or any of the things you have become involved in, you are not the right kind of person, you just get others to do your killing for you.

You see Parker, I think you are a fake, you have got lucky several times I must admit but you haven't got that inner strength, that ability to block out the death and destruction that your actions inevitably invite.

You can't sweep away the suffering from your mind, you worry too much about the those who die because of your actions. No, you will never make an effective Agent Parker, you are too soft, you don't really believe in what you are doing and most importantly of all, people matter to you, and they shouldn't.

So, you are facing me, pull the trigger and kill me if you can, end another life, more blood on your hands. Be sure to look into my eyes though as you shoot, make sure you remember me, another haunting image in your dreams"

"You know Sergeant, you are right, I will never make an Agent, but I have never said I would. I am a victim of circumstances, just trying to do my best for what I believe in. I never volunteered for this, I just found myself in this situation. I do have nightmares, I do remember what I have done and those who have died because of me. I will just have to live with that, in the sure and certain knowledge that I will not be the only person with those thoughts by the end of this war.

One thing you are very wrong about though is killing you. Whilst I wouldn't do it out of choice, I would do it out of necessity and there is where I find myself at this moment in time. So, if you have a God, please ask for forgiveness now before I pull the trigger"

"Mr Parker, we will make an Agent of you yet"

With that she took a step towards Peter, grabbed his Browning 9mm and with a jerk pulled it towards her. The gun immediately fired sending her crumpling to the ground like a lifeless rag doll. He looked down at her, her blood spreading out on the ground, it looked dark red in the light of the fire. He felt a degree of pity, not for her but for the family who would soon find out that they had lost a daughter, a sister, perhaps even a mother. He felt sympathy for those who would shed a tear, but most of all he felt numb at the thought of another wasted life, just another number in the final total of squandered lives in the madness of this war.

Clearing his throat, he addressed the dead soldier, "I have just realised Sergeant, I didn't even know your name"

Chapter 33.
Home
Nighttime, June 14th, 1943

They could hear the familiar noise of Lysander aircraft approaching. Its slow steady drone echoed into the night, it was strangely comforting, perhaps it engendered thoughts of home. The safety of their families, the familiarity of home and routine was a missed comfort, perhaps at last they would experience them once again.

Everything had returned to a calm and warm summers night, the occasional noise of an owl or fox, perhaps the odd cricket somewhere close by. How things changed so quickly, an hour ago people were dying, blood was spilled everywhere but now, nothing seemed out of place. In that time their lives had gone from utter madness to mundane normality.

The Resistance fighters were spread out across the field, torches at the ready, they would provide the guidance for the pilot landing the aircraft. Everything was in place, and ready for the evacuation back to England.

Madeleine was going to stay with Monique from the Resistance until she recovered. She would eventually go back to Belgium and would use Claude's silver Citroen for the journey. By that time, things would have settled down and perhaps the SS would presume that they had all escaped back to England.

Everybody had said their goodbyes, Richard and Claude were glad to be away and on their way to England. The local Resistance group were certainly very relieved to see the back of them all. Having so many fugitives in their area was proving difficult and dangerous for their other operations.

Peter and Madeleine limped off into the darkness, they were sore and swollen from the beatings they had received but they needed to have some privacy.

"So, this is it Peter Parker, I will never see you again. I can't believe I will live the rest of my life without you, I love you Peter, I always will, but I think you know that"

"We have experienced so much together in the short time we have known each other. I consider myself fortunate that I met you, I will never forget you Madeleine no matter how long I live.

I wish things could have been different, I wish I could stay here with you, spend the rest of my life working for your Aunt and Uncle in the bakery. We could spend our evenings in the Bar Saint Stephen in Chateau Du Beck.

But I have another life Madeleine, a life I have neglected for many months now, one that I need to get back to and re establish. I can't pretend that I have an easy choice but it's what I have to do"

"I do understand what you have to do Peter, but I can't pretend that I wish you had made a different choice. We could go to Chateau Du Beck and simply disappear, away from our past lives, away from this war. We could spend the rest of our time on this earth together, loving each other, laughing and being happy and no one would know our names!"

"I know Madeleine and don't think I haven't thought about that, don't for one moment assume I didn't want you, didn't dream about having exactly that life. Perhaps I will always regret not choosing you, maybe part of me already does, but I will have to live with that choice. I did consider that we had come so far together, we simply couldn't leave what we had behind, we had to stay together, I did think that Madeleine, I had that thought a million times over.

But I need to go home, restart my life, get away from this S.O.E business. The SS Sergeant was right, it's not me, I am not made for this kind of work, I am not strong enough. I just end up screwing things up, I let people down, people like you Madeleine"

She hugged him as tightly as their broken bodies would allow.

"You have not let me down Peter Parker, you have made my life wonderful and exciting. Despite you leaving, I would not have swapped that for anything"

The Lysander swooped in towards the landing area, the pilot touched down and with a slight bump and brought the aircraft to a stop. It immediately spun around and readied for the take off. He slowed the engine slightly but waved them over with an obvious sense of urgency.

Richard and Claude waved goodbye and sprinted over to the ladder and climbed inside. Peter shook hands with the Resistance fighters and thanked them for their help and sacrifice.

He turned to Madeleine, "so this is it, in reply to what you said before, I love you too and I always will. You will never know how much I wanted things to be different, how much I wanted to stay. Take care of yourself Madeleine, I will never forget you"

He turned and limped off towards the aircraft, staying any longer or saying anything more would have completely broken him. As he entered, he looked towards where Madeleine was standing, she waved, he waved back, just for a second, he thought about changing his mind, just for a brief moment he wanted to turn around and disappear with her, away from all of this, away to a life of true love.

The Lysander leapt into the night sky, and turned north, that was it, they were safe, Operation Red Book was over. He would never return but he would never forget the friends he had made, Laurent, Philipe and André. He would always remember Saint Aderald and the Bar Le Chat and so many adventures. Most of all, he would always remember the people who had died fighting for freedom.

There was one person who would always be in his thoughts though, that woman who had nursed him back to health after his crash. The person he had so many escapades with, that perfect soul with whom he had shared so many intimate moments, the one woman that he truly loved. That beautiful French girl, with stunning blue eyes and little dimples on each cheek, Madeleine.

Peter Parker will soon embark on his fourth and final mission, set in Abruzzo Italy.
The Beyondness of Peace,
Operation Mockingbird.